Kéntro

KÉNTRO

A Brandon McStocker Novel

TERRY STAFFORD

NEW YORK

LONDON • NASHVILLE • MELBOURNE • VANCOUVER

Kéntro

A Brandon McStocker Novel

© 2022 Terry Stafford

Published in New York, New York, by Morgan James Publishing. Morgan James is a trademark of Morgan James, LLC. www.MorganJamesPublishing.com

Morgan James BOGO™

A **FREE** ebook edition is available for you or a friend with the purchase of this print book.

CLEARLY SIGN YOUR NAME ABOVE

Instructions to claim your free ebook edition:
1. Visit MorganJamesBOGO.com
2. Sign your name CLEARLY in the space above
3. Complete the form and submit a photo of this entire page
4. You or your friend can download the ebook to your preferred device

ISBN 9781631954696 paperback
ISBN 9781631954702 ebook
Library of Congress Control Number: 2021934937

Cover and Interior Design by:
Chris Treccani
www.3dogcreative.net

Morgan James PUBLISHING **Builds** with... **Habitat for Humanity®** Peninsula and Greater Williamsburg

Morgan James is a proud partner of Habitat for Humanity Peninsula and Greater Williamsburg. Partners in building since 2006.

Get involved today! Visit
MorganJamesPublishing.com/giving-back

PROLOGUE

The 28th Amendment

The president of the United States walked into the chamber of the House of Representatives to thunderous applause from the joint session of Congress. It was the first time in many years the House was so united. There was not a single sign of reservation or division.

Once the chamber quieted, the Speaker of the House introduced the president. After another resounding welcome by the members of Congress, everyone sat except for President Andrew Richland.

President Richland looked over the chamber, scanning all of the attendees, then up into the gallery. Everyone sat still, waiting for him to speak. The president looked down to gather his thoughts. He finally looked up again.

"Ladies and gentlemen. I am happy, and so amazingly proud, to announce to you tonight that we have passed the 28th Amendment to the Constitution of the United States." President Richland raised both of his hands to form a *V* as the chamber once again erupted into pandemonium. Smiles lit up the room. When they quieted once more, the president continued.

"Ten years ago, this nation was in the throes of ripping itself apart, led by factions both within the government and from abroad—by those whose only objective was to instigate and celebrate our collapse. My fellow Americans, collapse we shall not." Everyone clambered to their feet in unanimous support.

"We have cleared the way, and our path is set to embark upon a journey of importance on a scale not seen in this nation since our forefathers first declared our freedom in 1776. Ladies and gentlemen, this nation has spoken loud and clear. We will no longer tolerate such corruption in our government. And since we can no longer trust this corrupt system to purge itself from our nation's capital, we will remove the nation's capital from the corruption." People sat again, and he continued.

"Our House Ways and Means Committee has given me a proposal that will reverse the course of our nation's demise once and for all. You will hear many announcements over the next several months that will take your breath away. We are taking the steps we have been discussing throughout this administration, ones that will rip our government from the hands of those who seek merely to destroy it. This amendment increases the size of the nation's capital beyond the previously allocated ten square miles. We now have twenty square miles at our disposal—twenty square miles that required our constitutional attention. Twenty square miles that will forever change the course of history. But more than the simple authorization of size, this amendment has served as the catalyst for solidarity."

Everyone in the chamber sprang to their feet. President Richland was able to do something that hadn't been done in years. He crossed the great divide in Congress, and the crucial work of the nation was on track once again.

CHAPTER 1

Brandon heard someone racing up the hall toward the conference room. He looked at the clock over the door. *No way is Bob running like that for a meeting*, he thought.

Jimmy crashed through the door, and Brandon jumped to his feet. Jimmy bent over and put his hands on his knees. He looked up. "Boss. Bob's dead," he said, trying to catch his breath.

Brandon's mouth fell open, and his head slanted like a confused puppy. "Wait. What?"

"Bob's dead," Jimmy gasped. "That's why he isn't here. They found him in the alley behind Tina's Grocery this morning."

"Do they know how? Has Anne been told yet?"

"I . . . I don't know."

"Well, get down there and find out what the blue blazes is going on."

Jimmy ran back out the door as Brandon sat in his chair at the end of the massive mahogany table. He lowered his head into his shaking hands. "God, help us." He sat in shock for several minutes, wondering what Bob's absence would mean for the company and what the loss of his friend would mean for him.

Brandon stood and wiped a tear from his cheek, then he walked out of the conference room, down the hall, and into Deborah's office. An attractive, middle-aged woman with straight, shoulder-length silver hair, Deborah Blanchard, one of Bob's project administrators, was sitting at her desk, eyes down, looking at a pile of papers. She looked up over the top of her black-rimmed glasses, tiny gold chains dangling to each side.

"Brandon, what's wrong?"

Brandon was silent for a moment, staring at his feet. "It's Bob, Deb. He's gone."

"Gone where?" Deborah looked past Brandon at the clock above her door. "I thought we were meeting in a few minutes."

"Deb, he's dead."

Deborah froze and locked her eyes on Brandon's. "No," she said as she sprang to her feet, slamming the chair against the cherry credenza behind her. She walked to the side of her desk. Brandon met her there. She looked up at him with tears welling. "How? Why?"

"Jimmy's trying to figure it out," Brandon said as he wrapped his arms around Deborah.

While she cried into his crisp white shirt and tie, Brandon scanned the hazy outline of the large project board on the wall behind her. Airport, Expressway Cross, Infrastructure, Federal Buildings, Monuments . . . all project titles that ceased to be in organized columns and swam before his eyes.

"Anne!" Deborah shouted as she pushed herself away from Brandon. "Does Anne know? That poor woman."

"Nobody knows anything," Brandon said. "Right now we need to stay calm and wait to hear from Jimmy. Stay here. I need to go back to my office and make some calls." He rushed down the hall toward his office. He felt jumpy, and his stomach began churning as he walked faster and faster. He threw his door open and spun the phone around on his desk, not wasting the time it took to walk around to his chair. He called the first-floor receptionist.

"Mary, have we had any visitors come in over the last hour or so?"

"No, sir."

"Good. Activate our controlled-access policy and lock the front door. Employees only!"

"Yes, sir. Will do. What's going on, Mr. McStocker?" Mary asked.

"Mary, just do it. I'll fill you in later."

"Of course. Yes, sir."

Brandon walked around his desk and sat down. He whipped the chair around and gazed out the window over the traffic lights at the intersection and down the busy street. The phone rang. He pivoted back around and picked it up.

"Yes."

"Mr. McStocker, it's Jimmy on line one."

"Thanks, Mary." Brandon pressed a button. "What have you learned?"

"Boss, the paramedics are telling me it looks like a heart attack."

"What would he have been doing behind Tina's?"

"I don't know. Apparently he always comes in here for coffee."

"I know, I know. But why in the back?"

"Hey, Boss, the police are headed over to pick up Anne now and take her down to the station."

"Oh, no. I better run down there. Call me on my cell if you hear anything else."

"Will do."

Brandon pressed another button. "Mary, get Senator Wilhelm on the phone, please."

"Yes, sir."

Brandon hung up and rotated his chair again and stared out of the window. The phone rang.

"Yes."

"I have Senator Wilhelm, sir."

"Thanks, Mary. Put him through."

"Senator, how are you, sir?"

"Fine here, Brandon. What's up? How's my favorite project manager?"

"Not so good, sir. I'm afraid I have some terrible news. Bob McClellan is dead."

"What? How?"

"Heart attack, apparently, on his way to the office this morning. I just wanted you to know so we can determine our next steps."

"Let me talk to some folks here and try to figure out what it might mean."

"Yes, sir. Of course. And Senator, I have our offices on lockdown."

"I understand, son. I don't blame you. Hopefully it's nothing. But we need to be sure. He's married, right?"

"Yes, sir. He is. I'm headed to the police station now to be with his wife. I'm sure she's devastated."

"Yes. By all means. Take care of that. I'll be in touch."

"Yes, sir. Thank you." Brandon walked by Deborah's office on his way to the elevator, putting on his long gray coat.

"Deb, I'm headed down to the police station to be with Anne. Mary has us on lockdown for the time being. Hold down the fort?"

"Of course. I can't believe this is happening."

Brandon exited the elevator on the first floor and knocked on the counter as he walked toward the front doors. "Mary, I'll be gone for awhile. Hold my messages, and lock this door behind me."

"Yes, sir."

Brandon headed down the walkway and into the parking lot. He stopped at his car and turned in the cold wind. His dark hair, normally well-groomed and parted on the side, lost all shape as it blew in the wind. He looked at the sign on front of the red-brick office building. *McClellan and McStocker Project Services, Inc.* "Oh, Bob. What in the world are we going to do without you, my friend?" Warm tears rolled down his frozen face as he slid his tall, slender body into his BMW and drove away.

Brandon walked quickly down the corridor at the Fairfax Police Station. He saw Anne sitting in a chair next to an officer's desk with her face in her hands. Brandon stopped and leaned against the wall. His lip quivered. As usual, she had overdressed. *She has always been such a classy lady*, he thought. Her gray hair glistened under the bright lights. More than a dear friend, Anne McClellan was the closest thing to a mother Brandon had known since both of his parents died when he was young. He straightened up and shook his head.

Anne heard footsteps and looked up. She smiled, relieved that it wasn't another policeman. "Brandon. Oh, dear God, Brandon." Her welcoming smile quickly turned to anguish as she stood to embrace him.

"Anne, I am so, so sorry."

"Brandon, he was just fine when he left the house this morning. What happened?"

"I don't know, Anne. We'll have to wait and see."

A police officer appeared and sat at his desk. "Can I help you, sir? Are you a member of the family?"

Brandon extended his hand. "I'm Brandon McStocker, officer. Senior partner at McClellan and McStocker and friend of the family."

"Oh, jeez, ma'am, you're *that* McClellan?" Anne nodded and sat back down.

The officer looked back up at Brandon. "Wow, I hear about you guys in the news all the time." Brandon pierced the officer with his glare. "Oh, yeah. Sorry. So, ma'am, when did you last see your husband?"

"This morning when he left for work."

"Did he have a reason to be at Tina's Grocery?"

"Officer," Brandon interrupted. "Bob stops at Tina's every morning for a cup of coffee and sometimes a bite to eat. Do we have to go through all of this right now?"

"It's Sergeant Turner, and yes, we do. Would you like to have a seat?"

"Thank you, Sergeant, but no. I need to go out in the foyer and make some calls. Can you tell me where they took Bob?"

"The deceased is with the medical examiner down in Manassas."

"Thank you. Will you be okay here, Anne?"

"I'll be fine, son. You go ahead."

Sergeant Turner continued to question Anne as Brandon went back out to the foyer in front of the station. He threw open the door and flipped his phone case open with such anger that he startled an elderly woman sitting near the exit door.

"Sorry," he said. Then, "Cassandra, it's me."

"Hey, babe. What's up?"

"Honey, Bob McClellan is dead."

"What?"

"Sweetheart, he's dead."

"No way."

"I'm afraid it's true."

"Oh, no! Where's Anne?"

"I'm here with her at the police station."

"What about the kids?"

"I don't know, hon. I need to get back in there with her."

"Of course. Call me when the dust settles, okay?"

"I will. Susan and Liv okay?"

"They're fine. Go. Go."

"Okay, bye. Love you." Brandon turned and started to walk back into the station. As he put his phone away, it began to vibrate. The display said *Unknown*. He pressed the answer button. "This is Brandon."

"Mr. McStocker, this is Senator Wilhelm's office. Do you have a moment to speak with the senator?"

"Yes. Of course."

"Brandon, where are you now?" the senator asked with panic in his voice.

"Uh . . . I'm at the Fairfax Police Station with Mrs. McClellan. Why?"

"How soon can you be at the White House?"

"The White House? What on earth for?"

"President Richland wants to meet with us."

"Us?"

"You and me."

"I can be there in about an hour, I suppose."

"Good. I'll meet you there." Senator Wilhelm hung up before Brandon had a chance to say goodbye.

"What in the world!" Brandon exploded.

The elderly lady sitting next to the door glanced at him again, looking irritated.

"Sorry," Brandon said. He walked quickly back into the station and down the corridor, where Anne was still answering Sergeant Turner's questions.

"Anne, I need to run. Will you be okay here?"

"I'm fine, dear. Please, do what you have to do."

"Good," Brandon said. "How about if Cassandra and I stop by your house later on. Would that be okay?"

"That'll be fine, dear. Now go on."

"Okay. Sorry I have to leave you like this," he said, leaning down to kiss her on the cheek. He rushed out of the building. As he drove through the busy D.C.-area streets, he was already ahead of himself, his mind crisscrossing between past and future. *What could the president possibly want with me? This project is huge, and the president must have trusted Bob immensely to turn it over to him. Bob and I built this company together. How will it even look now without him? This project was Bob's crown jewel. The poor guy doesn't even get to see it through.*

Brandon arrived at the White House. The security guard already had his name and quickly cleared Brandon through the gate, motioning him to the front doors, where Senator Wilhelm and some of his staff stood waiting.

"Come on with us, Brandon," the senator said, barely giving Brandon time to open his door. "This gentleman will take care of your car," he said, nodding in the direction of one of the White House staff.

Brandon reached back into the car and grabbed a leather notepad he kept on the front passenger seat. He turned into the cold, wet wind and rounded the back of his car to join the others on the sidewalk.

"Can I ask what this is about?"

"You'll find out soon enough," Wilhelm said.

CHAPTER 2

"The president will see you now," the receptionist said.

"Thank you," Senator Wilhelm replied as he and Brandon stood and entered the Oval Office.

"Senator. How good to see you. Come on in and have a seat. How's that golf game of yours?"

"As atrocious as always, I'm afraid, Mr. President. Sir, you remember Brandon McStocker, Bob McClellan's right hand at McClellan and McStocker."

"Of course. Pleasure, Mr. McStocker."

"Please, call me Brandon. It's an honor to see you again, Mr. President," he said as they shook hands.

The president continued to make small talk as he sat in his armchair. Brandon and Senator Wilhelm settled on the couch across from him. They filled the time as the staff brought a tray of drinks and snacks.

"So, Brandon, I'm so sorry for your loss. I guess things are pretty crazy at Mack & Mack. I hated to have to ask you to come in when I know you have so many other things to tend to."

"It's fine, sir. Yes, it's quite a shock for everyone. Not only was Bob my partner, but he was also a dear friend."

"Mr. President, Brandon placed his company facilities on lockdown this morning, not knowing what might be going on," Senator Wilhelm said. "Can you think of any reason why that would be necessary?"

"Not at all. The poor man had a heart attack, did he not?"

"He did, Mr. President," Brandon said. "That's what we're told. The whole thing gave me such an uneasy feeling. It was just a knee-jerk reaction, sir."

"Well, if there's anything to it, you will certainly have the full support of the White House to get to the bottom of it."

Brandon nodded his head and looked down at the floor. "Thank you, sir."

The president leaned forward in his chair, narrowing his eyes. "Gentlemen, as you probably know, I called you here to discuss the project. I know it's a painful time, and I'm sorry, but with so much at stake, I don't want to lose the momentum we've built up since passing the amendment. There is nothing more important to this country right now than the Kéntro Project."

"Yes, sir. I understand," Senator Wilhelm said.

"Brandon," the president continued, "I've met with Bob a number of times on this project and asked him to keep what he shares to a minimum. Did he tell you the full scope of it?"

"Well. Uh. No, sir. I don't think he did. I know we've been working on a massive number of plans for individual buildings and public works projects, but he told me how sensitive the project was and shared none of the details. Frankly, I always assumed it was for a new build-out of the District. That's what the 28th

Amendment did, right? Increased the size of D.C. to twenty square miles?

"Yes and no," the president said. "Brandon, before we go on, I need to ask you something incredibly important."

Brandon's already nervous jitters erupted into sheer panic. This was only the second time he had even been around the president. The first was at a gala he and Cassandra attended with Bob and Anne several months earlier. "Yes, sir?" Brandon said, not exactly sure how to respond.

"Bob told me that if we ever needed an alternate for him, or if anything ever happened to him, there is nobody on this planet more capable of taking over Kéntro than you. I know Bob was one of a kind—a hard man to replace—but I'd like for you to take over Kéntro. Can you do it, Brandon? It would be a great service to your country."

Brandon's first thought was that the president seemed overly dramatic about constructing a handful of buildings. He looked around the room as he thought about what the president was asking. The importance of merely being in the Oval Office was just beginning to sink in for Brandon, and now the president himself was entrusting him with a project that was apparently highly confidential.

"Of course, sir. I know I could never replace Bob, but whenever he asked me to do something, I always knew he had my best interest at heart. I suppose I should trust that he's still taking care of me, even though he's gone."

President Richland and Senator Wilhelm looked at each other, nodding, then looked back at Brandon. "Congratulations, Brandon," the president said with a smile. "Consider yourself the new executive project manager for The Kéntro Project. Mr. Wilhelm, will you please make arrangements for Brandon to meet with the Oversight Committee?"

"Of course, Mr. President."

"But, Mr. President, my board of directors might have something to say about this."

"Oh, let us take care of that."

"Of course, sir."

"Brandon, it's almost time for this news to break anyway, but please understand the gravity and the sensitivity of what I'm about to tell you."

"I understand, sir."

"You've heard the fearmongers and talking heads in the media predicting the end of time because of the 28th Amendment, right?"

"Yes, sir." Senator Wilhelm watched Brandon intently.

The president continued, "Brandon, much of what they are saying is true."

"Sir?"

"Yes, the foundation of the Kéntro Project involves moving the nation's capital out of D.C."

Brandon gasped and looked at the senator then back at the president.

"So, that's what you meant in your speech when you talked about ripping it out from under the corruption? But how? Is that even legal?"

"Yes. That's what I was referring to. I almost said too much in my exuberance. The Constitution doesn't specify the location of the nation's capital, only that it be limited to ten square miles. To proceed with the long-range plans, we need twenty square miles. That's why we needed the amendment."

"As far as how, that's where you come in," Senator Wilhelm said. "Bob had you guys working on developing plans, not for updating Washington, D.C., but for building a whole new city. A whole new infrastructure for our nation's capital."

"It sounds a bit insane if you don't mind my saying so, sir." Brandon looked back at the president.

"Perhaps," the president said. "But the people of this country are so tired of government corruption and are frustrated with their inability to do anything about it. It's time. What we want to roll out to them now is a more specific plan to rip the nation's capital out from under the power brokers and return it to the people. We think the people are ready."

"But sir, what will keep those same power brokers from relocating right along with the government?"

"I guess there's a two-part answer to that, Brandon. First of all, it will give us a fresh beginning and an opportunity to restart relationships with the lobbyists or simply sever ties with those whose interests aren't aligned with the good of the people. Secondly, and probably the bigger reason, is that this nation as a whole is so upset with our inability to get things done, I'm certain this will pull it together. Whether or not it is practical, getting the country back together for a purpose—any purpose—is reason enough to go down this path."

"Okay, so exactly how do I fit into this?"

"Brandon, we need you and your firm to lead this project. It's what Bob had you working on these past several months. Apparently, he had a firm doing a little survey work going on as well."

"Wait. Does this have anything to do with Bob's death?"

"We hope not," Senator Wilhelm said. "We think it was merely a tragic coincidence. Maybe the stress of it. But we're looking into it under the radar as a precaution. Brandon, is that why you locked down your facilities this morning?"

Brandon stared at the floor in silence for several seconds before looking at the senator and then at the president. "My gut just told me something was off. I knew Bob had been coming down here quite a bit, and I knew there were many things he wasn't telling me. As I said, Bob has been a close friend for years. I knew if he wasn't telling me something, it was because he couldn't. I let it go at that. But when I learned he was dead, I didn't want to take any chances with the safety of our employees. It just seemed prudent at the time. Was it a mistake?"

"No, you had to do what was right for you, Brandon," the president said. "I don't think the press picked up on it, so no harm."

"Excuse me. Let me text my receptionist to open it back up before they do catch on." The president and Senator Wilhelm got up and poured coffee for themselves. They walked over to the president's desk, eating pastries while Brandon contacted his office. Brandon slowly tapped out the words to Mary with his shaking hands.

Cancel lockdown.

Everything okay? she texted back.

Fine.

Brandon stood, poured himself a cup of coffee, and walked to the desk.

"Gentlemen, I . . . I just don't know what to do with all this. Dare I ask where you are building our nation's new capital?" The president and Senator Wilhelm looked at each other and smiled.

"Kéntro," the president said. "The name of the project. That's Greek for 'in the middle.'" He led the other two across the room and pointed to a map of the United States hanging on the wall.

He pushed his finger into the center of the country. "Right there. There's a little monument right outside of the town of Lebanon, Kansas, identifying the geographic center of the continental United States. There's plenty of room out there. That's where we're going to put it."

Brandon's eyes grew as he looked back and forth between each of them. "Uh . . . not to break up the party, sir, but does Kansas know about this?"

"They will," the president said. "We've been communicating with Governor Redman, and he seems supportive. Many people around the country have been advocating for something like this, but they've never made a big deal of it. Most everyone thought they were kooks, anyway."

"How in the world did you get Redman onboard? I thought he was against everything your administration stands for," Brandon said.

"He is, but we played to his greed," Wilhelm said.

"None of this is going to be easy," the president said. "While we had the support of most of Congress on the 28th Amendment, relocating the center of government was only conjecture. Once we roll this plan out, those that have their grip on D.C. will be all over the media spreading their usual poison. My communications director and her staff will handle all that. We want you to focus on getting the move done."

Brandon scanned the room until he let his gaze land on the bushes blowing in the wind outside the president's window. He wanted to get his eyes off of the other two men. His thoughts were on Bob. Senator Wilhelm started to speak but instead, turned his attention to the president clearing his throat. The president shook his head, signaling Wilhelm to remain quiet.

After a few minutes of silence, while the president and the senator sipped their coffee, Brandon turned to face them. "Gentlemen, is my family safe? Is Anne safe?"

"We have no reason to believe the opposition would do anything to hurt anyone over this, Brandon. But if your gut is telling you—"

"It is!" Brandon cut him off. "Since the moment I found out Bob was dead, I've been dealing with this gnawing in the pit of my stomach that something isn't right."

The president put his hand on Brandon's shoulder and looked into his eyes. "Brandon, I know you can do this. Bob knew you could do this. Look, I know you're a man of faith. Do you want to take some time to pray with your family about this?"

"First, what I need to do is figure out a way to explain all this to my wife. Then we need to get over and spend some time with Anne. I can't believe she has to go through this now."

Senator Wilhelm put his coffee on the table and joined the other two. "Brandon, why don't you take some time to gather your thoughts, and do what you need to do with your family and Anne. But I need you to come back tomorrow, so we can go over some details. I'll have my secretary set up a time and give you a call. Is that okay?"

"That's fine, sir."

The president walked around his desk and sat in his chair. "Brandon, I have an idea that I want to check out. Senator, when you're finished with your meeting tomorrow, bring him back by here for a few minutes."

CHAPTER 3

Brandon drove into the driveway of his two-story gray Cape Cod in Fairfax. He turned off the ignition and inhaled. He stared at the wraparound front porch with the white, accented trim that gave it its old farmhouse charm. All the shrubs in front of the porch shimmered in the cold wind. He sat thinking for several minutes before he finally got out of the car and walked to the front door.

"Daddy!" his girls shouted when he walked into the living room. Brandon's two daughters, Olivia and Susan, had been watching TV but hopped up from the couch and wrapped themselves around his waist.

"Mom! Daddy's home!" Olivia shouted.

"I heard, I heard," Cassandra said as she walked in from the kitchen. Her long, blonde hair, tied in a ponytail, was hanging over the front of her thick burgundy sweater. Brandon couldn't help but notice her red, puffy eyes and the unusual wrinkles on her forehead. She stood on the toes of her stocking feet and kissed him, then took his coat and briefcase and placed them on the loveseat.

"You girls stay in here and watch TV. We're going into the kitchen for a few minutes," Cassandra said.

"Can I go to my room and practice on my ukulele instead?" Susan asked.

"That's fine," Brandon said, smiling, first at Susan and then at Cassandra.

"Whatever," Cassandra said with a grin. As Brandon and Cassandra walked into the kitchen, they heard Susan gallop up the steps then slam her bedroom door. "That girl," Cassandra said, rolling her eyes. They stopped next to the small breakfast table and faced each other. Cassandra rubbed Brandon's arm and forced a smile. He leaned into her, wrapping his arms around her and resting his cheek on her head. He began to weep. They stood in silence for several minutes crying, in each other's arms.

"I can't believe he's gone," Brandon said, wiping his eyes.

Cassandra pulled a napkin from the holder on the table and handed it to him. "Come on, sweetheart. Sit."

"It's been a heck of a day," he said as he sat down across from her.

"I'm sure," Cassandra said. "What happens now?"

"I don't know. We need to go see Anne." They sat quietly for several minutes before Brandon stood and walked to the coffee pot on the counter. He poured a cup and leaned against the countertop. Cassandra stood, then walked over to his side to pour herself a cup. She turned around and leaned against the countertop next to him, silently reflecting a few moments before speaking.

"Let's go see Anne and make sure she's okay."

"Okay," Brandon said. "She was in shock this morning, as you would expect. She didn't look good at all. I don't know when their kids are getting into town, but I hope it's pretty soon."

"She's a strong woman."

"Yes, she is. Before we leave, I need to tell you something else that happened today."

"There's more?"

"Well, yes," he said, looking over at her. "I was called to the White House."

"What!"

"Senator Wilhelm took me there to meet with the president."

"Are you kidding me?" Cassandra said, turning to face him. "Senator Wilhelm? The president? Brandon, what is going on?"

"Apparently Bob had been singing my praises to the president. The president wants me to take over a project we've been working on. As it turns out, it's a heck of a lot bigger than I had imagined." They walked back to the table and sat down. Brandon explained the Kéntro Project to her. Her mouth hung open in disbelief the entire time.

"I don't know any more of the details right now," he said. "But I have to go back in tomorrow and meet with the committee they created, coming off of the 28th Amendment."

"Does Bob's death have anything to do with all that?"

"I don't think so. The president said they're looking into it. But it'll be okay."

"What do you mean, it'll be okay? Honey, are you in danger?"

"I'll be okay. I promise."

Cassandra got up from the table, poured herself another cup of coffee, then brought the pot back to the table to top off Brandon's. "So, I guess this means we'll see even less of you?"

"I don't know, honey. Things are changing so fast. I don't have a clue what's going to happen."

Cassandra saw the worry on Brandon's face and forced herself to relax. She sat down and reached across the table to hold his arm. "Sweetheart, if anyone can do this, you can. I'm sure that's why Bob spoke so highly of you."

"I sure hope so. I'm going to have to sit with Deborah and develop a strategy."

"Are you going to be able to do this from halfway across the country?" she asked, the pitch of her voice climbing as it occurred to her what might happen.

"I just don't know, hon. Let's go check on Anne."

Brandon rang the doorbell. They waited on the front porch, holding their collars up to shield their necks and cheeks from the cold wind.

"Well, look who we have here," Anne said as she opened the door. "Get in here out of the cold. Let me take your coats." Anne was still well-dressed—her tall, slender figure stood majestically in the doorway with her beautifully appointed living room spread out behind her. Brandon and Cassandra looked at each other, amazed at her ability to act as though nothing was wrong. Cassandra walked through the door past Anne, and Brandon followed her. They took off their coats and handed them to her. When she laid them on the back of a chair and turned to greet them, tears filled her eyes.

Cassandra rushed over and held her. "Anne, I am so sorry." Anne became limp in Cassandra's arms, and Brandon grabbed both of them, guiding them to the couch.

"Sit here, Anne," he said. Anne and Cassandra settled in on the couch and Brandon took a seat in a chair on the other side of a long coffee table.

"I'm sorry. Can I get you two something to drink?" Anne asked.

"No. We're fine. You just relax," Cassandra said.

"I don't need anything," Brandon said. "When are your kids getting into town?"

"I think sometime tomorrow." Anne fell silent for several moments while Brandon and Cassandra simply looked on. Anne continued, "You two have been such good friends. Thank you for coming over."

Cassandra met Anne's gaze. "We got here as soon as we could, Anne, and we wouldn't want to be anywhere else right now."

"Pastor Landry is on his way over," Anne said.

"Good," Brandon said. "I'd like to see Carl myself and talk to him a bit."

"He's a good man, that Pastor Landry," Anne said.

"Yes, he is." Brandon smiled at the sweet Southern belle drawl in Anne's voice. At the same time, he remembered that she was smart, with plenty of business savvy. She was very much a part of Bob's firm and was even his administrator in the beginning.

It was at Pastor Landry's church that Brandon and Bob met ten years earlier. They quickly became friends when Bob saw himself in Brandon. Brandon had also become close friends with Carl as he traveled along his spiritual journey. Brandon had always been skeptical about organized religion, but he was comforted by what Carl taught and enjoyed having one-on-one conversations with him over coffee.

"Brandon, honey, they keep telling me it was a heart attack," Anne said. "Bob did seem a little stressed lately."

"Anne, we don't need to talk about all that now," Brandon said.

"No, no. Now listen," she said, raising her hand toward him. "He just seemed uneasy. I knew that big project was riding high on him. Then that man came to see him a couple of weeks ago and got him even more upset."

Brandon and Cassandra looked at each other with raised eyebrows. Brandon looked back at Anne. "What man was that, Anne? Do you know who it was?"

"Denny something. He said he was from Senator Sanders's office."

"Did he say what he was doing here?"

"No. I let him in, and the two of them went back there to Bob's office. I just wanted to let you know about that before Pastor Landry gets here." Brandon filed it away as they chatted about old times and their memories of Bob. He noticed that the stories of the beginnings of McClellan and McStocker seemed to soothe Anne. She laughed, waving her hands around with every story. Brandon and Cassandra smiled at her and let her go on until the doorbell rang.

"I'll get it," Brandon said. He stood and walked to the door.

"Brandon!" Pastor Landry said when the door opened. "I thought that was your car out there. How ya been?"

"Doing well, Carl. Doing well. Come on in."

Carl Landry was a short, gray-haired man. He was the senior pastor at a large church that the McClellan and McStocker families attended together.

Anne began crying again when she stood to greet the pastor. He wrapped his arms around her and held tight. She let all of her pain drain out as if the pastor were a direct conduit to God himself. She wailed and went limp in his arms. Brandon and Cassandra both jumped to their side to steady Pastor Landry.

"It's okay, Miss Anne. Sit back down here," Carl said. He sat next to Anne on the couch and put an arm around her shoulders.

After several minutes, Anne quieted herself. "I'm sorry," she said.

"Anne, honey, you have nothing to be sorry about," Cassandra said, sitting on the side of the chair with her arm around Brandon's back.

"What a difference a day makes," Pastor Landry said as he squeezed Anne's shoulder.

"Yes. Yes, it does," she said. Anne brought Pastor Landry up to date on some of the stories she had been telling Brandon and Cassandra before he arrived. He smiled and listened. He knew that's all she needed at the moment. Later, the four moved into the kitchen, where Anne had baked homemade cookies. She served them, along with the fresh coffee she had made despite their half-hearted protests. She fussed around the kitchen to keep herself busy and continued to tell her stories about Bob.

"We met at the University of Alabama in Huntsville," she said. "He was an engineering student there while I was working on my accounting degree." She bragged about the time they got to meet Wernher von Braun and some of the members of his German rocket team at a dinner party. "Bob's days at the Marshall Space Flight

Center were short but very rewarding and formative in his career. He had always preferred construction over launching rockets, so that's the path he chose. It wasn't long after we left Huntsville and moved to D.C. that he started his engineering firm, McClellan Project Management Services." She looked at Brandon, and tears returned.

"Several years after you graduated from Harvard Business School and went to work for Bob, he asked you to become a full partner. He was so proud of you. Bob told me that he wanted your business acumen and project management skills. But I knew it was more than that. Not only were you a partner, but you were also a dear friend to him. Both of you have been such dear friends to us." Brandon and Cassandra barely held back the tears. Carl smiled at Anne's story. Anne continued to tell story after story of her days with Bob—funny stories. Tears of laughter filled the kitchen as the tales were told as only Anne could tell them.

The laughs once again turned to silence and tears when it was time for everyone to go home. Anne walked them to the front door, where they put on their coats and braced for the cold wind.

"Hey, Carl," Brandon said, leaning in while the ladies said their goodbyes. "Do you have time to meet for coffee in the morning?"

CHAPTER 4

Brandon entered the diner and saw Carl sitting at their usual booth, staring out the window with his hands wrapped around a cup of coffee. Brandon scooted himself into the seat across from him.

"Good morning, Preacher."

"Hey, Brandon. How ya doin' this mornin'?"

"Cup o' joe, hon?" the waitress shouted from behind the counter.

"That would be great, Dottie," Brandon shouted back. "I guess I'm okay," he said, looking back at Carl.

"Dang, son. A bit serious, aren't you? What's on your mind?"

"Oh, this thing with Bob, for one." Brandon gazed out of the window at the morning traffic. "I guess he was under a lot of stress that I wasn't aware of."

"How so?"

"Well, I was called down to the White House yesterday and learned a lot about the project we've been working on. I had no idea it was so big. I suppose it makes sense that Bob may have dropped dead from a heart attack."

"Are you doubting it?"

"Let's just say I have an uneasy feeling about it. I'm going back down there today to meet with the committee they formed out of the 28th Amendment ordeal. The president wants me to take over the project."

Carl's eyes widened as he leaned forward across the table. "The president?"

"Yes, the president," Brandon smiled, continuing to gaze out of the window.

"Brandon, I know you can't tell me all the details, or you would've by now. But brother, you've got this. You're like the most accomplished project manager on the planet. Whatever they need you to do, I know you can do it. Bob thought the world of you and trusted you. That didn't come easily for him. The fact that you were his friend and go-to guy speaks volumes."

Brandon dropped his gaze and shook his head, then slowly looked back up. "Thanks, Carl. I appreciate it. I just wish I knew how to process all of this. I miss him so much already. I could use your prayers."

Carl met Brandon's red eyes. "Let's start right now." The men lowered their heads, and Carl said a prayer. After the *amen*, they sat without saying a word for a few minutes. Brandon pulled his wallet from the breast pocket of his jacket and placed a $10 bill on the table.

"I've got this one, Carl."

"Thanks. How big is this project anyway?"

Brandon stood, then pulled his coat from the hanger and put it on. He turned and looked down at Carl. "Think along the lines of building a majestic city in the middle of nowhere. Think Dubai."

★ ★ ★ ★ ★

Brandon met Senator Wilhelm at his office in the Capitol building, and they walked together down the hall to an impressive wood-clad conference room. Five people sat around the table. There was a silver tray in the middle, piled high with pastries.

"Grab some coffee, Mr. McStocker," one of the ladies said. Wilhelm was already at the serving table filling his cup. Brandon joined him there.

The senator leaned over to Brandon. "Relax. This is the easy part." Both men sat at the conference table and pulled notebooks from their briefcases.

The committee chair at the head of the conference table cleared her voice. "Mr. McStocker, we've been informed by the White House that you have accepted the lead on Kéntro. Is that true?"

"Uh. Yes, ma'am. Apparently that's what Mr. McClellan would have wanted."

"Good. Let me explain what's happening. I won't take up much of your time. I know the president is waiting to see you."

"Senator Taylor, please, take all the time you need," Senator Wilhelm said.

"Thank you, Senator. Mr. McStocker, do you have any idea how big this project is? Did Mr. McClellan share any of those details with you?"

"No, ma'am. He did not."

"I see. You are familiar with the new 28th Amendment, are you not?"

"Of course."

"Good. I know there has been much speculation about what all that meant, so let me lay it out for you. Mr. McStocker, the citizens of this country are asking—no, begging—for us to make a major change here in the nation's capital. The problem for years has been that we've been unable to effect that change. The roots of corruption run too deep." Senator Taylor opened a folder and spread several papers around in front of her.

"We have to move it, Mr. McStocker. Since we can't take the corruption out of the capital, we will remove the capital from the corruption. We have the nation's support right now. And, as they say, we have to strike while the iron is hot." She took a drink, and everyone else around the table did the same. "The committee has determined that there is no better place for the nation's capital now than in the geographic center of the continental US."

"That way we can keep closer tabs on the left coast," another member interrupted with a chuckle. Everyone in the room laughed, releasing some of the tension.

"Mr. McStocker," Senator Taylor continued. "We need you to move our nation's capital to a little town called Lebanon, Kansas." Brandon looked at Senator Wilhelm. The senator nodded. Brandon looked back at Senator Taylor. She had confirmed the strange truth the president told him the day before.

"Sir, you might think there is nothing in Lebanon, Kansas. You would be correct. You will need to build us a new city and the infrastructure that goes along with it. I understand that Mr. McClellan already had your firm working on some of the early planning for such a city."

"Uh. Yes, ma'am. But we had no idea what we were working on. Frankly, I thought it was a plan to expand Washington, D.C."

"I'm sure that was part of the cover. All this is already in the rumor mill, so we aren't going to be able to keep a lid on it. Do you understand, Mr. McStocker?"

"Yes, ma'am. I believe I do."

"Good. There are several things we need to address to get the project off the ground. First of all, you will have the full support of this committee, who in turn has the full support of the White House. Whatever you need, bring it to this body. We also know that you aren't going to be able to lead a project of this magnitude from halfway across the country. We've negotiated with Kansas State University in nearby Manhattan, Kansas for an office complex. We would like you to operate from there. Can you make that happen, Mr. McStocker?"

"Yes. But, ma'am, this project is going to take years. And I have a board of directors to report to."

"Mr. McStocker—Brandon—I know this isn't going to be easy. Far from it, I would imagine. But what you are about to undertake is probably one of the most important things to happen to this country since the Constitution was signed. It's going to take all of us doing some pretty amazing things, breaking some long-held rules, and forging new paths to get it done. Do you understand?"

"Of course, Senator. I completely understand. I can make it happen."

"Good. Someone from the FTC will be contacting your board president directly to explain the gravity of the situation and provide a signed waiver to the corporation. You should pull together a special board meeting, and it'll all come out then."

"Yes, ma'am."

"We'll also need you to check in with the committee every few days with an update on the project plans. You can work out the details with Senator Wilhelm. He will coordinate any of the critical resources you might need. Do you have any questions for the committee?"

"No, ma'am. Not at this time."

"Okay, good. Now, sir, I think you better get over to the White House."

★ ★ ★ ★ ★

"Brandon. Please come in. Have a seat."

"Good morning, Mr. President. Thank you."

"Coffee?"

"No thank you, sir. I've reached my limit."

"Did you get a good briefing from the committee?"

"I did, sir. But I have to admit, it's a bit overwhelming."

"It is for all of us, I'm afraid," the president said. "This is the biggest thing to happen to this country since the Civil War."

"Well, Senator Taylor said since the Constitution was signed," Brandon chuckled. "But I get your point." They sat down. Brandon peered across the coffee table at the president, thinking how ironic it was that he should mention the Civil War. The president smiled, realizing he had struck a dissonant chord in the conversation.

"Oh, relax, Brandon. We aren't going down that road. I thought we might have been several years ago, but the country is in a fairly good place these days. Of course, the parties came together on a most unfortunate platform, but getting rid of the white-collar crime in D.C. is on top of everyone's list. Even private corporations are turning their backs on the free rides and want to invest their resources toward helping us out. The upside of all this is that we'll figure out a way to pay for it. The budget element of your project is essentially unlimited."

"Reminds me of the Apollo days at NASA," Brandon chuckled.

"That, and then some," the president said as he stood. "Brandon, I want to introduce you to someone." He walked around his desk and pressed the intercom button. "Send Mr. Langston in, please."

"On his way, sir."

The president walked toward the door, and Brandon stood, not sure what to make of the situation. A very tall, muscular Black man in a crisply tailored suit entered the room and reached for the president's hand.

"Good morning, Mr. Langston. Please, come in. Can I get you some coffee?"

"No, thank you, sir. I'm fine."

"Brandon McStocker, I'd like you to meet Sonny Langston. Sonny, Mr. McStocker and his family are your new assignment."

Brandon released Sonny's hand and raised his eyebrows as he looked at the president.

"Assignment, sir?"

"Brandon, you expressed concern yesterday about your safety, and considering the nature of this project, I think we all need to consider it. Mr. Langston is with the Secret Service. He and his team have been detailed to your family. Mr. Langston is assigned to you personally. I don't think it'll be full coverage. There's no reason to cause even more stress for your family, so I think keeping an eye on them from a distance would be adequate."

"Uh . . . okay . . . I guess. I know I brought it up, but do you really think all this is necessary, sir?"

"Probably not, Brandon. Especially now. But things might get hectic in the future. By then, Mr. Langston and his team will have been able to size up the environment."

"Well, okay. Just how many people are on this detail, sir?"

"Only three for now. Mr. Langston will introduce them to you and your family when it's convenient."

"Of course, sir. I guess I better call Cassandra and get her up to speed. Cassandra is my wife," he said, looking at Sonny.

"Yes, sir. I know."

"Okay," Brandon said. "Is there anything else, Mr. President?"

"Well, there is one more minor detail." He and Sonny smiled at each other. "Sonny is also your driver."

"My driver, sir? I know I probably sounded a little nervous yesterday. But again, is all this really necessary?"

"Brandon, you have now become an essential part of an unprecedented move by the nation. I think it's perfectly reasonable that we would take some precautions to ensure continuity in leadership going forward. Your car is waiting, and Sonny can take you wherever you need to go. The staff will make sure your personal vehicle makes it home safely."

CHAPTER 5

Brandon walked into Deborah's office with Sonny close behind.

"Deb, this is Sonny Langston. I'll explain later. Sonny, this is Deborah Blanchard, my new deputy project manager."

Deborah's look cut though Brandon like an arrow through the heart.

"What?"

"Will you accept the position, Deb? I don't have time to worry about the board on this, and you're obviously the person I need."

"Uh . . . sure. Listen, everyone is gathering down in the theater. They should be ready to go by the time we get there." The three of them left Deborah's office and walked to the elevator. A few minutes later, they entered the company's training theater packed with almost two hundred employees, meandering and chatting as they found their seats. Brandon didn't wait for an introduction. He went straight to the microphone stand in the middle of the stage as Deborah sat in a chair behind him. Jimmy was sitting in the front row, visibly confused. Sonny stood in the wing watching the proceedings from behind a curtain.

"Ladies and gentlemen, can you take a seat, please. This isn't going to take long." Silence fell over the theater. Brandon turned and whispered to Deborah, "The members of the board are being rounded up now. They should be here shortly. Please let Mary know."

"Of course."

Brandon returned to the microphone stand. "Ladies and gentlemen, you all know by now of Bob's untimely death yesterday morning. As far as anyone knows right now, it was a massive heart attack. My wife and I have visited his wife, and she is doing as well as can be expected. Yesterday, and again today, I was summoned to the White House. They briefed me on what Bob had been working on—what we were all working on quite unknowingly." A wave of whispers rose throughout the room. "Ladies and gentlemen, I'm just going to throw it out there. It turns out that the Kéntro Project has been chartered to relocate the federal government from Washington, D.C. to a completely new site in Kansas."

"Kansas?" someone shouted. The room erupted in chatter and laughter.

It took several moments for Brandon to regain their attention. "Look, I know. It seems impossible, but apparently, it's what the country wants. You've seen the news. People are fed up with what's going on down there. That's really what the 28th Amendment movement was all about. It gives the feds the power they need to get things done."

"Why Kansas of all places?" someone shouted.

"Good question," Brandon said. "The president and the committee assigned to this project decided it would make the most sense and be most efficient if the federal government operated from the center of the country. I guess they decided on a location that isn't debatable, the geographic center of the continental US. This so happens to be near a little town in Kansas called Lebanon. I researched it a little myself, and quite frankly, there isn't much of anything there." The noise rose again as everyone confirmed what they were hearing with those sitting around them.

Brandon pointed back behind him. "As the new senior executive project manager on Kéntro, I've asked Deborah Blanchard to be my deputy. We will be meeting with the board of directors shortly after we wrap up here. They'll need to go over the legal aspects of how this will affect the company." Jimmy's jaw dropped, and his face flushed red. He locked eyes with Deborah. She shook her head and shrugged off what Brandon had said. Jimmy then slumped down in his seat and crossed his arms.

"Over the next several days, I'll be meeting with the department heads to pull together a project plan for you all to use. We're talking a full infrastructure, federal buildings, an entire support structure, and transportation, up to and including an international-class airport. Of course, we'll be bringing on other design and engineering firms that specialize in each of those areas."

After Brandon quieted the rumble, he took the microphone off of the stand and paced back and forth on the stage, looking at individuals in the crowd. "Needless to say, our entire focus will be on this project. Everything else will be farmed out to other firms, and the GSA will reassign those contracts. Most of us on this project are going to have to relocate to Kansas. The committee has made arrangements for a temporary office space at Kansas State University. Obviously, I haven't had a chance to discuss a move with anyone. Once we get the details, I'll have your department heads discuss the arrangements and determine who can and cannot go. We'll keep this facility open as a D.C. liaison office for as long as possible and should be able to keep some part of the design team here." The room was silent and in shock. Fear came over the faces of the audience. Brandon dropped the microphone to his side and walked over to Deborah.

"I'm sorry, Deb. I'll explain all this later. I just have to get ahead of any potential leaks."

Deborah's body was stiff as she and Brandon walked toward the front of the stage.

"I know this is nuts, but try not to worry about it," Brandon reassured the crowd. "Everything's going to be okay. The project itself has been held in secrecy to this point, but the White House is about to release it to the public. Remember, our work in this company is sensitive—nobody else's business, and I expect it to stay that way."

Brandon handed the microphone to Deborah and walked off stage. "Sonny, let the folks at the White House know the cat is out of the bag."

"Okay, ladies and gentlemen," Deborah said, "that's it for right now. Your department heads will pass further instructions to you when they become available. We would like to keep this information in-house for now. Please return to your workstations and tend to the tasks you've been working on. Thank you for all of your excellent work. You are dismissed." She looked at Jimmy. He hadn't taken his glare off of her. She placed the microphone back on the stand and walked off stage to meet Brandon and Sonny. She looked at Brandon when she got closer.

"Jimmy is irate," she said.

"Well, he'll just have to be that way. I'll try to talk to him later on."

Brandon, Deborah, and Sonny got off the elevator on the fourth floor. Sonny stepped to the side and remained standing next to the elevator as Brandon followed Deborah into her office. She looked at the schedule on her wall as she walked around her desk.

"So, all this was for Kansas," she said.

"Apparently so. Who would have guessed?"

"Brandon, I can go out there with you." She sat in her chair. "But I'm not sure how long I can stay. You know I've been thinking about retirement, right? I've got grandbabies here."

"I know, Deb. But I need you with me on this." Deborah's intercom buzzed.

"Yes."

"Ms. Blanchard, is Mr. McStocker in there with you?"

"Yes, he is. Go ahead."

"Mr. McStocker, the directors are in the conference room, ready to start."

"Thanks, Mary. Tell them we'll be right there."

"Yes, sir."

Jimmy joined the two of them walking toward the elevator. "Boss, can we talk?"

"We'll talk after the board meeting."

Sonny remained standing outside the conference room as Brandon and Deborah went in and sat on the side of the table next to the windows. Brandon looked out and noticed the wind was still blowing. Mary closed the door on her way out. Don Greene, the chairman of the board, sat at the end of the long table under the large brushed aluminum McClellan & McStocker logo and called the meeting to order.

"Ladies and gentlemen, I assure you, I can keep this meeting short."

A chuckle went around the room. Brandon and Deborah looked at each other with the same thought. *How in the world is he going to keep this short?*

Mr. Greene continued. "I received a call from Senator Taylor, head of the Kéntro Project Oversight Committee. I've had my office follow up on all this, and it's legit. The senator informed me that because of the massive size of this project, the White House made the unprecedented move to obtain a court-ordered waiver of the Federal Acquisition Regulations to allow the federal government to have direct oversight of the lead contractor on this project. What this means folks, is that Mack & Mack is going to be reporting directly to the committee and all liability will be transferred accordingly. Is there any discussion?"

Sharon Smith, one of the board members sitting across the table from Brandon and Deborah, smiled and spoke up. "I don't think this comes as a surprise. We all knew that being involved in a project of this size and complexity was going to cause some strange things to happen." Brandon and Deborah noticed that all of the board members were smiling in an eerie show of unity.

"The board will entertain a motion to disband itself until further notice," Don said.

"So moved," Sharon responded.

"Seconded," came another voice from the other end of the table.

"All in favor, say aye."

"Aye!"

"All opposed."

Silence fell over the room. "Motion is approved. Ladies and gentlemen, this board of directors is hereby disbanded until further notice, and this meeting is adjourned." Everyone stood and began shaking hands, talking, and laughing. Some filed out of the door through the foyer and into the cold wind. Brandon and Deborah remained sitting at the table. Brandon leaned back in his chair and smiled at Deborah.

"What the heck just happened?"

"I have no idea."

"Brandon! Brandon!" Don shouted from across the room, motioning for him to make his way through the crowd. They rose from the table and walked to the front to speak with him. "Look, I know this makes no sense right now, but after speaking with Senator Taylor, it was clear that having a board in the middle of the plans and decisions this is going to require would be a massive bottleneck. As Sharon said, it comes as no surprise. The feds will compensate us with future contract awards, I'm sure. I just want to wish you all the best of luck on this. It's an amazing opportunity, and if anyone is up to the task, it's you guys."

There it is again, Brandon thought, looking up at the ceiling.

"If there's anything any of us here on the board—ex-board—can do to help on the project, please don't hesitate to ask."

"Thanks, Don," Brandon said. "We appreciate that." Brandon and Deborah shook hands with Don and a few of the other members then eased their way out of the conference room.

"Mary, will you call the department heads, please?" Brandon requested as they walked by the reception desk toward the elevator. "Have them meet in my office in fifteen minutes."

★ ★ ★ ★ ★

Brandon and Deborah sat at the small conference table in Brandon's office as the department heads filed in and took their seats. After everyone seemed to be in, Sonny reached for the doorknob and looked at Brandon. He nodded, and Sonny closed the door.

"Okay folks, what questions do you have?"

After several seconds of silence, a voice came from the corner. "Is Bob's wife okay?"

Deborah's eyes welled up, and Brandon lowered his head to hide his own watery eyes. After all the chaos going on around them, the gravity of what had happened finally came rushing back to him. Hearing that this was what his team wanted to know reminded Brandon of the culture and the family Bob had created there.

He scratched his nose and cleared his throat. "Anne is doing fine. I've seen her a couple of times and will continue to check in on her. Their kids are on their way into town, so she'll be fine. Thank you for asking. What else?"

"Considering that we don't know anything," another department head said, "you should probably do all the talking."

"Yes, yes. I know."

Jimmy stood in the back corner, raising his hand. Deborah looked at Brandon, shaking her head.

"What, Jimmy?"

"Boss, does all this have anything to do with our lockdown yesterday?"

"Not really. That was just a precaution. When you told me about Bob, I got a case of the jitters. That's all there was to it."

"It sounds like the company might be growing," another manager said. "Is this going to give us an opportunity to grow as well?"

"It's possible," Deborah said. "But as always, we'll continue to work those issues through HR." She looked across the table and nodded at the Human Resources director.

"What other changes can we expect to see?" yet another voice asked.

"Well, to start with, Ms. Blanchard and I just returned from the quickest board meeting in the history of this company." He sat up straight and pulled on the lapels of his jacket to regain his composure. "Because of the complexity of this project, the board members voted to disband. We're now working directly for the feds—the Project Committee."

"Dang! That's huge," someone said.

"Speaking of huge," one of the ladies questioned, "who's that standing outside your door?" Everyone chuckled and looked at Brandon.

"Well, the president saw fit to assign a Secret Service detail to me."

"The president?"

"What?"

Chapter 6

Brandon explained what he knew about the project to date as everyone in the room took notes. "Ms. Blanchard had been working with Bob on a rough plan for the project. I'll let her go over what she knows about schedules."

"What I have is obviously very high-level," Deborah said. "I do know that we're building a city, literally from the ground up, out in the middle of nowhere. Kansas State University is in Manhattan, Kansas. Lebanon is about 150 miles northeast of there. That's Kéntro, the center. Lebanon is a small town, barely more than a ghost town, and will likely be consumed by the construction. There's a small geodetic survey monument just outside of town marking the geographic center of the continental US. We have to preserve that little park at all costs." The room remained silent. Everyone was listening intently and taking notes. Deborah took a sip of her coffee and continued.

"As Brandon mentioned down in the theater, we're going to have to build everything. There is basically no infrastructure in Lebanon. The very first thing we need to do is work with the

Department of Transportation to get a major road approved and built between Manhattan and Lebanon. That will have to happen quickly."

"The committee assures me that they will support us in whatever we need," Brandon said. "They've even promised to eliminate all of the usual government red tape to get the companies we need on contract."

"Once we have a way to get equipment up there," Deborah stated, "we can start working with the FAA to get an airport approved and under construction east of town."

"Seriously?" a voice came from the group.

"Not just an airport—an international-class airport," Deborah said.

"Holy crap."

"We can't build a metropolis until we can get equipment and supplies on site, now can we?" Deborah said with some tension in her voice.

"Keep in mind," Brandon interrupted, "that new road from Manhattan to Lebanon is just the beginning of a network of roads around the new capital. There will eventually be two major spurs between Interstate 70 and Interstate 80 crisscrossing through and centered on Lebanon. There will also be a beltway around the city—maybe even two, an inner and an outer."

"In the beginning, though," Deborah continued, "we need to stay focused on that first road between Manhattan and Lebanon and then out to the airport."

"We're already getting a lot of questions about relocation requirements," one of the department heads said. "Who is going to be required to move, and who will be able to stay here?"

"That's going to be tough to answer," Brandon said. "Ideally, we could pick up this whole building, along with all of the occupants, and drop it out there. Right now, I can see leaving a small contingent of engineers and staff out here to keep the communications going. But most of the design staff is going to have to move. I know people have lives, and honestly, if someone can't make the move, I'll have HR help them find new employment. I don't want that to come across as callous; I hope we can keep everyone. But the reality is, I don't think that's going to happen. Any more questions on that topic before we move on?" Brandon paused. "Good. Let's go through the stakeholders so we know what we're dealing with. We need to get that in the project plan upfront," Brandon said.

"I've been jotting notes about that," Deborah said. "The obvious stakeholders are the White House and the Project Committee. We also need to make early contact with the head honchos at the university. We need to make contact with the governor's office in Kansas and see what they know and what they expect. I hope the committee can streamline any bureaucracy we'll need to deal with there."

"My brother lives in Kansas," chimed one of the department heads. "He's not very impressed with the governor out there. Apparently he's a real piece of work."

"We'll have to cross that bridge when we get there," Deborah responded. "We've also got a whole laundry list of federal offices to add to the lineup. DOT, FAA, GSA, DOE. You name it. A veritable alphabet soup." The group laughed.

"Who's against us?" someone asked loudly, above the noise. The room fell silent.

"What's that?" Brandon asked.

"Who's against us? You've got a bodyguard standing outside your door. Who's against us?" Everyone's head rose from their notebooks and looked at Brandon.

"Look, you guys have heard it all on the news. Most of the D.C. insiders don't want this to happen. The lobbyists and other power brokers in town are livid. It's the Committee and the rest of the country demanding this change. Well, except for much of California and New York. But you know how that goes."

"Is this firm in danger?" a department head asked.

"I don't think so," Brandon said. "The FBI is watching things closely, I'm told. Sonny was assigned to me mostly because of Bob and my family. Bob died of a heart attack, but I guess they don't want to take any chances. We're fine. I'll keep checking back with the White House."

"Okay, you guys," Deborah said. "Go back to your offices and start brainstorming on this stuff. What are you going to need? What do we need to consider for each of your elements? Jimmy, start developing a work breakdown structure for the plan. I'll have HR get to work on arranging any transfers we need to make and coordinating housing. We might be able to pull some employees from the engineering school out there at the university. Okay, let's go!" Everyone left the room with a buzz.

"Brandon, can I speak to you for a minute?" Jimmy asked.

"I suppose. Deborah, will you close the door behind you, please?"

"Sure." She smiled back at Brandon as she left.

"What's up?" he said as the door latched. "Have a seat."

Jimmy returned to his chair and leaned his back against the table. "Well. Uh, you know that Bob was grooming me for that deputy position, right?"

"Jimmy, look. I have no idea what you and Bob had worked out for your future. Apparently, you had earned his trust. But my trust is in Deborah. She has already been working on the plans for this project, and we've worked closely together for a long time."

"You don't think I've earned it?"

"Maybe you have, Jimmy. I don't know. We're all going to be busy. Just keep your head down, and do your job. There are going to be plenty of growth opportunities in this company in the very near future. Hang in there, okay?"

"That job is rightfully mine, Brandon."

"I'm sorry, Jimmy. Let's stay focused on the project, okay?" Brandon stood and reached for Jimmy's hand.

Jimmy stood and shook it half-heartedly. "Okay. That's fine. Thanks, Brandon. But Bob respected me, you know. He wanted me to play a bigger role here." Brandon nodded. Just as Jimmy left Brandon's office, the intercom buzzed.

"Now what?" Brandon growled as he walked around his desk and pressed the button. "Yes, Mary."

"Sir, Senator Sanders's office is on the line."

"Sanders? Oh, jeez, put 'em through."

"Mr. McStocker, please hold for Senator Sanders," a voice requested. Brandon sat and turned to gaze out of the window.

"Mr. McStocker?"

"Yes, Senator. What can I do for you today, sir?"

The senator wasted no time getting to the point. "Brandon, I understand the president has you chasing down one of his ridiculous pipe dreams."

"Well, I don't know about all that, sir. But we've been contracted to lead the Kéntro Project, if that's what you mean."

"I wouldn't waste much time on it, son. We're gonna stop this madness."

"Sir, that's way above my pay grade. All I know is what my marching orders are from the Committee. I intend to press on accordingly. I hope you understand, sir."

"This is going to stop."

"Sir, since I have you on the phone, do you have someone on your staff named Denny?" Brandon recalled the man Anne had mentioned visiting Bob a while back.

"This is going to stop, McStocker. You can see it all on the six o'clock news."

The line went silent.

CHAPTER 7

Brandon and Cassandra sat in a quiet booth and placed their order. The lunch crowd had already come and gone, so it was a good time to relax and catch up.

"I didn't see your car when I came in. Where did you park?" Cassandra asked.

"Oh, yeah. That." Brandon smiled.

"What?"

"See that black limousine out there with the big guy sitting behind the wheel?"

"Uh, yeah."

"That's me."

"What?"

"Yeah. Now that the president has me heading up this project, he thought it would be prudent to assign a Secret Service detail to us."

"Prudent," she repeated. "Us? Who's us?"

"Well, Sonny out there is assigned to me. Apparently he has two others on his detail to keep an eye on you and the girls from a distance."

"Get out. Are you serious? You mean we're going to have strangers in suits following us around everywhere we go?"

"No, the president assured me that it wouldn't be like that. I'm not sure how all that's going to work. Sonny will introduce the others whenever we can get together at the house."

"Oh, I'm sure the girls will think it's the greatest thing since sliced bread, but I, for one, am not interested in the least. Are we really in danger?"

"No. The president simply sees it as a precaution. No big deal." Brandon told Cassandra about his hectic day while they ate their lunch, save the part about Senator Sanders calling and giving him a hard time. They walked to the cash register, and Brandon paid the check.

"Follow me out, and I'll introduce you to Sonny." They put on their coats and walked out to the parking lot. Sonny saw them coming and got out of the car to greet them.

"Hey, Sonny. This is my wife, Cassandra. Honey, this is Agent Sonny Langston."

"It's a pleasure to meet you, Agent Langston," Cassandra said. "Welcome to the family?" They chuckled, and their breath was visible as it escaped in the cold air.

"The pleasure is mine, ma'am. Thank you. Please, call me Sonny."

"Of course, Sonny. Listen, would you and the other two members of your detail like to join us for supper tonight? Say around six o'clock?" Brandon looked at her, amused.

"That's very nice of you, ma'am, but highly unusual and certainly against protocol."

"Honey, they can't do that," Brandon said.

"Nonsense! I'm not going to have strangers hanging around my house and my children. I don't think that's asking too much. Do you?" She looked at Brandon with tears welling in her eyes.

"That would be very nice, ma'am. Yes. Thank you." Sonny glanced at Brandon then turned and walked to the back of the car. He opened the door for Brandon. "Back to your office, sir?"

Cassandra elbowed Brandon in the side, her tears turning to laughter. "Impressive."

"Oh, hush." He leaned over and kissed her. "I'll see you later this afternoon."

"Okay, babe. Good to meet you, Sonny."

"You as well, ma'am."

★ ★ ★ ★ ★

"Six o'clock on the nose," Cassandra said when the doorbell rang.

Six o'clock. That's right, Brandon recalled. *Sanders mentioned I'd see something on the news tonight.*

"We'll get it, we'll get it," Olivia and Susan shouted, running recklessly to the front door. They both froze when Susan pulled the door open.

"Whoa," Olivia said. She and her sister stepped back and looked up at two men and a woman, all very tall, impeccably well-dressed in black, and not smiling . . . at all.

"And who might you be?" Sonny asked, reaching down to shake Olivia's hand. He finally smiled a bit.

"Uh, I'm Olivia. This is my sister, Susan. You can call me Liv." She reached up and shook his hand.

"Hello, Susan," Sonny said, reaching over to shake her hand.

"No. That's not happening." Susan pulled her hand behind her back, turned, and walked back into the house.

"Susan, you little brat," Cassandra shouted as she walked into the entryway. "Hi, Sonny. Don't mind her. Come on in. I'm so glad you were able to get permission to join us." The three agents entered the house. Olivia ran into the kitchen to join her sister.

"Hi, I'm Cassandra McStocker." She extended her hand to each of the two other agents. "Welcome to our home."

"Mrs. McStocker, this is Agent Natasha Simpson and Agent Gary Davis," Sonny said.

"It's a pleasure to meet you both. Thanks for coming."

Everyone retreated to the dining room, where Cassandra introduced the other two agents to Brandon. After several minutes of small talk, they sat at the table.

"Isn't that TV a little loud?" Cassandra asked Brandon over the noise.

"I just want to find out what Sanders is talking about. Sorry about the TV, you guys. I'm trying to get a handle on some news. Do you mind if we say grace over the food?"

"Oh, not at all, sir. Please do," Sonny said.

Everyone held hands. Susan was sitting next to Sonny. She looked up at him and furrowed her brows, trying to make a mean face, then tentatively put her hand in his and bowed her head.

"You better stop it, young lady," Cassandra demanded. Sonny smiled down at Susan then lowered his head. After the prayer, they began passing the dishes of food around the table.

"Have you ever shot anyone?"

"Susan!" Cassandra shouted. Olivia could barely control her snickering.

"It's fine, Mrs. McStocker." Sonny said. "How about we save all that for another day?" he said to Susan. How old are you girls, anyway?"

"I'm thirteen," Susan replied.

"I'm fifteen," Olivia followed.

"Wow, two teenagers," Agent Simpson said, finally smiling. "Have you decided what you're going to be when you grow up?"

"A project manager, like my daddy."

"Really? Do you even know what that is?"

"Yes," Olivia said. "He makes things happen." Everyone laughed and continued to eat.

"How about you, Susan?" Agent Davis asked.

Susan looked up from her plate with a deadpan stare. "I want to be president . . . or a musician."

"Really now?" Sonny said. "Maybe you could be both."

"Listen!" Brandon shouted. "There it is." He jumped up from the table and ran to the living room.

"Brandon, please!" Cassandra begged. Everyone else remained at the table but sat quietly, listening to the news report.

"They're all standing out on the steps of the Capitol," Brandon shouted. "It's Sanders, of course."

"We have it on reliable insider information that the president and his henchmen are planning to abuse the powers provided by the 28th Amendment to rebuild the entire federal government," Sanders said. "This is madness. The president has clearly lost his mind and is using his office to perpetrate one of the biggest crimes ever against this nation."

"Okay. Whatever." Brandon pressed the Off button on the remote control. "Sorry, you guys. I just wanted to see if he had anything up his sleeve. Same old rhetoric, don't you think, Sonny?"

"Yes, sir."

"Mom, can I be excused to go upstairs and do my homework?" Susan asked.

"You mean play your guitar, don't you?" Olivia laughed.

"No. I don't mean that," Susan retorted.

"Girls, stop!" Cassandra scolded. "Susan, you go upstairs. Liv, it's your turn to do the dishes."

"Oh, Mom!"

"Don't do it," Cassandra said holding her index finger up to Olivia. She looked at Brandon, and he smiled.

Olivia looked at her dad, hoping for an override, but he simply turned his head.

"Oh, alright," Olivia relented. Susan sprang to her feet and ran up the steps. The agents laughed and continued to eat.

Brandon's cell phone started vibrating on the cabinet, where he had placed it. He looked at Cassandra and shook his head.

"You better get it," she said.

CHAPTER 8

Brandon and Deborah had been summoned to the capital the following Monday. They were to make a presentation to a combined session of the Kéntro Project Committee and the House Ways and Means Committee to go over the project plan.

Once they were around the table, Brandon introduced Deborah. "She will walk us through the project charter and plan."

"Thank you, Mr. McStocker. You may proceed, Ms. Blanchard."

"Thank you, Senator Taylor." Deborah flipped over the cover page of the six-inch-thick unbound document in front of her. "I've asked several of the interns to pass around copies of this plan. When we wrap up here, you can leave them on the table, and we will make sure they get to each of your offices." Deborah stood so she could more easily look down onto the massive project plan and began flipping the front matter over onto the table. After several minutes of preparatory comments, killing time while the copies got passed around, she started her presentation.

"On page two, you will see a map of the area in Kansas where the construction will take place. On the screen, we are projecting the same map where we will zoom in so you can see an animation of the time-lapse construction progress in a few minutes. The project will require four phases. Construction is Phase Two. Phase One will be the layout and basic infrastructure development so we can get equipment and supplies to the site. It will include the first roadway from Manhattan into the area and the first runway of a new airport. Phase Two begins construction of the city itself. Phase Three is the physical relocation of all federal agencies to their new homes—"

"Wait!" a member interrupted. "Madam Chair, we aren't just taking the rotten apples out of one barrel and putting them in the new barrel, are we?"

"No, Henry," Senator Taylor said. "All of the elected members of Congress and their staff will obviously have to move. The president and most of the staff from the White House will go as well, along with all of his administration. Unelected offices will be up for discussion. We have to do all we can to eliminate the apples you are concerned about, but that's going to take the help of the White House and the citizens of this country."

"Yes, ma'am."

"Ms. Blanchard, please continue."

"Thank you. During the move in Phase Three, there will still be a lot of construction going on around the city. We will be coordinating with the private sector to ensure that the construction of retail space and services is accomplished with as little interference as possible. Once the office complexes in D.C. are vacated, Phase Four will be the orderly dismantling of Washington, D.C."

"Wait, what?" One of the members jumped to her feet. "How can that be? Who approved that?"

"Shirley, please be seated," Senator Taylor said. "It was determined early on by the White House that there would be no logical purpose to keep the federal infrastructure intact in D.C. We will keep the historical markers in place along with their associated park areas and, of course, the museums and other tourist sites. But it would be impractical to try to find a new purpose for the White House, the Capitol building, and the Pentagon—the core government facilities. All of those old buildings are falling apart anyway and need to be taken down. The country needs to know with complete clarity that this administration is resolute in getting this shift done. The shift they demanded. Beyond that, Shirley, the decision is not within the jurisdiction of Ways and Means."

The joint committee continued to meet for five days as Brandon and Deborah went over different parts of the project plan in detail. A few of those days went late into the evening. Shortly after 9:00 p.m. on the fifth day, Deborah flipped over the last page to the back cover of the document and took her seat.

"Thank you, Senator. To close, we would like to run a simulation on the front screen. This is a view of the infrastructure that has to be built before construction of city center can even begin." She pressed her remote, and the map of northern Kansas and southern Nebraska appeared. A red line began to squiggle its way from Interstate 70 at Manhattan to the northwest and stopped at Lebanon, where a small circle appeared. Brandon explained, "This is the first stretch of the new interstate that will enter in to gain access to the site. The circle is the first beltway around the city. The airport will go in just east of there."

Deborah pressed her remote again, and the red line continued to travel northwest until it stopped at Interstate 80 in Lexington, Nebraska. Brandon continued, "This is the first leg of the major throughway." Once again, Deborah pressed the remote, and a new red line popped up in Lincoln, Nebraska and proceeded southwest from Interstate 80 to meet up with the beltway in Lebanon. The line then continued southwest until it stopped at Interstate 70 in Colby, Kansas.

"Well, *X* indeed marks the spot," one of the members shouted. The room filled with tired laughter.

"It sure does," Senator Wilhelm said. "Turns out, it's a cross, marking the center of the country."

"A national cross like this is the most efficient way for all parts of the country to gain access to the new capital," Deborah pointed out.

"National cross. I like that," Senator Taylor said. "National cross it is. Ms. Blanchard. Mr. McStocker. The work you and your firm have done here is nothing short of amazing. I can see why the president has placed his trust in you." Brandon and Deborah nodded and started packing away the material they had amassed on the table in front of them. "Before we adjourn, there are a few important items I need to share with everyone, including our guests from Mack & Mack. Please, can I get everyone's attention?" The members thought they were finished, and the buzz of completion and handshaking had already begun. Those standing returned to their seats, and the room quieted once again.

"Ladies and gentlemen, this will just take a few more minutes of your time, and it is important. Thank you. This committee met several times in closed session before we started this review of the project plan. Then we met with the president last night after our session here, where we have agreed on several major issues that will be declared under executive order. It is clear from the plans that Mr. McStocker and Ms. Blanchard shared that the little town of Lebanon is going to be swallowed up by this construction. Therefore, we think it is only fitting that the twenty square miles authorized by the 28th Amendment will be called Lebanon, Kéntro District or Lebanon, K.D."

"What does Kéntro even mean?" one of the members asked.

"It's Greek," Senator Taylor said. "It means *the center*. The president also agrees that because of the size and complexity of the Kéntro Project, this committee's status should be elevated to an office in his administration. It will be the National Transition Office. Sometime during the next week, this committee will be disbanded, and all documents in our possession will be turned over to that office. We should also congratulate Senator Ron Wilhelm, who has been named to head that office." The room managed a tired applause as everyone stood. Brandon and Deborah looked over at Senator Wilhelm and added nods and smiles to their applause.

Senator Wilhelm acknowledged the accolades and motioned for everyone to stop. He then leaned toward Brandon's shoulder. "Can you two hang around for a few minutes after everyone's gone? I'll fill you in a little on what's going on." Brandon and Deborah both nodded.

Senator Taylor finished, "Ladies and gentlemen, thank you for your time and your service to this committee. We are adjourned, and you are dismissed." A dull roar came over the room as everyone returned to shaking hands and conversing as they filed out of the double doors into the hallway. When the room had cleared, Senator Wilhelm walked from the door back to the conference table and sat down. His smile left him. Brandon and Deborah already had their coats on and were standing with their packed briefcases next to the cart Deborah brought in.

"Sorry I didn't tell you guys that whole National Transition Office thing was coming. The president is working hard to keep this project close to the White House. He was already starting to lose faith in this committee. Even Senator Taylor encouraged him to disband it."

"We're glad you have the reins in a more official capacity now," Brandon said.

"You guys did a great job on this project plan. I'll be using it as the foundation to build out the charter for my office. For now, though, you two get some rest. You deserve it." Brandon pulled the vibrating phone from his coat pocket and read the text out loud.

"Reinforcements." He smiled. "It's Cassandra. That's our code for there's an issue with one of the girls. That usually means Susan, our youngest."

Deborah put her hand on Brandon's arm. "Is everything okay?"

"It's fine. If it were urgent, she would have added a 911 to it. But still, I should probably get home."

"Go," Senator Wilhelm said as he stood and picked up his briefcase. "Get home and take care of your family."

Sonny was waiting outside the front door with Brandon's car as the three of them exited the building together.

"Good night," Brandon said. "Deb, let's just take the weekend off and try to clear our heads. You did a fine job in there this week. I'll see you at the office bright and early Monday morning."

"Thank you. Sounds good," she said as she took her car keys from the valet.

Shortly after leaving D.C., Brandon noticed Sonny watching his rearview mirror with unusual intensity. "Everything okay?" Brandon asked.

"Fine, sir. It's nothing." The drive home was quiet, but Sonny continued to stare into the mirror. Brandon trusted that it was nothing to be concerned about. He laid his head back and closed his eyes. "Here you go, sir," Sonny said as he pulled into the driveway. Both of them walked to the front door. A car drove by the house and slowed down but then rushed off.

"What the heck was that?"

"I don't know, sir, but I'll hang around out here for awhile before I head home. Would you like me to post a car out here?"

"No. We'll be fine. I plan to be in all weekend, but if we decide to go anywhere, I'll let you know."

"Yes, sir. Goodnight." Brandon walked in the front door and heard Cassandra and the girls talking in the kitchen.

"I told you that you couldn't just do that," Cassandra said as Brandon entered the room, laying his coat and briefcase on the countertop.

"Daddy, I need your help here," Susan said.

Cassandra dropped her jaw and looked at Susan then over at Brandon. She was shocked yet almost smiling in amusement. Susan's face was dead serious.

"Oh, do you now?" Brandon said.

"I want to take guitar lessons. Mom says I can't take guitar lessons until I start doing my homework without a fight. Why do I need to do homework if I'm just going to be a musician?" Brandon looked at Cassandra. She peered at him with her eyebrows raised.

"Honey, it's good that you want to learn to play your guitar better, but you have to do your homework. Liv always does hers as soon as she gets home from school. If you do it that way, you'll have it out of the way and can practice your guitar all you want."

"Liv is a nerd," Susan said with a laugh.

"Hey!" Olivia picked up a wet dishcloth from the sink and threw it across the kitchen at Susan. Susan raised her arms, but the cloth made its way through and splatted her on the face.

"Olivia!" Cassandra yelled.

They all laughed as Susan cocked her arm to throw it back. Brandon grabbed the cloth from behind her and tossed it back into the sink. "Stop, you two." He looked intently at Susan and pointed toward the chair. "Sit down here. Have you done your homework yet today?"

"She has not," Cassandra chimed in. Susan shook her head no.

Brandon continued. "Go up to your room and do your home-work—"

Olivia stuck her tongue out at Susan, and they both smiled.

"—and tomorrow morning, I'll play guitar with you a little bit. If you show your mom that you can do your homework with-out giving her a hard time for one month, we'll talk about guitar lessons. Deal?"

"Okay, Daddy. But I still don't know why I have to go to school. They aren't teaching me anything I need to know."

"Now you're just being silly. Do we have a deal?"

"Okay, Daddy." Susan left the kitchen and ran up the stairs to her room.

"Liv, you go on upstairs too, sweetie. Your mom and I need to talk."

"Okay, Daddy."

Olivia was barely out of the kitchen when Cassandra asserted, "Brandon, I'm not moving these girls to Kansas. It's insane." They went into the living room and talked for over two hours. Brandon explained what had transpired at the meetings earlier that day.

"Can't they find somebody else to do this?"

"Honey, you know they can't. We're already up to our ears in it, and the White House wants to get moving."

"I know. I know. But I love this house, Brandon, and I love this town. I just can't do it. If we move these girls to Kansas, Susan is going to check out altogether."

Then they fell silent. Brandon looked at the ceiling trying to think of a solution. "I guess I'll just get an apartment out there and go back and forth for awhile until we see how it's going to work." The text chime went off on Brandon's phone. Cassandra rolled her eyes and stared into the flames dancing in the fireplace. "It's from Senator Wilhelm," Brandon said.

"Of course it is."

"It just says, 'turn on the news.'" Brandon stood and picked up the remote control from the coffee table and turned on the TV. It was a scene shot from the steps of the Capitol building once again. Senator Sanders was talking, but the voice was that of a commentator.

"Sources from inside the firm tell Channel 8 News that meetings are already underway to plan this move of the capital to Kansas. Let's break in and listen to what Senator Sanders has to say."

"What the heck," Brandon murmured.

"Senator Sanders! Senator Sanders! What can you tell us about this announcement?" The reporter pressed in through the crowd, extending a microphone into the senator's face.

"This is an insane move by the White House and its administration to destroy this country once and for all. We will take this to the Supreme Court, if necessary. They've taken the new amendment completely out of context and are using it to relocate the nation's capital in its entirety. This move is not what the amendment was about. We will stop this!"

"Senator, did your source at McClellan & McStocker tell you where exactly they plan to move to?"

"I think we'll be getting more information early next week," the senator answered with a subtle grin.

"What a jerk," Brandon said. "I don't get it. What in the world is going on? What source?" Brandon's phone chimed. "Wilhelm again. The president wants to see us first thing Monday."

Cassandra took the remote from Brandon and turned off the TV. "Honey, I'm scared."

CHAPTER 9

The next morning, Brandon did his best to keep his mind off work but with little success. After breakfast, he went to Susan's room and taught her some chords on the guitar. The sun had come out, and the wind finally died down. The family spent that afternoon in the backyard, stacking a load of firewood dumped there earlier in the week. Saturdays were movie night, so that evening, they gathered around the large flat-screen TV to watch hours of old classics on Netflix.

After church on Sunday morning, Cassandra saw Deborah standing in the foyer near the front door.

"Hey, girl! Cassandra shouted.

"Hey, Cass, how are you doing?" Deborah hugged her then turned to Brandon. "Good morning," she said. "Are you getting rest?" She reached up for a hug.

"I suppose."

"Have you been watching the news at all?"

"Not since Friday night."

"It scared me too much to keep watching it," Cassandra said.

"I understand," Deborah said. "What the heck is all that about calling us out?" She looked back at Brandon.

"I don't know. I'm going with Wilhelm to see the president in the morning. I suspect he's going to want to move quickly."

"I need to go get the girls," Cassandra said. "I'm sure their class is out by now."

"Well, you guys enjoy your Sunday. I'll see you back at the office in the morning, whenever you get there."

"Okay, Deb," Brandon said. "You get some rest, too. It's going to be a long week."

★ ★ ★ ★ ★

"Good morning, Mr. President," Brandon said as he walked into the Oval Office.

"Brandon. Come in." The president stuck his head out the door before Brandon had a chance to close it. "Would you have Ms. Whiting come in, please," he said to his secretary. He then closed the door.

Brandon went to the couch, where Senator Wilhelm stood to shake his hand.

"Thanks for coming, gents. Please, have a seat. What do we know about that media fiasco Friday night?"

Wilhelm looked at Brandon.

"Oh, uh . . . I don't know what to make of it, sir," Brandon said. "But I'll see if I can figure out what's going on when I get to my office."

"It's time the public learns about what's going on," the president said. "But those guys were using some pretty specific language, don't you think?"

"Yes, sir. They were." Wilhelm scowled at Brandon. Brandon shrugged his shoulders. There was a soft knock on the door to the Oval Office, then it opened.

"Sir, Ms. Whiting."

"Angela. Please, come in." The president stood and walked to greet her. The other two men stood as well. "Gentlemen, this is Secretary of Education, Angela Whiting. I asked Ms. Whiting to come down and brief you on your accommodations at Kansas State. Angela, what have you learned?"

"Sir, the school has been very cooperative and quite generous," she said. "They have agreed to vacate the top floor of Rathbone Hall on campus. It's a major facility within the College of Engineering. They've also agreed to share lab space and even some faculty if needed. They will block off one of the parking lots and reserve it for your people." She looked at Brandon. "I'll have my office send you a floor plan with the total square footage and the office and conference room dimensions."

"Thanks. I appreciate that," Brandon said. "How long can we stay?"

"Indefinitely. The president of the school said you can stay as long as you need. They're just finishing up a new engineering building and have already started moving in there. We'll pick up the tab for your rent."

"Thanks, Angela," the president said. "I appreciate your help."

"My pleasure, Mr. President." The president walked with her to the door and returned to the conversation.

"Mr. President," Brandon began, "have we learned anything about Bob McClellan's death?"

"I haven't heard anything, Brandon. As far as I know, it was a heart attack. I've heard nothing more. We're still waiting on the pathology report. Why do you ask?"

"Something has been eating at me," he said. "Something his wife Anne told me. Apparently, not long before Bob died, he had a visitor to their house. I mean, he had clients and employees to their house all the time, but for Anne to notice this one particular visitor and then tell me about it just feels off. Is there any investigation going on?"

"I'll have someone check into it."

"Thank you, sir. I guess his name was Denny. I asked Senator Sanders about him, but he dodged the question."

"How's Sonny and his team working out for you?"

"It hasn't been the strain that I thought it might be. My youngest, Susan, is giving them a run for their money, but they seem to be taking her in stride."

"Good. Have you started preparing for the move yet?"

"Not really, sir."

"Are you going to buy a house out there for your family? We can help with that."

"Well, sir, Cassandra and I aren't thrilled about the idea of pulling the girls out of school and uprooting them. We may just leave things the way they are and see how the project unfolds out west."

"I understand. I'm sorry you have to go through all this. Just know that your sacrifice for this country is deeply appreciated. Of course, we'll cover any accommodations you need out there."

"Thank you, sir."

★ ★ ★ ★ ★

"Sonny, I need to get over to the Bob's memorial service. Are your people with Cassandra and the girls?" Brandon asked.

"Yes, sir. They're meeting us at the church."

Brandon pulled his phone from his coat pocket and called the office. "Mary, put me through to Ms. Blanchard, please."

"Deb, is everyone going to the memorial service?"

"Pretty much."

"That's good. Let's go ahead and shut it down. Give everyone the afternoon off."

"Okay. I'll get the word out. How was your meeting with the president?"

"Well, everyone seems anxious to get us moved out to Kansas." Brandon noticed Sonny's concentration on the rearview mirror. He held the phone to his chest.

"Again?" he said to Sonny, looking at him in the mirror.

"Afraid so, sir."

"Deb, we've got someone tailing us again. Go ahead and lock the place up, and I'll see you at the church."

"Okay, Brandon. You guys be careful."

Brandon hadn't had time to put his phone back in his pocket when it vibrated. It was Cassandra. "Hey, honey. What's up? Are you on your way?"

"We are. We're in the car with Natasha and Gary."

"Who's driving?"

"Gary is."

"Okay, let me speak to Natasha."

"Here she is."

"Yes, sir?" Natasha said.

"Natasha, we're being followed again. I know you don't want to freak out the kids, but have you seen any indications?"

"Uh . . . yes, sir. We are, too."

"Okay. Just get my family to the church, and keep it low-key."

"Yes, sir. We're only about ten minutes out." She handed the phone back to Cassandra.

"We'll see you there," Brandon said.

"Okay, honey."

Agent Simpson raised her wrist to her mouth and whispered into the sleeve of her coat. "Is he nervous?"

"Maybe a little," Sonny answered in a low voice. He looked into the rearview mirror and watched Brandon return the phone to his coat pocket.

When they arrived at the church, Sonny pulled the car up to the front door where Cassandra and the girls were standing and talking to Pastor Carl. Sonny tried to get around the car to open Brandon's door, but he was already getting out.

"It's okay, Sonny," Brandon said. "I can open the door myself. I'll text you when we're almost ready to go."

"Yes, sir."

Cassandra and Carl were chuckling at Brandon when he joined them.

"What?"

"Oh, you," Cassandra said. "He's just trying to do his job, opening your door."

"Oh, that. I know, I know. I just can't get used to this whole driver thing. Hi, sweet girls," he said, stooping to hug Olivia and Susan. He then hugged Cassandra and shook hands with Carl. "Have you seen Anne yet?"

"No," Cassandra said. "We just got here a minute ago."

"She's up in the front pew," Carl said.

Brandon, Cassandra, and the girls entered through the massive front doors of the church building and walked the center aisle toward the front. Brandon looked around to see who he knew but couldn't escape the notion that he wanted to see if there was anyone suspicious in the sanctuary. He wasn't expecting to see a Secret Service detail in the room. There were four, what he presumed to be agents, posted around the perimeter of the room. *Could they be any more conspicuous?* he thought. The family walked around the front pew and greeted Anne and her children. Cassandra kneeled in front of Anne and held both of her hands.

"I love you," she said. "And we loved Bob. He was such a good man."

Anne couldn't speak, but she smiled at Cassandra and then looked up at Brandon as he leaned down to kiss her on the forehead.

"We'll be right behind you," Brandon said.

Anne nodded, still unable to speak. Olivia and Susan laid their heads in Anne's lap and wrapped their arms around her waist. She rubbed their heads and dabbed her upper lip with a handkerchief.

The McStockers sat down in the pew behind Anne. Carl walked up to her and leaned down to greet her again before climbing the steps to take a seat behind the pulpit. A vocalist sang, standing at the edge of the platform. When she finished, Carl stood and walked to the pulpit.

"We have gathered here today to celebrate the life of a great man, friend, and member of this congregation: Bob McClellan."

The service continued a little over an hour as family and friends shared eulogies and funny stories. Brandon couldn't help but watch the two agents sitting at the far right and left ends of the front pews. His thoughts then turned to his friend, Bob. What a journey they had traveled together, building the company and enjoying the friendship his family shared with the McClellans. *The truth is*, Brandon thought, *Bob was like a father to me and a grandfather to Liv and Susan.* Bob had created a company based on integrity, and Brandon expected nothing less of himself. He shook his head then looked straight up at the ceiling of the sanctuary, tears welling in his eyes. Cassandra took his hand and gently laid it in her lap, then wrapped her other arm around both girls.

CHAPTER 10

B randon and Deborah walked up the sidewalk to Anderson Hall, a grand, stone, castle-like facility at Kansas State University. Their appointment was at 9:00 a.m., and they arrived with several minutes to spare. They walked in the front door, and the receptionist pointed them to the president's office. Another receptionist sat outside his door. She greeted them then picked up the phone to report their arrival.

"Mr. Freeman will see you now. You can go right in." The door opened and out walked a tall, gray-haired man. He extended his hand to greet Deborah and then Brandon. Their attention was immediately drawn to his bright purple tie.

"Come in. Come in," he said. "Daniel Freeman. Welcome to K-State."

"Thank you for meeting with us, Mr. Freeman. I'm Brandon McStocker, and this is my deputy, Deborah Blanchard."

"Please. Call me Dan. Have a seat. My assistant is on her way. Coffee? We have tea or water out there, too."

"No, thanks," Brandon said. Deborah smiled and shook her head no. Freeman began telling them about the campus. They looked around his office at the photos and banners. There was purple everywhere. They heard a tap on the door, and a younger blonde woman walked in wearing a purple dress suit and carrying a notebook and pen.

"Come on in, Sandy," Dan said. "Brandon McStocker, Deborah Blanchard, this is my assistant, Sandy Laughlin." Everyone shook hands then sat at a small, round conference table in the corner of the office.

"Let me just say what an honor it is to be hosting this historic project right here at K-State," Dan said. "When the secretary of education called me several months ago, I was tickled at what she was asking me. This is a win for everyone."

"We agree wholeheartedly," Brandon said.

"Thank you so much for allowing us to set up shop here," Deborah said. "We'll try not to be a burden. I'm not completely sure yet how many personnel will be moving here, but it could be a substantial number."

"Think nothing of it," Sandy said. "The top floor of Rathbone Hall has already been vacated, and there is plenty of office furniture up there. We can walk up there and have a look around when we're finished here. Is there anything specific you think you might need that we can help with?"

"Well, we're going to need an admin assistant first thing," Deborah said.

"I'll get you in touch with a temp agency," Sandy said. "They can set up a temp-to-hire if you like, or however you want to do it. We've had good luck with them." Dan and Sandy continued telling the visitors about the campus and the town of Manhattan for over an hour before finally drawing the meeting to a close.

"Ready for a stroll over to Rathbone?" Sandy asked.

Deborah closed her notebook and stood. "Sounds great."

"Well, I'll leave you three to it," Dan said. "Enjoy your visit. Sandy will be your point person for the university. She'll set you up with whatever you need. But if I can help in any way, just give me a call."

As the three slowly walked down the sidewalk toward Rathbone Hall, Sandy described the campus layout and shared some of the history of the school.

"If you want some awesome ice cream, you'll want to pay a visit to Call Hall." She laughed when she explained that they shouldn't be surprised when they hear "Wabash Cannonball" being sung somewhere on campus. "It's a thing," she said as they all chuckled. They arrived at Rathbone Hall with its vast concrete and stone columns holding a massive array of glass. They entered the main doors and rode the elevator to the top floor.

"This is still home base for the College of Engineering," Sandy said. "The students know you're coming and are pretty excited about it. You'll find that it's a mixed bag of political leanings, but pretty much everyone supports the big move."

"That's good to hear." Brandon let out a sigh of relief. The elevator doors opened on the third floor, and Sandy led them down the hall to a corner office complex.

"You can look around, but I assumed you would want this area for your executive offices.

"It does seem to be laid out well for it," Deborah said. She looked at Brandon. "I think we should set up a reception area back down there in front of the elevator door."

"Good idea."

"Our Maintenance Department is standing by to assist you in any way they can. I'll give you the name and number of the supervisor. If you give him a diagram of the layout you want, his crew can relocate the wall dividers and furniture however you like. We're going to split off the phone system and put a call server up here so your phones will be completely independent of the school's. The IT guys will reset the phones once the floor layout is finished."

"You folks are being so gracious," Brandon said. "We appreciate the warm welcome and all of your help."

"Mr. McStocker, this is the biggest thing to happen around here in years. The support will grow, I assure you. I know this is going to be your home for several years, so when you leave here, we want you to go with fond memories."

When their visit was over, Brandon and Deborah bade farewell to Sandy, climbed into their rental car, and drove off campus. Sonny wanted to go to Manhattan with them, but Brandon insisted that they go alone so as not to draw unnecessary attention to themselves. The two compared notes and shared their excitement about their new temporary home as Brandon drove around the streets of Manhattan.

"That was a little weird, don't you think?" Brandon asked.

"What do you mean?"

"It all just seemed a little too sweet and perfect for my taste."

"Maybe. But we're in the Midwest now. This isn't the beltway."

"I suppose. Hungry?"

"I'm starving," Deborah said. "Let's check out one of the local places." They were nearing the north end of town when Brandon saw a flashing EAT sign ahead and on the left side of the road. As they got closer to the restaurant, Deborah read another sign on the front of the building.

"Barney's Diner. Looks interesting. What do you think?"

"I think we're almost out of town. We better take what we can get."

Brandon pulled the car into the small parking lot on the edge of the road. The chrome facade looked like something right out of the fifties. The age of the building and all the fixtures made it entirely likely that it was. A bell rang overhead as Brandon opened the front door for Deborah to walk inside.

"Afternoon, folks," an elderly lady said from behind the long counter. "Just grab a seat anywhere. I'll be right with you." Three men sat on round stools at the counter, and eight or ten other people sat at the chrome and Formica tables. The two wandered to the end of the restaurant and sat at the table next to a window. The old vinyl-covered chairs squeaked as they sat and adjusted their weight.

"There's a jukebox over there," Brandon said. "We can dance."

"Shut up," Deborah grinned.

"What can I get for you folks today?" the waitress asked.

They each ordered BLTs with fries and iced tea and continued to discuss the move as they ate. Brandon drew a rough floor lay-out on a napkin based on what they had just seen on campus. An hour had passed, and the table had already been cleared when they decided to leave.

"What's the quickest way to Lebanon from here?" Brandon asked the waitress.

"Hon, there ain't no quick way to Lebanon from here. What in the world you goin' up there for, anyway? You got family up there?"

Deborah smiled. Brandon grinned as well. "No, ma'am. We just want to take a drive and check that area out."

"I suppose," she said. "Get on 24 out here, and head up toward Turtle Creek Lake then out to Riley. Highway 24 splits off out there somewhere. You'll have to turn left. I think the sign says Clay Center. Go way on past that, and after you pass Waconda Lake on the left, you'll take a right when you get to Downs. That'll take you right into Lebanon. Only thing there is that old monument. Center of the country, you know."

Brandon looked at Deborah and chuckled. "Oh, we know." They returned to their car, and Brandon drove back out onto Highway 24, turning left to go north. It wasn't long before the four lanes reduced to two, and they were driving off into the vastness of the Midwest—slow rolling hills of empty fields, sand and gravel pits, and crops—a mix of barren brown dirt and lush green wooded areas.

After two and a half hours on the road, they arrived at the town of Lebanon. At first, the only sign of any business activity at all was the grain bins and silos south of town.

"Oh my," Deborah said as they passed by rows of tired, old houses, clearly lived-in but with sagging rooftops, doors, and windows barely hanging on. "I had no idea." They turned off the main road and followed the sign that said "Business District." They drove toward some silos and began to see activity. They turned left onto Main Street and went through the downtown area. All of about 800 feet of it—a bank, a post office, a market, and a few more old buildings—mostly boarded up. They didn't say a word as they drove through town. It wasn't long before they were back in a residential area. Once again, big and mostly tattered houses lined the streets. Only a couple were freshly painted and well maintained. At the end of Main Street stood a couple of old schoolhouses.

Brandon drove back out onto the main road and continued north of town until he saw the sign he was looking for—"Geographic Center of the Continental U.S.A." He turned left and headed toward the monument. When they arrived, they got out of the car and walked the grounds.

"And here we are," Brandon said. "The center of the center."

"Kéntro," Deborah said in a quiet, reverent voice, barely audible over the howling wind. A brass plaque embedded in a ten-foot-high stone monument had been installed by the US Coast and Geodetic Survey and marked the center. There was a flagpole on top, flying both the US and Kansas flags. There was also an awkwardly tiny chapel on the grounds that appeared to be converted from a shed. A small pulpit sat in the front, and several tiny pews lined two of the walls inside.

"Why is this chapel even here?" Deborah asked.

"Beats me. This is on private property." Deborah's silver hair was blowing back and forth in the breeze as she turned in a circle to take in the slowly rolling hills and fields of green grass that surrounded the site. The monument sat on a rise in the terrain, so as she continued to turn, she could see for miles—horses and cattle grazing in the distance and a few barbed wire fences disappearing over the horizon.

"This is perfect," she said. We need to make sure to remind everyone that we will maintain this little spot just as it is, forever."

Brandon looked up at the flags blowing in the wind when he heard them popping. "Yes, let's build a nice stone fence around this first thing, so there is no question," he said.

"You got it."

CHAPTER 11

After several months of planning back in Fairfax, Brandon was finally arriving for his first day at the new office complex on the campus of K-State. The elevator door opened, and he stepped into the new reception area, which was complete with a new receptionist. She stood and greeted him. He smiled and walked directly to the counter.

"Well, good morning. I'm Brandon McStocker." He reached across the black, chest-high counter to shake her hand.

"Yes, sir. I know. I'm very pleased to see you finally. I mean, it's a pleasure to meet you, sir. I'm Cindy Graham, your new receptionist."

"I gathered." He smiled. "Sitting at this desk was a dead giveaway."

"Yes, sir. Of course. I'm sorry, sir. I guess it was obvious."

"Hey, Cindy. Relax. Here's your first bit of on-the-job training. We're all friends here."

"Yes, sir. Of course."

"Are you from here in Manhattan?"

"Yes, sir. Born and raised. My parents have a small farm just outside of town."

"Good to hear. Has Ms. Blanchard arrived yet?"

"Yes, sir. She's in her office."

"Good. It was a pleasure meeting you, Cindy. Welcome to the team."

"Thank you, sir."

He walked past empty cubicles, kitchen areas, and conference rooms to the end of the third floor, where the executive offices were set up. He looked around to study the arrangement. There was an empty desk in the waiting area and several seats and a coffee table with magazines strewn over it. Four offices surrounded the common area, one in the corner with Brandon's name on it and one with the door standing open. That one appeared occupied. The doors to the other two offices were closed.

"Good morning," Brandon said, assuming the opened door was Deborah's.

"Hey there," Deborah said. "How was your trip?" She greeted him with a hug.

"Not bad, really. Now that things have warmed up, it was a pleasant drive."

"Have you checked out your apartment yet?"

"I stayed there last night. I couldn't tell much about it, other than it's full of boxes."

"Well, there's your new digs, my friend." She pointed to his office door.

"Yeah, let me throw this stuff in there. I see we still don't have our secretary."

"The agency is sending someone over this afternoon. They insist we'll like her and that she's a perfect fit. That always makes me nervous. Get settled. I'm updating some schedules. Come on in when you're ready for an update."

Deborah returned to her office, and Brandon walked into his. He threw his briefcase on a chair and hung his coat on a tall hanger that stood behind the door. He glanced around at the dark wood bookcases and large cherry desk, which sat in front of a matching credenza. He walked over to the massive window that looked out over the campus and took in the sights. His mind began to race. *The project. Cassandra and the girls. Senator Wilhelm and the White House. Why did Bob have to die?*

He sat in the tall, plush chair at his desk and looked at the blank computer screen then at the phone on the other corner of the desk. He leaned back and stared at the ceiling, where he saw something unexpected. He smiled. It was a roughly round pattern of small holes in the acoustic ceiling tile. The previous occupant obviously enjoyed tossing pencils into the ceiling during times of boredom. He continued to stare at them, then his smile faded. He closed his eyes. He prayed silently for a few minutes before rocking forward and standing up in a single motion. He pulled his notebook from the briefcase and walked back out of his office.

"I guess we can call this the commons out here," he said as he walked into Deborah's office.

She looked up with a half smile. "I suppose."

"What have we got?"

"Sit," she said. She picked up a pile of documents and drawings from her desk and carried them over to the conference table. As Brandon sat, she spread them out in front of him. "Jimmy will be here tomorrow. I have him set up to meet with a local real-estate attorney, so they can start the process of getting right-of-way agreements with landowners for this first road." She traced a line on a map with her finger from Manhattan, roughly following the route they drove when they went to Lebanon months before. "It's mostly open range; I don't think they'll have much trouble."

"Good. I hope not," Brandon said. "I want to start moving dirt, like, yesterday."

"I understand. We have several contractors lined up with bids. They're all very experienced and seem to do good work."

"Well, shoot, let's use all of them."

"That's kind of what I was thinking. We could partition off the road and build each section simultaneously. Our designers are almost finished getting it on paper. The state and the feds are expediting the permits. We'll be skirting the little towns between here and there to ease the burden."

"Good. And the airport?"

Deborah pulled a small stack of papers from the pile and spread them out. "We've already done the rough designs and put out some RFPs to the airport construction community. We'll see what we get. We're going to clear a staging area just north of town, here, so the contractors can get ready with their equipment. As soon as the road is passable, including the east side of the new beltway, they'll be able to caravan up to start clearing."

"Sounds like quite a parade."

"Oh, it'll be something to behold."

"What about the FAA?" Brandon asked. "Are they engaged yet?"

"Administrator Slattery and his entourage will be out next week to go survey the area and start the process of expediting permits and licensing. I think they're going to put inspectors up there full-time, so there are none of those kinds of delays."

"Where are we putting Jimmy?"

"I think right here next to me." They heard Brandon's intercom from across the common area.

"Mr. McStocker?"

Deborah walked over to her desk and pressed the button on her phone. "Cindy, he's in here with me. What is it?" Several extraneous beeps and noise on the speaker followed for a few seconds. Deborah smiled at Brandon and shook her head. The two then heard a crash that sounded like Cindy dropped her handset on the desk. Deborah covered her mouth and closed her eyes in amusement.

"Um. I'm sorry, ma'am. Can you hear me okay?"

"Just fine, Cindy. You're doing fine. What's up?"

"It's the governor's office on the phone for Mr. McStocker."

"I'll take it in my office," Brandon said as he stood and took a last look at the maps in front of him.

"Yes, sir," Cindy said.

He walked back to his office through the common area, picked up the handset, and pressed the blinking button. "This is Brandon McStocker."

"Hold for the governor, please."

After several seconds, the governor of Kansas came on the line. "Brandon. Governor Redman here. I heard you were in town. How are things going?"

"Well, sir. I'm just barely catching my breath and going over some plans with my staff. How can I help you?"

"I'd like to meet with you here at the statehouse as soon as you can manage it. You know, to get familiar with the details of the project. I have some vendor recommendations for you—some companies around the state that I trust and with which I do business. When do you think you can make it?"

"Uh . . . can we shoot for next week, Governor? I'd like to get things here up and running."

"I suppose that's fine. If you can make it sooner, that would be better."

"I'll see what I can do, Governor. I'll have someone set it up with your people."

"Okay, McStocker. We'll talk later." The governor hung up before Brandon could say anything else. He placed the handset back on the phone and spun his chair to look out the window. He scanned the budding trees and flowers around the campus and watched the birds gathering materials to build their nests. He didn't know how much time had passed when he heard Deborah tap on his door frame.

"You okay, buddy?" she said.

He slowly turned his chair and looked at her. His eyes were red. "I don't know, Deb."

She walked into the office and closed the door behind her. "What is it, Brandon?" She sat in one of the two chairs in front of his desk.

"I'm thinking about asking Wilhelm to find somebody else for this job."

"Why?"

"Cassandra. The girls. I don't know. This is just too big."

"Brandon. Nobody is better suited for this than you. Bob knew it. Senator Wilhelm knows it. And the president knows it. Besides, I'll be danged if I'm going to let you leave me stuck with some other subpar manager like Bob."

"Whoa. Wait. What? What are you talking about?"

Deborah lowered her head and thought. She stood, walked over to Brandon's window, and looked out over the campus. He turned his chair to follow her.

"Brandon, look. I know Bob was a dear friend of yours. He was mine as well. But I'm still here because of your leadership. Of course, Bob was an outstanding project manager, but he could never get the performance out of this company that you do. The way you treat your people and respect what they do. Bob got some pretty amazing things done, but you're able to get things done, too—impossible things. And people do them because they want to get them done for you. Everybody in this company respects you, Brandon."

Brandon's mouth hung open. He was speechless. She broke her gaze, turned, and looked at him.

"Brandon, this is your company now. And we're all the better for it. You've got the leading role for the biggest show this country has ever seen. God is finally taking this country back, and you are the Moses he chose to do it. You can't ignore that."

Brandon was still stunned. "Uh . . . I had no idea. I thought everybody loved Bob."

"Of course I loved Bob, goober. Everybody did. But when he barked orders at the department heads, they all nodded with enthusiasm but then waited for you to make sense of everything. It's you who led them. I think Jimmy may be the only one you need to keep an eye on."

Brandon shook his head. "Oh, yeah. Jimmy."

"I thought we should keep him close. That's why I wanted him next door."

Cindy's voice filled the office through the intercom. "Mr. McStocker, Ms. Wilson is here to meet with you and Ms. Blanchard."

"We'll be right there, Cindy. Thank you." He stood and hugged Deborah. "Thank you. You've always been such a good friend."

"I'm always here for you. Are Cassandra and the girls going to move out here with you?"

"I don't think so. She can't get comfortable with any of this." Brandon reached across his desk and pressed the button on the intercom again. "Cindy, we've had a slight change of plans. Have Sonny bring the car around. I think we're going to take Ms. Wilson to lunch first."

"Yes, sir."

"Do you mind, Deb?"

"Not at all. I'll grab my purse. Barney's?"

Brandon smiled. "Yep."

★ ★ ★ ★ ★

Brandon and Deborah introduced themselves to Mena Wilson at the front desk and made small talk in the car on the way to Barney's Diner. Mena was a tall, serious-looking woman in her forties with short, sandy blonde hair. She wore a conservative business dress suit and walked with confidence, her eyes always straight ahead as if she were on a mission. Once they were seated at Barney's, she finally smiled.

"Mr. McStocker, Ms. Blanchard, thank you so much for meeting with me. I certainly didn't expect lunch."

"For starters, call me Brandon. Treating you to lunch is my pleasure. Can we call you Mena?"

"Of course, sir."

Deborah pulled a folder from her briefcase. "We've gone over your resume, and I must say, it's impressive."

"Well, thank you."

Brandon smiled and sat back in his chair. "Tell us a little about yourself. Are you from here in the Manhattan area?"

"Yes, sir," Mena said. "My parents are farmers, and we've lived in different parts of the state, but we always managed to end up back here. I love it here."

"Where do your parents farm?" Brandon asked.

"They have quite a few acres north of here. Barely hanging on I'm afraid, but I'd hate to see them lose it. I'd do anything to help them avoid that."

Brandon's face went blank, and he looked over at Deborah.

"What else can you tell us?" Deborah asked.

"Well, let's see. I'm a single mom, now an empty nester with a granddaughter. I've built up my administrative skills through the years and thought it might be time to get back in the workforce. When I heard what you guys are doing, I jumped at the chance to help, like I was called to be part of it." Brandon looked at Deborah and raised his eyebrows with a smile.

"How are you folks doin'?" the waitress shouted. "What can we cook up for you today?" The three placed their orders and continued the conversation over a two-hour lunch. Much of it had little to do with the job and much to do with Manhattan, farming, parenting, and grandparenting.

CHAPTER 12

Sonny pulled the limo into Brandon's driveway in Fairfax. After months of meetings and design work, Brandon was able to take some time to go home. As he got out, the front door of the house flung open, and Olivia ran out on the porch and down the steps.

"Daddy!" she shouted. She ran into his arms.

"Hey there, sweetheart," Brandon said. "You're getting so big."

"Hi, Sonny," she said. Sonny nodded.

Cassandra came out of the front door but wasn't quite as excited. She stood and waited for them to come up on the porch. She hugged Brandon.

"Hi, Sonny," she waved.

"Ma'am," he said, leaning against the front fender.

"Where is she?" Brandon asked.

"Up in her room, where she always—"

Before Cassandra could get her words out, Susan walked out of the front door and past them without saying a word. They watched her continue down the steps and out to the limo.

"Hi, Sonny."

"Well, hello there, Boss."

"Shot anybody this week?"

"Uh, no. Can't say that I have. You?"

She smiled. "No." They spoke for a few more minutes before she returned to the porch and hugged her dad, still not saying a word, then proceeded back up the stairs and into her room. Cassandra shook her head.

"I'll go talk to her," Brandon said.

Cassandra nodded and put her arm around Olivia. "Let's me and you go in the kitchen and whip up some lunch. What do ya say?" They all went in, and Brandon closed the door behind them. He took his suit jacket off and threw it across the back of a living room chair then walked up the stairs to Susan's room. She was sitting in the middle of her bed with her legs crossed, her ukulele in her lap, and papers scattered all around her.

"What are you working on?" Brandon asked. He looked around at the papers and moved some to sit down on the edge of the bed.

"Oh, nothing." She lowered her head and stared at the neck of her ukulele.

"You okay, honey?"

"I'm fine. Why? What did Mom tell you?"

Brandon smiled. "Your mom didn't have to tell me anything for me to see that something is bugging you. So what's going on? Why are you staying in your room all the time?"

"Daddy, all I want to do is play music. Is that so wrong?"

"I suppose not, unless it starts impacting your grades. What's happening there?"

"Oh, that. It's just so boring. They aren't teaching me anything I want to learn."

"Sweetheart, you can do better than that. You know you have to do the work." He picked up one of the sheets of music in front of her and turned it around for her to see. He placed two fingers on the page. "What's this between here and here?"

"A measure of music?"

"Right. And these?"

"Notes."

"What kind of notes?"

"Two quarter notes and a half note."

"And if you add all of those up?"

"Four beats."

"What would it be if all four of those beats were in one note? What would it be then?"

"A whole note."

"Good. How did you know that?"

"Because the time signature says there are four beats in a measure."

"Right. Honey, this is math. Everything you learn in school right now is laying the foundation to help you with other parts of your life. Maybe even something you love doing. Like music." She looked up at him with a hint of a smile on her face. Brandon turned and slid further up on the bed to face her directly.

"What about your friends?"

"My friends?"

"Your mom told me that you've stopped hanging out with your friends here in the neighborhood, and you won't introduce her to the kids she sees you with at school."

"The kids around here don't get music. They're just stupid."

Brandon pulled his head back. "Whoa. Who is this? Honey, what if I said you were stupid because you don't get project management, or your mom said you were stupid because you don't get law?"

"I don't care. Can I practice now?"

Brandon stood. "You need to reel it in, young lady. I don't know what's eating at you, but I'm going to go have some lunch. I'd like you to cool off and come down to join us, but the attitude stays up here. Got it?"

She looked down at a sheet of music and nodded.

"We're going to talk more about this later."

He turned and walked to the door. Then he stopped and slowly turned back around.

"No. You know what, sweetheart, let's talk about this now."

He closed the door and sat back down on the bed. "This is all my fault."

Susan rolled over and looked up at him. "What?"

"I'm not here for you like I should be. I am so sorry."

Susan sat up and threw her arms around Brandon's neck and started crying.

After they talked it out for several minutes, Brandon went down the stairs and into the kitchen, where Cassandra and Olivia were putting the finishing touches on some sandwiches and potato salad. He took a glass from a cabinet, filled it with ice, and poured tea from a pitcher. Cassandra watched his every move.

"What the heck happened?" he said. Brandon and Cassandra both sat down at the table.

"I can't figure it out, Brandon."

After several minutes, Susan came into the kitchen and joined them. She didn't say anything about the conversation with her dad—she barely said a word at all. Brandon talked about his time in Kansas and a little about the project. After lunch, Olivia went upstairs, and Susan went out on the front porch. Brandon and Cassandra cleared the table and did the dishes. Brandon sensed that she didn't ask the girls to clean up because she wanted to talk. The girls sensed it as well.

"This is making me crazy," Cassandra said, standing next to Brandon at the sink.

"Honey, I think she's just going through some kind of a phase. Music isn't the worst thing to be consumed with."

Cassandra shook her head, staring at the plate in her hand. "Brandon, I'm not talking about Susan. I'm talking about us. I'm talking about you being gone. I'm talking about raising these girls like I'm a single mom."

"Honey, I'm sorry. Why don't you just come out there with me?"

"Brandon! I'm not jerking them out of school and leaving everyone we know." They both fell silent for a few moments as Brandon mulled over what was happening. He looked out the window and saw Susan sitting on the step of the front porch next to Sonny but couldn't hear the conversation.

"What are you doing?" Susan asked.

"Oh, just soaking up some sun. You?"

"Just ate lunch. You hungry?"

"Not really. I can grab something later."

"I really hate being a kid."

"I think you're too young to know what you hate."

"Why can't I just play music?"

"Mainly because you're a kid."

"It sucks."

"Sweet girl, you don't know 'sucks.' You think you've got this adulting thing all figured out? Why can't I just play football?"

"You want to play football?"

"I did."

"You should play football."

"How would I be sitting here talking to you if I was off somewhere playing football? Besides, I wanted to defend my country more than I wanted to play football. I went into the Navy right after high school."

"Oh. Well, I can't join the Navy, and I can't stop thinking about music."

"I understand. Your dad says you're really good, you know."

"He does?"

"Yes, he does. So what's bugging you?"

"I don't know. I hate school. I don't understand most of it. Liv is the one with the brains."

"I'm sure you have a few brains, yourself."

"Mom and Daddy are mad 'cause I don't hang out with the neighborhood kids anymore."

"Why is that?"

Susan turned and locked eyes with Sonny. "Keep a secret?"

"Sweetie, I work for the Secret Service. Secret is practically my middle name."

"I don't like it when my friends around here keep asking me where my daddy is and why isn't he home. It's like they think he left us or something."

"Mmm. That must be tough. You know your daddy loves you, right?"

"I know." She turned back around, dropping her gaze.

"He's doing great things for this country, and you should be proud of him."

"I don't even know what to tell them when they bring it up."

"Well, tell them just that. Your pop is off working on an important project for the president of the United States. That's pretty huge."

Susan looked up at him with a questioning eye, like she didn't believe him. She returned her gaze to the concrete steps and sighed.

"So, you didn't shoot anybody this week?"

"Nope. Nary a one."

They sat quietly for a few minutes before the front door opened. They turned in unison to see who it was.

"Here's a plate for you, Sonny. You're welcome to come in and eat," Cassandra said.

Susan stood and walked around her and into the house.

"Well, I was going to eat later. But no, I can have a little picnic right here on the porch. Thank you."

Cassandra went back into the kitchen and sat at the table, where Brandon was sipping on another glass of iced tea. "I went to visit Anne a couple of nights ago," she said.

"Yeah? How is she doing?"

"She's fine. Strong woman. She asked about you and the project."

"I'm sure she's curious about Bob's baby."

"I just needed to talk to someone who gets what I'm dealing with. It was sad that I had to go looking for support from a woman who just lost her husband."

"Well, she is your friend."

"She's more like a second mom."

"I'm sorry I wasn't here for you."

"I guess it's just the way it's going to be, Brandon. I've about concluded that I don't have a husband anymore, and I guess I can live with that. Everyone sees you as a hero. So, I don't have much of an argument. You're married to this project. But I worry about the girls. They miss you. And Lord knows they need you."

"Honey, I don't know what to do. I told Deborah that I wanted to ask the president to replace me."

"No!"

"No?"

"You can't do that. You can't quit this project. You can't betray Bob and Anne. You can't shake the foundation of the company he left you with or all those people who depend on you there. You just can't."

"Now you're confusing me," Brandon said. He took Cassandra's hand and led her into the living room, where they sat on the couch. He put his arm around her, and she burst into tears.

"Honey, I am so sorry you have to deal with all this." He let her cry into his chest for several minutes until she sat up straight.

"I'm sorry. I'll deal with it. But I don't want you feeling like you have to keep coming back here. You need to focus on what you have going on out there."

"Sweetie, what are you talking about?"

"Just don't. Of course, you should keep in contact with the girls, but keep your mind out there."

"Cassandra, you know I love you, right?"

"I do. And I love you. But right now, I need to focus on these girls."

"What can I do?"

"I'm worried about Susan and the kids she's starting to hang out with. I don't know who they are or anything about their families."

"Well, if my talk with her earlier is any indication, they must love music, too. The kid is consumed with it. I don't know that there can be much harm in that. Maybe if you take more of an interest in her music endeavors, she'll bring her heart back home. I don't know. Is Liv helping any?"

"Oh, you know Liv. She's the mini-you. As far as she's concerned, you hung the moon. She seems to understand Susan and talks to her all the time. I don't sense a rift there at all."

"I'll take the weekend off. We'll do a cookout in the backyard," Brandon said. They sat quietly on the couch for a while before Brandon went out on the front porch to check in with Sonny.

"Everything okay out here?" he said as he closed the front door behind him.

Sonny stood up on the steps. "All is well, sir."

"Have a seat. I just wanted to come out and get some fresh air." They sat on the white wicker chairs that surrounded a small tea table, and they stared across the front yard in silence, watching the birds and smelling the freshly cut grass from the neighbor's lawn.

"How's your family, Sonny?" Brandon asked, breaking the silence.

Sonny turned and narrowed his eyes, wondering what Brandon was getting at. "Don't have much of a family, sir. Nobody I care to keep up with, anyway. I lost track of most of them years ago. My folks weren't too big on the parenting thing."

"Sorry to hear that."

"No. Don't be. It's been for the better, I suspect. I've been able to build myself from the ground up."

"From what I can tell, you've done a fine job with it."

"Thank you, sir."

"I'm afraid our little Susan is determined to do just that."

"Cute kid. She's a little spitfire for sure."

"That she is, Sonny. That she is."

CHAPTER 13

The elevator door opened. Brandon and Sonny stepped into the reception area, both out of breath.

"Good morning, Cindy. Is Ms. Blanchard in her office?"

"No, sir. She's in your conference room."

Sonny moved to the side and stayed in the reception area while Brandon rushed toward the executive offices. He glanced over as he entered the conference room and noticed someone sitting at what had been the empty secretary's desk. He closed the door behind him, threw his briefcase on the conference table, and sat at the end.

"What happened?"

Deborah was stunned. "Uh . . . good morning? Welcome back?"

"Sorry, Deb. Good morning. Jimmy, good morning. I thought we had all the land agreements through to Lebanon buttoned up."

"Brandon," Deborah said, "I called you because one of the landowners we were negotiating with is a firm called Midwest

Holdings. They are refusing to budge on a ridiculous price they're demanding for a right-of-way.

"Midwest Holdings? Rings a bell."

"You got it. Rumor has it Governor Redman is a major stake-holder."

"Under the circumstances, Boss, I think we should just give it to them and move on," Jimmy said.

"Well, hang on. Let's think about this a minute. Is there any way to skirt the property?"

"Not unless we completely change the direction of the road. Maybe move the I70 interchange down to Junction City."

"Deb, you know that's not going to happen. We're too far into this design now. Are there any growers or cattlemen leasing out there?"

"Nope. Open range."

"Naturally. I guess I'll go out to Topeka and throw eminent domain in his face. What is it, Jimmy?"

Jimmy had been staring out the window, not saying a word. He turned to the table and rocked forward in his chair. "I just think it would be a lot easier to pay the price and avoid getting tangled up in court with a bunch of lawyers."

Brandon gazed at Jimmy for a few seconds and turned to look at Deborah.

She grinned and said, "I'll have Mena set up an appointment with the governor."

"Good plan. I thought that was her that I saw sitting out there. So, she works for us now?"

"Yep. Brought her on a couple of days ago."

Jimmy shook his head and turned his stare back out of the window. Brandon was finally able to cool off and slow down after several more minutes of strategizing. The three left the conference room and walked toward their offices.

"Welcome, Mena," Brandon paused at her desk.

"Thank you, sir."

"You got a minute?"

"Of course, sir." Mena stood, picking up a notebook and pen, and followed Brandon into his office, closing the door behind her. Brandon set his things aside and walked over to sit at the small conference table.

"Have a seat. Make yourself comfortable. Ms. Blanchard is going to talk to you about a meeting I need to have with the governor, but I just wanted to chat a bit first. Congratulations on your new position. I hope you'll be happy here."

"Thank you, sir. I'm excited about it. I feel so honored to be part of such an important project, even if it is in such a small way."

"Oh, I wouldn't consider it a small way at all. I suspect you will play a pretty big role. You'll be privy to a lot of very critical and often sensitive information. You know that, right?"

"Yes, sir. Ms. Blanchard spoke to me in great detail about that."

"Good. I don't want you to be paranoid about talking to your friends and family about the project in general. It's obviously all over the headlines now. Just keep it pretty high-level. I think you'll be able to understand what's sensitive once you've been around here awhile. So how are those grandbabies?"

"Oh, they are just wonderful, sir. Thanks for asking. My son and his wife are doing such a wonderful job raising them. Such a joyful little family."

Brandon smiled and shook his head. "Unfortunately, mine hasn't been so joyful lately."

"Sir?"

"My wife and two daughters back in Fairfax. Cassandra, my wife, is having a hard time with my youngest, Susan. Susan wants her entire life to be about nothing but music. She's neglecting pretty much everything else."

"Does she have a shot at it?"

"She does. She's very talented."

"What does she play?"

"Guitar mostly. But she has a ukulele she carries around with her and uses to write songs. She keeps saying she wants to learn how to play the fiddle."

"Funny you should mention that," Mena said, smiling. She put her pen and notebook on the table. "My cousin, Darcy, and her husband recently moved out here from Kentucky. She's an awesome fiddler. She's even won a bunch of awards and contests. They're pretty big in the bluegrass and old-time music circles. Maybe Susan can come out and work with her awhile."

"You never know. That might be just the ticket."

"They're trying to start up some music jams out at Barney's."

"I'm a bit of a guitar player myself. Let me know when they get something going. Who knows, I may pop in for awhile myself."

"Yes. I'll let you know. So, what does your other daughter like to do?"

"Oh, Liv. She's probably going to be an engineer. That kid knows everything about everything but is as sweet as they come. Luckily, she watches over her little sister. She loves what Susan does."

"That's nice."

"Yeah. It's a pleasure to watch those two together. So, Mena, is there anything you need to get started? Have they taken good care of you?"

"Oh, yes, sir. Cindy and Ms. Blanchard . . . and Mr. Dillon. They've all been very helpful."

"Good. I need to make some phone calls, so go over and see Ms. Blanchard about the details on my visit with the governor. We'll chat again soon, okay?"

"Yes, sir. Thank you. And thanks so much for this opportunity."

Brandon noticed that Mena's smile vanished as soon as she stood to leave his office.

"The governor will see you now."

Brandon stood and walked by the secretary sitting outside the governor's office. "Thank you."

The door opened from the inside. "Brandon. Come in, come in," Governor Redman said.

"Thank you for seeing me, sir."

"Of course. Have a seat. How can the great state of Kansas help you? How's that little project going?"

"It's going well, Governor. That's why I came to see you."

"Of course it is."

Brandon ignored the sarcasm. "It seems that one of the landowners isn't happy with the agreement we've given them. Are you familiar with Midwest Holdings?"

The governor smiled and looked at Brandon. "Well, yes I am. I happen to be on the board of directors."

"So you're familiar with the agreement, then."

"I am. Let's cut to the chase, Brandon. Under the circumstances, I think that property is worth much more than you're offering."

"Sir, the preliminary meetings that our real-estate department had with all the owners indicated that the terms were satisfactory."

"Brandon, we both know this project comes to a complete standstill unless you meet all the terms of the owners. Just because some are willing to cave for the good of the president's agenda doesn't mean everyone is. Now, you can try that eminent domain game, but I've got so many lawyers at my beck and call, you don't stand a snowball's chance in you know where. At the very least, I can lock horns with the feds and keep it tied up in court until we're all dead and gone. You might as well just buy the land for the asking price."

"You mean pay the ransom."

"Call it what you will, son."

Brandon wondered what conversations Deborah and Jimmy might have had that led to the governor lawyering up for an eminent domain fight.

"Brandon, I know the president is willing to do whatever it takes to get this done. I don't think it'll be so difficult for you to sweeten the pie."

"I'm surprised the state isn't demanding toll roads."

"Well, now there's a thought," the governor said with a satisfied grin.

"Thank you for your time, Governor. Your people will hear from my office soon."

"I'm sure they will. Come back and visit anytime, Brandon. Always good to see you."

As soon as Brandon got to his car, he started punching numbers into his phone. Sonny closed the door for him as Brandon climbed into the back seat.

"Senator Wilhelm, please. Brandon McStocker calling."

"Brandon! What's up?"

"Senator, we're going to have a problem with Redman. He's pretty much holding us hostage on some land he's controlling in the middle of the southeast spur."

"That S.O.B. He's been crossways with the president since he moved into the White House. He owns the land?"

"Not directly, sir. He's on the board of a company that owns it. Midwest Holdings."

"Why does that name sound familiar?"

"You know what, Senator, I thought the same thing."

"I don't feel good about this, Brandon."

"It's probably nothing. If I come up with anything, I'll let you know. So, what are we going to do about Redman?"

"Eminent domain?"

"I was going to use that myself, but he was already prepared for it. Sounded to me like he was getting ready for a full-on fight."

"Okay. I'll have my people look into the relationship he has with Midwest to see if we might have an angle there. Dang it!"

Brandon heard a beep on the line and Wilhelm's secretary. "Yes, sir."

"Missy, get DOT on this call, please."

"Yes, sir."

"Brandon, we'll see if we can get any help on this from Tony Simpson in Transportation."

Another voice came on the line. "Hold for Mr. Simpson, please."

"Transportation. Simpson."

"Tony. Ron Wilhelm. How are things over there?"

"Busy, as usual, Senator. How can I help you?"

"Tony, I've got Brandon McStocker on the line with us. He's the Exec PM on Kéntro."

"Good afternoon, sir," Brandon said.

"Dang," Tony said. "I finally get to talk to the man who's got America by the horns. How's it going out there?"

"It was going pretty good until now," Wilhelm said. "Brandon, tell Tony what you just told me." Brandon explained his conversation with the governor. Overhearing Brandon's side of the conversation, Sonny looked back and forth at him in the rearview mirror and the traffic on I70.

"Brandon, let me get my people looking at it. I don't know if we've got anything to leverage, but we can try."

"Thank you, sir. We need all the help we can get."

"Hey, Tony," Wilhelm said. "How are things coming along on the airport?"

"It's top priority around here, Ron. I don't see any problems on the horizon, except the lack of a road to get to it."

"Yeah. Crap," Wilhelm said. "We'll get past this."

Another beep on Brandon's phone. "Gentlemen, if we can wrap this up here, I have another call coming in. I need to take it."

"Okay, Brandon. I'll be in touch," Wilhelm said.

"Good to finally speak with you, Mr. Simpson," Brandon said.

"You as well, Brandon. I'll let the senator know as soon as I get something."

Brandon switched calls. "Hey, honey, what's up?"

"Your daughter."

"Oh, jeez. Now what?"

"Not that one. Little miss Olivia has won the grand prize at the science fair."

"What? Really! Well, good for her. What was her project?"

"You ready for this? She led a group of students to design and build a model of the new city in Lebanon."

"What! Are you serious?"

"You heard me right, honey. They built Lebanon. And if you ask me, they did a pretty darn good job."

"How funny. I'm so proud of that kid."

"Here, she wants to talk to you."

"Hi, Daddy."

"Hey, sweetheart. I am so proud of you. Nice job!"

"Thanks, Daddy. It was fun. Susan helped a little. She named the airport."

"She did? What in the world did she name it?"

"Amelia Earhart International Airport."

"Wow. That's good. There might already be one of those, but we'll check. I'm so proud of you guys. And I'm so sorry that I wasn't there to see it. Put Susan on."

"Hi, Daddy."

"Hi, sweetie. That was a great thing you did, helping your sister with the science project."

"It was fun. But I didn't do anything. Liv was drawing on the floor, and I was playing my guitar. She started getting all worried about the name for the airport. I Googled famous people from Kansas and boom! There she was." Susan giggled.

"Well, still. It was good of you. Maybe I can put that in front of the committee. Hey, I spoke to someone today who has a family member who plays fiddle out here in Manhattan."

"Really?"

"Yep. She thought that you might come out some day, and she'll teach you how to play."

"Oh, Daddy, can I?"

"Well, not right now. But your mom and I will talk about it and see what we can work out. Okay?"

"Okay, Daddy. But let's not dillydally, okay?"

Brandon laughed. "Okay, sweetheart. For now, you just keep the peace at school and do good."

"Okay, Daddy. Bye."

CHAPTER 14

It was Mena's first anniversary with the company. Sonny stopped the car in front of Rathbone Hall, and Brandon got out of the car carrying flowers and a box of candy for her. The road to Lebanon was nearing completion—except for the stretch going through the property owned by Midwest Holdings—and clearing had begun for the new airport.

"Good morning, Cindy," he said as he and Sonny walked out of the elevator.

Sonny stepped to the side, and Brandon went toward his office. He stopped at Mena's desk on the way.

"Happy anniversary."

Mena laughed and stood to hug Brandon. "Oh, thank you so much."

Deborah, wondering what the commotion was about, walked out of her office. "Oh, that's right. I completely forgot. Happy anniversary, Mena."

"Thank you."

"Good morning, Brandon," Deborah said. "Listen, we've got to stop ignoring Midwest and get them off dead center. We've been messing with this for a year now."

"I'll give Wilhelm a call in a bit. Mena, got a minute?"

"Yes, sir." She picked up her notebook and pen and followed Brandon into his office.

"Have a seat. Remember when I told you about my daughter, Susan, and the issues she was having back in Fairfax?"

"Yes, sir. Of course. Is she okay?"

"Yeah. She's fine. But it looks like she's going to be moving out here with me to finish school after all."

"Is that right?"

"I guess she's been getting crossways with her mother a lot lately. I get the impression they both need a break. I'm a nervous wreck trying to smooth things over from out here. I keep wondering what the heck I'm going to do to keep her busy."

"Sir, there's a great music scene here in town. I think with the right guidance she can get hooked up with some talented new friends. Is she still interested in learning to play the fiddle, or is she doing that already?"

"I don't think she has pursued it yet."

"Okay. Let me know when you think she might be coming, and I'll get in touch with my cousin, Darcy. She and her husband, Trevor, are doing really good things around here with their music. I'm sure she'd love to take Susan under her wing. She misses her granddaughters terribly since leaving Kentucky."

"That's a great idea. I like it. I'll mention it to her the next time we talk. It'll give her something to look forward to. Thanks, Mena."

"Is that all, sir?"

"Yeah, that's it for now. Any idea where Jimmy is?"

"He hasn't been in yet this morning and hasn't left any word."

"Okay. Will you get Senator Wilhelm's office on the phone for me, please?"

"Of course, sir."

"Brandon. What's going on out there?" Senator Wilhelm said.

"Great progress, sir. I just called to talk to you about Redman. We've ignored that land issue about as long as we can. We've got to get that road connected or come up with an expensive alternative."

"Have you heard from him lately?"

"Not lately. He was still asking for ten times what it's worth, then he got the environmentalists all spun up so it would get on the front pages of every newspaper around here. We've had plenty to do elsewhere, so I ignored it."

"I'll try to get in to see the president and see if he has any ideas."

"Okay, Senator. Thank you."

"So you guys have settled on Amelia Earhart International?"

"I think so, if it's okay with the folks out there."

"Turns out, there's already an airport that holds that name out near Atchison, but they've agreed to a renaming in order to honor Earhart with this international airport. So it's all good. The FAA tells me AEI is available, so we'll get the paperwork started."

"That's great, sir. My kids will be ecstatic. I think they've probably forgotten about it."

"It's a great story. It gives us a good laugh here in the halls."

"I bet. Please let me know what we can do about Redman."

"We'll get it kicked off dead center one way or another, Brandon. I'll be in touch." Brandon disconnected the call then pressed the intercom to the reception desk.

"Yes, sir."

"Cindy, have you seen or heard from Jimmy?"

"I think he must have been here very early, sir, before anyone else was here. He left the lights on down there."

"Okay. Thanks."

Brandon put on his coat and walked across to Deborah's office. "Wilhelm is going to try to shake Redman loose. We'll see if he makes any headway."

"It makes me crazy to think we've got both ends of that road nearing completion with that big gap in the middle," Deborah said. "It's nuts."

"I know it is. Listen, I'm going up to the diner for awhile. I need to think."

"You okay?"

"I'm fine. Susan is probably going to be moving out here, and I'm trying to wrap my head around it."

"Well, you know I'm here to help where I can."

"I know. Thanks. I'll see you shortly. Call if anything comes up."

"Will do. Bring me back one of Barney's cinnamon rolls, would ya?" They both smiled as Brandon walked out of her office.

"Sonny, just take me to the apartment so that I can get my car," Brandon said when he got to the elevator. "I'm going to visit the construction site. You can have the morning off."

"Yes, sir."

Brandon visited the south end of the road construction often so he could smell the dirt and see the progress. But he never took his limo. He thought it would be too much of a distraction to the workers. He got himself a four-wheel drive SUV for site visits.

After Sonny left him at this apartment, Brandon drove to Barney's Diner.

"Hey there, hon. Take a seat anywhere, and I'll bring that coffee."

"Thanks, Edna." Brandon walked to the corner table, as far from anything as he could get. He tossed his journal on the table and sat down. He stared out the window until the waitress arrived with his coffee.

"You eating this morning, Brandon?"

"I don't think so. Not today. I'll need a cinnamon roll to go for Deb, though."

"You got it."

It was during off hours, so there was hardly anyone there. Brandon noticed a slim gray-haired man sitting at the counter drinking coffee and reading a Bible. Brandon tried to remember the last time he had been to church. He missed his chats with Pastor Carl back in Fairfax. He opened his journal and began writing down some thoughts.

"Need a refill there, Emmett?" Edna asked, standing behind the counter. Brandon looked up to confirm that Emmett was the man he had seen.

"That one's on me," Brandon shouted across the diner. He even surprised himself.

Emmett looked up from his Bible and smiled at Brandon. "Thank you, neighbor."

"You're quite welcome."

Brandon shifted his gaze back to his journal. He wrote awhile and stared out the window. He could see the many graders, bulldozers, and excavators that had been staged across the road. Men in hard hats walked back and forth, climbing into those rigs and heading north onto the new road that paralleled 24 going out of town. The south end that went down to meet 170 skirted around the edge of town.

"Edna tells me that's all yours over there."

Brandon was startled out of his daydream and looked up to see the man talking to him.

"Emmett. Emmett Cleveland. Thanks again for the coffee."

"Brandon McStocker." He shook Emmett's hand. "Oh, you're welcome. Not mine, really. We're just managing the project."

"Pretty big project."

"Tell me about it," Brandon said. "Care to join me?"

"I don't want to interrupt anything."

"Oh, no. I was just jotting down some thoughts." Brandon closed his journal and slid it to the side of the table.

Emmett took a seat across from Brandon, and Edna brought a fresh pot of coffee over for refills. "I heard on the news this morning that the governor was threatening to shut down the project because of some property disputes."

"What? How in the world did they get that idea?"

"I don't know, son. I imagine you have to deal with a lot of that kind of stuff in your line of work."

"More than makes sense these days. What do you do, Emmett, if you don't mind me asking?"

"I pastor the community church down there on the right," he said, pointing over Brandon's shoulder.

"Really?" Brandon smiled. "I was just sitting here thinking about the chats I used to have with my pastor back in Fairfax, Virginia."

"You're from Fairfax?"

"Yeah. I have a wife and two daughters still back there, though my youngest has about decided that she wants to move out here with me."

"How long have you been in Manhattan? I don't think I've seen you in here before. And I'm in here way too much."

"I've been here a little over a year now. I've been coming to this diner for about that long, I guess. But never at this time of day. This is a little unusual for me. I stopped to gather my thoughts before I drive up to check progress on the road."

Brandon and Emmett chatted for a while before Brandon asked Edna for the check. She placed it on the table as both of the men stood.

Brandon grabbed the check. "I've got this one, Preacher."

"You sure?"

"My pleasure."

"Here's your cinnamon roll, hon," Edna said, handing Brandon a white box. "You tell Ms. Deb hey for me. Okay?"

"Will do, Edna."

"Pleasure chatting, Brandon. Hope to see you again soon."

"Yes, it was." Brandon shook Emmett's hand. "I'd like that."

The two continued to make small talk as they entered the parking lot then parted ways. Brandon drove north, and Emmett drove south, back toward town and his church. Brandon went slowly past the staging area across from the diner and watched the activity. He then went around the barricades onto the new road. He passed several graders along his way to the front lines, as they called the leading edge of the road construction. After driving some twenty minutes and topping the high point, Brandon saw the hordes of equipment moving dirt in every direction. The work was going on as far as he could see ahead of him. He pulled the car over to the side of the road, put his white hard hat on, and got out.

Brandon leaned against the front fender of his car and gazed out over the construction, scanning from side to side. He looked up to the sky, closed his eyes, and took in the smells of dirt and diesel exhaust.

"Bob, my friend. I hope you can see this." He looked over the fields again and thought about the progress they had made. He wondered how they were going to get through the Midwest Holdings gap. His phone started buzzing.

"Hey, Deb. What's up?"

"Where are you?"

"I just left the diner. I'm up here at the front line. Why?"

"Wilhelm just called. Apparently, Senator Sanders is on the warpath again."

"Of course he is. I'm guessing the president is stirring things up with the whole Redman ordeal."

"Well, they're all over the news feeds claiming that President Richland is building a road to nowhere."

"I haven't heard back from the White House. He was going to take care of it."

"Well, Sanders seems to be pulling together quite a following."

"Okay, Deb. I'll be heading back down to the office shortly." He put the phone back in his coat pocket. *What in the world is going on*, he thought.

Brandon got back in his car and started south on the new road. He hadn't traveled far when his phone buzzed again.

"Hey, Deb. Now what?"

"Brandon, I hate to be the one to tell you this, but Senator Taylor is dead."

"What?"

"It's true. It'll be hitting the newswire shortly."

"Dang it! What happened?"

"All I've been able to scrape together is natural causes."

"Yeah, right. Crap! Aside from Wilhelm, she was our biggest Senate supporter."

"I'm sorry, Brandon. We'll talk when you get back."

"I'm on the road now. I have another call coming in."

"Okay, bye."

"This is Brandon."

"Mr. McStocker. This is the governor's office. He would like to speak to you."

"Put him through."

"Brandon. Governor Redman here."

"Good morning, Governor. How can I help you today?"

"Brandon, I'm gonna let you go through that gap, but dang it, I want my people working on it."

"Your people, sir?"

"I want some of the contractors around Kansas on that project. I want you to stop importing the labor on Kéntro. You hear me?"

"Governor, I don't think there are enough bulldozers in Kansas to pull this off. But I'll have my folks contact the statehouse and get the details. If they do quality work, of course we'll put them on the project."

There was silence on the other end of the phone.

"Governor?"

Silence.

"He hung up on me."

CHAPTER 15

"Mena, get Senator Wilhelm on the phone, please," Brandon muttered as he walked by her desk into his office. He was standing behind his desk pulling files from his briefcase when Deborah walked in.

"I don't know what you've done, Brandon, but I just got a call from Midwest's attorneys. They're going to sign off on the gap agreement."

"All I did was bring in the president. I have no idea what he did. Any news on Senator Taylor?"

"It's all over the newswires now. Mostly speculation. Sonny called in. I think he was about to come looking for you. He also checked in with his team in Fairfax. No activity there."

"Mr. McStocker, Senator Wilhelm's office is on the phone."

"Thanks, Mena. Put him through."

"I'll leave you to it," Deborah said and went back to her office, closing Brandon's door behind her.

"Senator, sorry to bother you. What's going on back there?"

"Well, you know. Another day at the office."

"Have you had a chance to speak with the president about Redman and Midwest?"

"I did. Great news. We can finally close that gap."

"Did he have something on Redman?"

"I suspect he did. But he also told the governor that he would talk to you about bringing some of his cronies into the project."

"Yeah, Redman beat him to the punch on that."

"He may have sweetened the deal a little, as well, with other bills coming to the floor," the senator speculated.

"I'm just relieved that we can finally start moving the dirt out there and get that equipment up to the airport site."

"Good."

Brandon ventured, "Are you hearing anything on Senator Taylor? Deb said it's all over the wire."

"Not really. I just keep hearing natural causes. What a terrible loss. She was a good woman and a great senator. The whole thing makes me want to throw up."

"Such a tragedy."

"Yes, it is, Brandon. What are you up to?"

"I was just out looking at the construction on the south end of the spur and couldn't help thinking about Bob McClellan. Just then I got the call about Ms. Taylor. I'm sure her family is devastated."

"We have people headed over to her home in case they need anything. Her husband is a professor at Georgetown. They sent someone over to pick him up as well. They have three kids, but I don't know their ages or their status."

"You know, Senator, I still don't have a good feeling about Bob."

"I know. We haven't closed the books on that yet, either. Brandon, I think we're going to beef up patrols around your house back here—you know, just to be on the safe side. You might want to let Cassandra know."

"I understand, sir. Thank you."

"I don't think they're in any real danger. It's just a precaution. Sonny and his folks are working on some ideas. Apparently, he wasn't crazy about your taking off without him this morning."

"Yeah. I guess I'll stop doing that."

"He'll be discussing it with you. Listen, I need to run. We have a vote coming up."

"Thanks, Senator. I'll be in touch."

Brandon walked out into the commons and shouted, "Jimmy, let's get the equipment moved to the gap!"

Jimmy walked out of his office with a puzzled look. "Really? It's a go?"

"It's a go. We need to move quickly."

Deborah walked out of her office with a smile on her face. Mena stood, and they all raised their arms in celebration. "Woohoo!"

Brandon walked back toward his office. "Mena, I guess you better get Cassandra on the phone."

"Yes, sir."

Deborah met Brandon's look, and her smile vanished, knowing the news he had to share with his wife. She walked back into her office and closed the door. Brandon returned to his office and spoke to Cassandra for almost an hour, explaining what had happened and what Senator Wilhelm wanted to do about security.

"The good news is, we got the gap out of Redman's hands and have the go-ahead to start construction," Brandon said.

"Honey, this is nuts," Cassandra said. "Who's doing this?" Brandon, watching a nest of birds in a tree outside his office window, wanted to forget everything. But he knew he couldn't. "Brandon?"

"Honey, it could be pure coincidence. It probably is, but if there's something going on, you can bet Senator Sanders and his wife are behind it."

"I see Natasha and Gary walking around outside. I hate this."

"I know, honey. I am so sorry. But you and the girls are safe. I promise. The senator just added the patrols as a precaution. Has Susan said any more about coming out here?"

"It's pretty much all she talks about, especially since you told her about that fiddler lady. Are you sure you would be able to deal with her out there?"

"We'll figure it out."

"It breaks my heart that she doesn't want to stay here in Fairfax. But Brandon, she is so disconnected and seems so miserable. There are times when she's in her room I think the house could be burning down, and she wouldn't know it. I'm not even sure she would care."

"Is she being disrespectful?"

"No, not really. She's just such a little introvert. If it wasn't for Liv, I don't know what I would do."

"We have to be careful not to make Liv think this is her responsibility."

"Oh, I know. I know."

Brandon turned his chair back around to face his desk and leaned forward, resting on his elbows. "Honey, I have to run. You hang in there, okay? Everything's going to be fine."

"I suppose."

"Bye, hon. Love you." Brandon hung up the phone. He stood and walked over to the massive whiteboard on the wall at the end of his office. He picked up a marker and scribbled at the top of the board, "How?" He stared at it for several minutes and then placed the marker back on the tray. He sat at the conference table, continuing to stare at the board. Mena walked in and put a folder on Brandon's desk. She noticed him gazing at the whiteboard. She saw the word *How?* and wondered what he was doing. But he was a million miles away. She stood motionless for several seconds, wondering if she should interrupt.

She finally spoke. "Are you okay, sir?"

"Mena, ask Ms. Blanchard to come in, please." Brandon didn't break his gaze.

"Yes, sir." She left the room.

Brandon smiled. "Of course," he said under his breath, continuing to brainstorm his idea.

"Brandon, what is it?" Deborah asked. "Mena said you're acting weird."

"I'm fine, Deb. Have a seat. I think I have the answer for getting caught up on the cross."

She pulled a chair out, sat at the conference table, and looked at the board. "Well, bud. All I see is 'How?'"

"Too many thoughts to write down. We need to crash this thing, Deb."

"Brandon, it's too early to be crashing the project, don't you think? That's nowhere in sight yet."

"I mean the cross." He jumped to his feet, picked up the marker, and drew a large X across the board with a circle around the center. At the bottom right corner of the board, he drew another small circle.

"Look. We've been staging the equipment for the southeast spur here, across from Barney's, right?"

"Uh, yeah."

"Let's get all of that equipment up to the gap and make a push to get a path cut through to the north end. Meanwhile, let's start staging everything that needs to get up to the airport site there in that staging area. I mean everything. I'm just talking about crashing the cross. Throw everything we've got at it. Let's get the surveyors out to start laying out the other three spurs."

"What? Now?" Deborah narrowed her eyes and cocked her head, still staring at the board.

"Let's find every road construction firm this state has to offer and get them staged on all four corners to pull this cross in simultaneously. That'll scratch Redman's itch, and it'll get us back on track."

"Brandon, that's a little crazy, don't you think?"

"Hey, Jimmy!" Brandon yelled at the top of his lungs, startling Deborah and Mena both. He didn't have time for the intercom. Jimmy came out of his office and looked at Mena, who merely shrugged her shoulders. He continued into Brandon's office.

"Come on in, Jimmy. Have a seat. We're going to crash the cross."

"Crash the cross? Boss, what does that even mean?"

"Jimmy, I need you to get three more construction teams together and get them out to Lincoln, Lexington, and Colby. Clear staging areas at each site. Deb is getting the survey teams out as soon as she can to get the other three spurs laid out. As soon as we get the southeast spur punched through, I'm going to add another team to start on the beltway. We're going to pull the national cross in from all four corners at the same time."

"Boss. Are you serious? Don't you think you've got a little bit of scope-creep going on there?"

Deborah looked at Brandon and smiled. "Yeah, Boss. Don't ya?" she mocked.

"No. It's not scope creep. Schedule creep, perhaps. But it's to the left. We'll get ahead of schedule if we can pull this off. Redman's been complaining about us not using his henchmen, so let's play his game and get this done."

"Can we trust anyone he puts on the table?" Deborah asked.

"Of course we can," Jimmy said. Brandon and Deborah froze and looked at him. "I think we can," he clarified.

Brandon shook his head. "Jimmy, get the department heads together and make the cross their priority. Break the site managers up into four teams, get the specs out and get rolling on contracts. By the time you award, Deb will have the spurs surveyed and staked. If you have any issues, let me know."

Deborah leaned over and grabbed Jimmy's arm on the table. "Give them a few minutes to get past the idea that you're a lunatic, so maybe they can embrace the madness." The three laughed, releasing some stress. Even Mena smiled when she heard them.

"Look," Brandon said. "I keep thinking about something. Our '*why*.'"

"Our '*why*?'" Deborah asked.

"Yeah. After staring at the '*how*' up there for so long, I think we need to get clear on why we're doing this project and lean on that until it's complete."

Jimmy scratched his head and looked at Deborah then back at Brandon. "What do you mean, Boss? We're doing this because the president told us to do it."

"No. It's more than that. Why are we moving the capital to the center of the country? It's a new beginning. We have front-row seats to watch this nation get a fresh start. I never want us to forget that. It needs to be our 'why.'"

"I guess that's true," Deborah said.

"We may all have our 'whys' to answer to while we come to work every day. But we all need to be aligned on this one. What do you guys think about a big banner down there behind Cindy that says, 'Mack & Mack: Working together to give the nation a fresh start'? Maybe even put one in the lobby at the Fairfax office."

"I like it," Deborah said. "I'll work with Mena. She can take the lead on that."

"Thanks, Deb. Jimmy, you better get to Topeka. You've got a bunch of right-of-way agreements to button up and a bazillion permits to file."

"On it, Boss." The three stood and broke from the impromptu meeting. Brandon followed the other two to his door and looked out at Mena.

"Now, I guess we need to get Susan on a plane. She's champing at the bit to get out here."

"Yes, sir. I'll get it booked. Would you like me to coordinate it with Mrs. McStocker, as well?"

"Yeah, go ahead and do that. Thanks, Mena."

CHAPTER 16

Brandon waited in the terminal of the Kansas City airport, watching for Susan to come from the gates. He kept looking at the arrivals monitor and back down the concourse then at his watch. He caught a glimpse of her in the distance. As she made her way through the crowds, he saw the green suitcase she pulled behind her and the guitar gig bag on her back. An airline attendant was walking beside her, smiling and chatting. Susan didn't appear to be engaged in the conversation. When the two were near enough, Susan locked eyes with him and smiled. She walked straight into his arms.

"Hi, Daddy." She spoke with a calm, cool sigh of relief.

"Sir, I'll need to see some ID. We don't want this sweet little girl to get into the wrong hands now, do we?"

"Of course." Brandon pulled his wallet out and flashed his driver's license.

"Thank you, sir." She turned and bent down to Susan.

"You take care of yourself, sweetie. Okay?"

"I will, Ms. Carla. Thank you."

The attendant walked away, and Brandon took Susan's suitcase. They started their journey to baggage claim.

"So, how was the flight?"

"It was fine."

"You want me to take your guitar?"

"No. I'm good."

"Your mom and Liv doing okay?"

"They're fine."

They walked in silence for awhile.

"You hungry?"

"No."

"You want a punch in the nose?"

Susan looked up at him and smiled then nudged her shoulder into his side. He put his arm around her, and they continued down the concourse to retrieve her checked suitcases. Once they had everything rounded up, they walked out of the terminal building to the curb, where Brandon's car was waiting.

"Sonny!" Susan shouted as she walked faster to get to him.

"Hey, baby girl. How are you doing? It's so good to see you."

"You too, Sonny." She wrapped her arms around his waist. Then she pulled away and looked up at him. "You shot anybody lately?"

"Not lately. Now shut up and get in the car."

Brandon shook his head and loaded the suitcases into the open trunk as Susan jumped into the back seat. The two-hour trip back to Manhattan was quiet. Susan was tired, and Brandon didn't want to put his little girl through an inquisition, though the thought had crossed his mind. They arrived at the apartment and carried everything in.

"This is your room, right here," Brandon said. "You like it?"

"I do, Daddy. This is nice."

"I know it's plain right now, but we can fix it up however you like."

She slid the gig bag off of her back and leaned it in the corner. She walked into Brandon's arms again and squeezed his waist. He smiled and squeezed back.

"You okay, honey?"

"I'm fine, Daddy. I'm just glad to finally be here."

"I'm glad too, sweetheart. It'll be a little adjustment for us, but we're going to be fine. You think you better give your mom a call?"

"Okay." While Susan was on the phone in the living room, Brandon's cell phone started buzzing. He walked into the kitchen to answer it.

"Hello, this is Brandon."

"Mr. McStocker, listen closely," the voice on the other end said. "You need to shut Kéntro down, and shut it down now."

"Who is this?"

"That doesn't matter. Shut Kéntro down. If we don't see a shutdown in the headlines in thirty days, you're going to pay. Got it?"

"Look, I don't know who this is, but . . . hello? Who is this? Hello?"

The caller had already hung up. Brandon walked back into the living room.

"Who was that, Daddy?"

"Oh, nobody, sweetheart. Wrong number. Your mom doing okay?"

"They're fine. But I don't think Liv is going to like me being out here."

"I bet she isn't. They're both going to miss you. I'm sure of it. Listen, I need to go to my office for a little bit. You can go with me. There's someone I want you to meet."

When they arrived at Rathbone Hall, Susan was turning her head in every direction, trying to take in the sights of the campus.

The three rode the elevator to the third floor, where Sonny stepped out and to the side as he always did.

"Hi, Cindy. This is my daughter, Susan."

"Hi, Susan. It's so good to meet you."

Susan smiled and waved her hand. "Hi."

"Sonny's going to stay here while we go down to my office."

Susan reached over and punched Sonny in the stomach. He bent over to fake pain and laughed.

"Don't shoot anybody," she said. Cindy looked at Brandon.

"Don't even ask," he chuckled.

As soon as they rounded the corner into the commons, Deborah shouted out of her office door. "There's my girl! Get in here."

"Aunt Debbie!" Susan ran into her arms.

"You're getting so big," Deborah said.

Mena looked on with a smile as Deborah and Susan walked back out of her office.

"Hey there, Suze."

"Mr. Jimmy. Hi."

"So this is the famous little Ms. Susan. Hi. I'm Mena, your dad's secretary."

Susan walked over to Mena and politely shook her hand. "Hi, Mena. You're the one who has a friend who plays the fiddle?"

"It's my cousin actually, but yes. That's me. We'll get you two together sometime really soon, okay?"

Susan smiled. "I'd like that."

"Your dad didn't tell me what a pretty girl you are. How old are you?"

"I'm almost fifteen. My birthday is in a few weeks."

"Well, then. We'll need to celebrate."

"I don't care much for parties," Susan said, looking down at her feet.

"How about a bluegrass jam, then?"

Susan raised her head and grinned, then looked at Brandon. "Can we do that, Daddy?"

He laughed. "Of course we can. I wouldn't mind breaking out a guitar myself for that."

"Well, I'll set it up then," Mena said.

"Don't you guys even think about doing that without me there," Deborah said.

Mena nodded at her with two thumbs up. "I'll let you know."

"Mena, will you take Susan on a tour of the place?" Brandon asked. "Maybe run down to Call Hall for ice cream. I need to make some phone calls."

"Of course. It'll be fun. What do you say, kiddo?" Mena asked.

Susan smiled. "Sure!"

Mena stood, turning off her computer monitor and picking up her purse.

"Bye, Daddy," Susan said as they disappeared around the corner toward the elevator.

"Have fun, sweetie."

Brandon looked at Mena's monitor wondering why she thought it was necessary to turn it off.

"Well, they sure hit it off in a hurry," Deborah said.

"They sure did." He turned his focus to Jimmy. "Do you know if Wilhelm is in his office?"

Jimmy looked up from gazing at the floor. "Sorry. What?"

"Senator Wilhelm. Is he in his office in D.C.?"

"Oh. I don't think he had any trips planned. He should be there." Jimmy walked into his office.

Brandon looked at Deborah and shook his head as he walked toward his own office. Deborah smiled and retreated into hers. Brandon closed the door behind him.

"Good afternoon, Senator."

"Brandon. Good to hear from you. How's it going out there?"

"Now that we're closing the gap, things are starting to speed up. We came up with a plan to expedite the cross, so you may see our expenditures spiking."

"That's fine. I think that's just what the NTO needs to see."

"Any news on Senator Taylor?"

"Not really. That's just a sad ordeal. I don't know if they'll ever get to the bottom of it."

"Senator. It just feels like they could connect the dots and get back to Senator Sanders and his wife. It seems like the press keeps giving them a pass."

"Oh, yes, they are the darlings of the media. Luckily nobody's paying any attention to the media these days. If they were, Kéntro would be dead on arrival."

"That's for sure. Listen, Senator, apparently, they're on me now. At least, somebody is."

"What do you mean?"

"I got a call earlier today. Somebody was demanding that I figure out a way to shut the project down."

"Well, they took long enough."

"Yeah. That's what I thought."

"Is Sonny staying close by?"

"Yeah, but I haven't told him about it yet. I guess I should."

"You most definitely should," Wilhelm said, raising his voice. "What are you thinking?"

"I know. I will. Susan was in the car with us, and I didn't want to scare her."

"Oh, she's out there now?"

"Yes, she arrived this morning. She's out gallivanting around town with Mena now."

"With Mena, huh? How did you get her to take off with a complete stranger?"

"It was a little bizarre how quickly she warmed up to Mena. They talked about fiddling and bluegrass music. At that moment, I think they sealed the deal. Something tells me they're going to be inseparable. Mena doesn't get to see her grandkids as often as she wants, so this is going to be good for both of them. Unexpected but good."

"Well, good for them. Listen, Brandon, I'll let the investigators know about your phone call and see if they can shake something loose. In the meantime, you need to bring Sonny in on it. If we get anything on the Taylor investigation, I'll let you know."

"Thanks, Senator. I just can't get past the thought that Senator Taylor's death and Bob's death are connected." Brandon ended his call with the senator and dialed his home in Fairfax.

"Hello."

"Hey, hon. It's me. I guess you heard, she got here safe and sound. She's out with Mena now, getting some ice cream."

"Really? Are you serious?"

"Crazy, isn't it."

"Oh my goodness. That didn't take long. How funny."

"It was pretty neat to watch how quickly they hit it off."

"Well, we miss her already. Liv has been gloomy all day. But she knows Susan needs a change, so she'll be fine."

"Yes, they both will. Honey, so that you know, I got a threat today. I don't think it's anything to worry about, but I didn't want to keep it from you. Just be a little more vigilant when you're out and about. I haven't told Sonny about it yet, but when I do, I'm sure Natasha and Gary will be the first ones he calls."

"Brandon, this sucks. I don't think I can take it anymore. I didn't sign up for this crap!"

"Cassandra, come on. It's going to be fine. Maybe I shouldn't have told you after all."

"Don't," she said. "Don't you dare keep secrets from me."

"Of course I won't, honey. I'll tell Sonny right now. That way they'll be on guard back there as well."

"Have you heard any more about Senator Taylor?"

"Not yet. Wilhelm has his people all over it."

"Yeah, right. I hate this."

"I'm sorry, honey. Hang in there with me, okay? The NTO will get to the bottom of it. I have to go. I'll have Susan call you again tonight, okay?"

"Yes, please do. I know Liv will want to hear from her, too."

Brandon hung up the phone and spun his chair around. He looked out over the campus and watched the birds flying in and out of the trees.

"Brandon. Got a sec?" Deborah's voice boomed over the intercom.

"Scared the crap out of me," he said, spinning his chair around to his desk.

"Sorry," she chuckled. "I just had a bit of an epiphany about the schedule and wanted to run it by you."

"Be right there."

CHAPTER 17

"What do ya have?" Brandon said as he sat down at the small round conference table in Deborah's office.

"After you decided to bring in all four spurs of the cross simultaneously, it got me thinking about other things we might be able to do to speed things up."

She walked to the whiteboard at the end of her office and wrote at the top center of the board, "Dubai."

"Dubai? I wondered when that might come up," Brandon said with a smile. "So we're going to build skyscrapers now, to tickle the sun."

"Shut up. No. But there was some genius there. Those guys went into that project thinking outside the box in a big way. They didn't limit themselves to what they knew about construction."

"True. And?"

"And we've had our teams working day and night trying to engineer K.D. based on what they know about D.C."

"I suppose that's true. We assume that what was created to run the country evolved that way for a reason."

Deborah pointed the marker at Brandon and pierced him with her eyes.

"Exactly!" she shouted. "We assumed that. So think Dubai. We need to get out of the box."

"Uh . . . build up not out?"

"No, Brandon. We need to start designing with genius. Our engineers and architects are great at what they do, but they only know what they know—what's within their discipline."

"Well, that is what we pay them for. Your point?"

"My point is, we need to match them up with other disciplines—those guys sitting outside the box. Those guys who are constantly complaining about the poor facilities and infrastructure they're forced to work in."

Brandon leaned forward in his seat, putting his index fingers together over his lips. He stared at the whiteboard as Deborah began listing some of the largest and most successful technology companies in the country. She continued her speech as she wrote.

"We've been contracting construction firms and road builders. We need to start hiring the great minds in this country. Not only do we start asking technology partners how to best create this city, but we also serve it up to the public, like getting the citizens involved in it. Congress had to sell it as a mission to take back our government. So let's help Congress by showing the people that they are a hands-on partner."

Brandon leaned back again in his seat. "Dang."

"Are your wheels beginning to spin?"

"Well . . . yeah. So what do you have in mind?"

"I think we get the cross done as quickly as possible, then have an industry day where we invite the geniuses of this country to participate in a bus tour of the entire area. We invite the heads of only those companies on the bleeding edge of their respective industries—telecommunications, renewable energy, green building designs, transportation, and operations research. Maybe even check in with K-State and other universities to see what kind of studies they are doing in infrastructure these days."

"Deb, that's awesome. We should have thought of this a long time ago."

"I think we would have all gotten here eventually."

"I'll get in touch with Wilhelm and see if we can get some time with the NTO so we can have their backing on this. I think they'll want to go full-court press on it."

They heard the phone ringing at Mena's desk. Knowing she wasn't there, Deborah pressed the speaker button on her phone.

"McClellan and McStocker. This is Deborah Blanchard."

"Ms. Blanchard, this is the governor's office. Is Mr. McStocker available to speak to the governor?"

Brandon nodded.

"Yes. Mr. McStocker is right here. Put him through."

"The governor is on the line now," the voice on the speaker said.

"Brandon. Governor Redman."

Brandon stood and walked over to Deborah's desk. "Hello, Governor. Good to hear from you." He rolled his eyes and smiled at Deborah. "How are you today?"

"Doing fine. Doing fine. Listen, I'll cut to the chase. I hear you folks have decided to start building all four spurs at the same time. Have you brought Nebraska in on this yet?"

In shock, Brandon reached across Deborah's desk and punched the mute button.

"What the heck!"

Deborah shrugged her shoulders and shook her head. Brandon took the phone off of mute.

"We're considering it, Governor. Just a conversation so far. Has our office been in contact with you, sir?"

"No. No. I just heard it through some permitting sources. Is Nebraska involved yet?"

"Not yet, Governor. It's still very early."

"You've been working with the road-building outfits I sent you?"

"Yes sir, we have."

"Good. I don't want all that work going to Nebraska. Ya hear?"

"I can't make any promises there, Governor. You know they're going to want a stake in this as well."

"Listen, Brandon. Don't start that crap with me. You gave me your word."

"We're probably going to be meeting with the NTO soon, Governor, on other issues. I'm sure I'll get some direction on how to proceed. You might want to express your concerns to Senator Wilhelm."

"Wilhelm's an idiot. This is between me and you, McStocker. Don't mess with me."

Deborah looked up from her desk and dropped her jaw. Brandon rolled his eyes again.

"Governor, I have to run, but I'll see what I can do. We'll be in touch soon."

The line fell silent.

"Governor?"

Deborah shook her head and pressed the disconnect button.

"What a jerk," she said.

Brandon stuck his head out of Deborah's office door. "Jimmy! Got a second?"

Jimmy walked out of his office and into Deborah's. "What's up, Boss?"

"Have you been communicating with the governor's office about us expediting the cross?"

"Uh . . . no. Why?"

"Well, he is miraculously in the know. Somebody in this office is feeding the statehouse, and it has to stop."

"Wait a minute, Boss. What are you saying? Do you think I'm leaking information to the governor's office?"

"No. Of course not. I just can't figure out what's going on. Never mind. Go on back to work. Sorry to interrupt."

Jimmy walked out of the office and turned to look at Deborah just as he went out of her sight. She shook her head.

"What?" Brandon asked, noticing her anxious look.

"I don't know, Brandon. I just don't know."

"Okay . . . well, let's focus on a trip to D.C. I'll get Mena on it as soon as they get back."

Brandon and Deborah walked into the committee chambers to address the NTO, their arms loaded with briefcases and documents. Senator Wilhelm sat in the center of the long table at the front of the room. It was daunting to them since neither of them had ever addressed a committee of that magnitude in that kind of environment. In a conference room, yes. But never sitting face to face with the entire committee.

"We will call this session to order," Senator Wilhelm said, slamming his gavel to get everyone's attention. "Mr. McStocker, Ms. Blanchard. On behalf of all members of the National Transition Office, I welcome you and thank you for taking time from your busy schedules to address this body. I understand you have a significant recommendation for us regarding Kéntro. Is that right?"

Brandon leaned forward and spoke into the microphone. "Yes, Senator. That is correct."

"Excellent. I congratulate you and your firm for getting the Kéntro Project moving in such an expedient fashion. I understand you're already in Nebraska surveying and working out the details for the two northern spurs of the cross."

"Yes, sir. That's correct."

"Does anyone else have any opening comments for Mr. McStocker?"

"I do," a voice came from the far left side of the table.

Brandon looked over and was shocked at who he saw. Deborah quickly scribbled on a piece of paper and slid it in front of Brandon. "What the heck is he doing here?"

"You may proceed, Senator Sanders. Welcome to the NTO Committee."

"Thank you, Senator. Thank you, Mr. McStocker, Ms. Blanchard, for being here. Can you tell me what kind of budget you've been assigned for this project?"

"Uh, I don't actually have one, Senator. Due to the size and complexity of the project, our direction is to do what needs to be done until and unless we're told to slow down or stop."

"And who gave you that direction, sir?"

Brandon looked at Wilhelm. The senator nodded.

"The president did, Senator."

"The president. Are you accustomed to taking orders from the president of the United States for construction projects, Mr. McStocker?"

"Of course not, sir. But again, due to its nature, there are many aspects of this project we aren't accustomed to."

"Mr. McStocker, has anyone ever told you that this project is doomed to failure, and you should shut it down?"

"Sir?"

Wilhelm interrupted. "Senator Sanders, might I remind you, this is not an inquisition. Nor is it a referendum on the project. We invited you to join this committee to provide opposing views, not to intimidate or undermine our guests."

"Senator, I just wanted to know if these guests were aware that this so-called move of the nation's capital is a sham and the pet project of an out-of-control president."

"That's enough, Senator!"

"I have no further comments." Senator Sanders punched the button on the base of the microphone in front of him. The tone of the meeting was set, and it was nothing like Brandon and Deborah expected.

"I'm sorry, Mr. McStocker. You may proceed," Wilhelm said.

"Thank you, Senator. I will yield to my deputy on this project, Deborah Blanchard."

He slid the microphone across the table toward her. They looked at each other and grinned.

"Good morning, members of the committee. I want to thank you for letting us address you this morning about this project. While it is certainly a gargantuan undertaking, headed up by the federal government, this is a project of the people. As such, we think it would be a boon for the people to get involved with Kéntro's development."

"Sounds intriguing. How might we do that?" Wilhelm said.

"Well, sir. I think we need to build the new city with leading-edge technology. As an architectural and engineering firm, we're not completely aware of all the technology available to us. We have so much genius in this country that we could and should tap into—bringing it to the front line so to speak. We would like to form a team of experts from all the disciplines surrounding the design of the city. We want to tap into the best there is in construction techniques, telecommunications, and transportation using queue techniques by the leading operations research analysts—even the new physical and digital library-management systems and the best in environmentally friendly landscaping techniques. We want to find those people that will inevitably say they wish things had been built better and put them to work before they have a chance to say it."

"How do you propose to do that?" Wilhelm asked.

"We will identify those geniuses who can add value to the project and send them personal invitations to participate. We will bring them all to Manhattan to meet with our engineers to get a feel for the design. Then, we will load them up on buses for a tour of the construction site. We believe this will get their senses engaged and the ideas flowing. We will create discipline-specific teams led by our engineers to start incorporating the leading-edge technologies into all areas of the design. We call it genius pods."

"Sounds like something our constituents might appreciate," Wilhelm said, looking up and down the table to his right and left.

Everyone was nodding in agreement except Senator Sanders.

Deborah continued explaining the concept and answering questions from the committee. When the members were satisfied, they all agreed that getting the country involved like that would be a public relations windfall. Except for Senator Sanders, they all gave their blessing to proceed with *genius pods*.

"Great job in there," Brandon said to Deborah as they walked down the hall outside the chambers.

"Hey, Brandon. That was awesome stuff. I'll be in touch," Senator Wilhelm said as he rushed by them, clearly on a mission.

"Thanks, Senator!" Brandon shouted as Wilhelm disappeared into the crowd.

"I'm headed to the house. I just got a text from Cassandra. You want to join us for supper?"

"Sure. That would be nice," Deborah said.

CHAPTER 18

Sonny turned the car into the driveway in Fairfax. Deborah saw Natasha and Gary sitting in another car across the street.

"Dang. Some serious security around here."

"Yeah. They just keep an eye on the place," Brandon said. "Cassandra doesn't much care for the arrangement."

"Better to be safe than sorry, I suppose."

"Thank you," Sonny said, making eye contact with Deborah and smiling his agreement in the rearview mirror.

Susan came out of the front door and down the porch steps as Sonny opened Deborah's car door. Brandon got out on the other side. Susan hugged her daddy, said hi to Deborah, then looped her arm around Sonny's. He patted her hand, and they walked up the steps to the front door, where Cassandra was standing to greet them.

"Come in. Come in," Cassandra said. "Our early supper is just about ready. Sonny, those two can come in and join us if they want."

"Thank you, ma'am, but no. We really can't."

"So, how has everything been going here today?" Brandon asked.

"It's been nice having this one home," Cassandra said, putting her arm around Susan. "But she keeps telling me how much she loves it out there, so I guess we'll send her back."

Susan smiled at her mom then walked into the kitchen.

"It seems that she has found a new friend out there," Cassandra said.

Brandon looked puzzled.

"She hasn't stopped talking about Mena all day. Apparently, there's a fiddle in her future."

They all chuckled and followed Susan into the kitchen.

"Where's Liv?" Brandon asked.

"Upstairs doing her homework. She's taking her senior year pretty seriously. You guys make yourself comfortable at the table," Cassandra said.

Susan climbed the stepstool and took some glasses from the cupboard and a pitcher of iced tea from the refrigerator.

"Make yourself at home," Brandon said to Deborah. "I'll just be a few minutes."

He went up the steps and into Olivia's room, where she was lying on the bed with several books open all around her.

"Hey, kiddo. What are you working on so hard?"

"Hi, Daddy. Math at the moment. How did your meeting go?"

"Oh, it was fine. They seemed to like Deb's proposal. Is school going okay?"

"Couldn't be better."

Brandon sensed sadness in her voice.

"What's wrong, sweetie?"

"Nothing. I just miss Susan being around to talk to."

"Oh, I know, honey. It must be hard for you. But she seems to be happy out there."

"She is, Daddy. She's been telling me all about it. I guess I'm a little jealous."

"Well, maybe after school is out, you can come visit."

"That would be fun. Do you think Mom would be okay with it?"

"I think so."

"Daddy, how long do you think Kéntro will last?"

"Oh, jeez, honey. I think we'll be building on that for years. Why do you ask?"

"I want to apply to Harvard and become a project manager like you. I want to get a job working on Kéntro. Do you think I can do that?"

Brandon smiled. "Sweetheart, you can do anything you set your mind to. I'd love to have you on the team. But you should talk to Aunt Deb about it while she's here."

"I will, Daddy."

"We'll be eating soon," Brandon said. "Finish up here and come on down."

"Okay. I'll be down shortly."

Brandon walked back into the kitchen, where everyone was sitting around the table and chatting.

"Everything okay up there?" Cassandra asked.

"Oh, she's hard at it. That girl amazes me."

"I know. She's something else."

"Did you know she wants to go to Harvard so she can come out and work with me?"

Susan smiled. "Honey, that doesn't surprise you, does it?" Cassandra asked. "The child worships the ground you walk on."

"She'd be a great addition," Deborah said. "Maybe she can be my replacement."

Brandon pointed his finger at her. "Don't even think about it."

★ ★ ★ ★ ★

On their way back to Kansas, Susan sat between Brandon and Deborah on the plane, reading articles in *Acoustic Guitar Magazine*. Deborah was thumbing through the in-flight catalog, and Brandon was clicking away on his notebook computer, while Sonny sat with his eyes closed across the aisle from them.

"Daddy, do you think Liv will come out and stay with us?"

"I don't know, sweetie. Do you miss her already?"

"Yeah. I do."

"Well, I just happen to know she misses you, too. Did you want to stay in Fairfax?"

"No. No. I mean, I miss Mom and Liv, but I love being in Kansas. Mena promised to set up that jam. I can't wait to meet her cousin, the fiddler. That's going to be so much fun."

"I think so, too," Brandon said.

Deborah looked up from her magazine and smiled at him. "You know, Liv and I chatted for a good long while last night. She had so many questions about project management—really smart questions. She knows her stuff."

"Yes, I told her to talk to you about it. You didn't scare her away?"

"Heavens no. She's determined. I think this is serious, Brandon. I think she has a passion for construction. She even sees Kéntro as a patriotic service to her country. What seventeen-year-old thinks that way?"

"That's your first mistake." Susan laughed.

"What are you talking about?" Brandon chuckled.

"She's more like the age of you and Mom than a kid."

Deborah smiled at Brandon, raising her eyebrows. "That's probably true."

"When did you get so smart?" Brandon asked.

"Hey. I know stuff," Susan said with a smirk.

Brandon and Deborah laughed and went back to what they were doing, shaking their heads.

"Did you know Mena's sister works in the governor's office?" Susan asked.

Brandon and Deborah froze, staring at each other.

"What?" Brandon asked. "How do you know that?"

"She got a call when we were out, and I asked her about the caller ID I saw on her phone that said *State of Kansas*. She seemed pretty matter-of-fact about it. I didn't know if she had told you guys or not."

The morning after returning to Manhattan, Brandon and Sonny walked off the elevator into the office complex. Sonny stood to the side.

"Good morning, Cindy," Brandon said.

"Good morning, sir. Welcome back."

"Thank you. Ms. Blanchard in?"

"Yes, sir. She's in her office."

"Sonny, can you check in at the school now and then. You know, make sure Susan isn't threatening the teachers."

"Of course, sir."

Brandon walked to the commons, where Mena was working at her desk.

"Good morning, sir. Did you have a good trip?"

"We did, Mena. Thanks. Everything okay around here?"

"Nothing major that I'm aware of, sir. There is a stack of messages I left on your desk. I didn't sense any panic in any of those calls. There was a call from the governor's office late yesterday. I forwarded that one to Mr. Dillon."

"From the governor's office, huh?" Brandon noticed Jimmy's door was closed, and the lights were out.

"He's not in yet?"

"No, sir. I haven't seen him yet this morning."

Brandon stuck his head in Deborah's door. "Hey, Deb. Did you get rested?"

"Yep. I slept pretty well."

"Good. Hey listen, that was a good show you put on in D.C. Thank you."

"You're quite welcome. I think genius pods are going to be good for the team."

"I'll be over here if you need anything." Brandon walked toward his office. "Mena, let me know when Mr. Dillon shows up."

"Yes, sir. Oh, I forgot to mention—I've been talking to my cousin, Darcy, and her husband. They've set up a jam at Barney's this Friday night. You think you and Susan can make it?"

"I'm going!" Deborah shouted from her office.

Brandon laughed. "Good deal. Of course we'll be there. If we didn't go, Susan would never forgive me."

"Great. I'll let them know."

"Hey, Mena, why haven't you mentioned that your sister works in the governor's office?"

She blushed. "Uh, I didn't think it was that important, sir. I'm sorry. Is it an issue? I guess I thought there might be a conflict of interest in some way."

"No. Not that I can see so far."

After about an hour, Mena tapped on Brandon's door and stuck her head in.

"Sir, Mr. Dillon is in his office."

"Thanks, Mena."

He got up from his desk and walked across the commons and into Jimmy's office.

"Hey, Boss. How was the trip?"

Jimmy looked tired. His hair was out of place, and it looked like he'd slept in his clothes.

"It was fruitful. You okay, Jimmy?"

"Fine. Why?"

"Well, you look like crap, for starters. What's going on?"

"I'm fine. I just had a late night last night."

"Have you been home at all?"

Jimmy ignored Brandon and took his notebook computer and other materials from his briefcase.

"Jimmy, I don't know what's going on, but go home—at least long enough to take a shower and put on some fresh clothes."

"I'm fine, Boss."

"Jimmy, *go!*" Brandon said, walking out of Jimmy's office. He glanced at Deborah leaning against her door frame, staring back at him. He continued into his office shaking his head.

★ ★ ★ ★ ★

Sonny turned the limo into the parking lot at Barney's Diner and into one of the few remaining spots. He popped the trunk, jumped from the car, and opened the back door for Susan. Brandon got out on the other side and walked around to the back of the car.

"Daddy, listen," Susan said as she reached into the trunk to pull out her guitar case.

They all three stood still. The air was full of old-time fiddle music coming from inside the diner.

"Oh my," Brandon said. "Listen to that fiddler."

Susan's eyes were wide open; her brows peaked into her forehead. "That is so amazing. I wonder if that's Mena's cousin."

"Let's go find out," Brandon said. He pulled his guitar case from the trunk and walked toward the front door of the diner.

Sonny closed the trunk lid. "I'll stay out here awhile, Mr. Mc-Stocker."

"You sure?"

"Yes, sir. I want to watch the parking lot for a bit."

"Okay, then. We'll see you inside."

Susan slapped Sonny's stomach with her free hand and pointed her finger in his face. "Try not to shoot anybody."

"Go," he said. "Get in there and play pretty."

Brandon held the front door open, and Susan walked into a wall of sound. She stopped and stared across the room as Brandon walked in after her, letting the door close behind him. Several of the tables had been moved into the corner on the other end of the diner, and a circle of chairs had been formed in the open space. Susan saw Mena sitting at a table in the corner and waved. There was a bass player standing to the side of the circle, a couple of guitar players, a banjo player, and two mandolin players. And there she was. A fiddle player, sitting in the middle of them looking toward them at the door. She smiled at Susan as she continued to play, her long golden hair shimmering in the late afternoon sunlight beaming through the front windows.

The music stopped. "Hey, you two. Get over here and pick," Mena shouted. "I've got some folks I want you to meet."

"Hey, Barney," Brandon said as he walked to the counter and across the room. "Hey, Preacher," he said to Emmett who was sitting at the counter. "Didn't expect to see you here."

"I love these things," Emmett said.

"This here is my daughter, Susan."

"Well, hello, Susan," Emmett said, reaching to shake her hand. "I'm pleased to finally meet you."

"Good afternoon, sir. Good to meet you as well. You aren't playing?"

"Oh, no, honey. I'm a listener. I keep a safe distance." He smiled. "But I'm sure looking forward to hearing you tonight."

"Hi, Susan," Barney said. "Can I get you two anything?"

"Just a couple glasses of water, for now, Barney. Thanks."

They walked to the corner near Mena's table and set their guitar cases down beside the wall under the window. The fiddler continued to smile and watch Susan.

"Well, sweetie," Mena said. I'd like you to meet my cousin over there. That's Darcy. And over there on the banjo is her husband, Trevor."

Susan slowly walked into the middle of the circle and extended her hand. "Hi, Ms. Darcy. I'm so glad to finally meet you." Darcy's smile grew, and she held Susan's hand, resting her fiddle on her knee with her other hand. "This is my daddy."

"Well, hello, Daddy," Darcy said.

"Brandon," he said extending his hand. "Brandon McStocker."

Brandon then turned to Trevor and shook his hand.

"Pleased to meet you guys," Trevor said. "Those guitars aren't doin' a bit of good in them cases. Break 'em out."

"It's been a long time," Brandon said.

The two of them went back to the table and took their guitars from the cases. They sat at the two empty chairs that had been waiting for them and tuned up.

"Y'all go ahead. We'll catch up," Brandon said, his old accent sneaking its way back out after years of hiding.

Darcy kicked off another fiddle tune, and the other musicians fell in behind her. Susan stopped tuning and stared at Darcy, her mouth hanging open. Darcy's bow jumped up and down, the rosin from the horsehair creating a little cloud in the last remaining streaks of sunlight peeking through the curtains.

The tune ended, and Darcy looked at Trevor. "Let's sing one. Let's do something slow and easy."

Trevor put his banjo in the case lying on the floor next to his chair and picked up a guitar on the other side. He began strumming, and Darcy started to sing.

"Hey, I know this song," Susan whispered, poking her elbow into Brandon's side.

"Sing with 'em."

When it got to the chorus, Trevor started singing harmony with Darcy. Then Susan started singing a second harmony line. Everyone in the room gasped. Darcy smiled and nodded her head for Susan to keep singing. Mena's eyes opened wide, and her jaw dropped. She looked at Brandon, and he shrugged his shoulders. The song the trio sang was breathtaking.

They all continued playing and singing late into the night.

CHAPTER 19

After the jamming came to an end, the diner emptied. Brandon, Susan, Deborah, Mena, Darcy, and Trevor sat around a table chatting while Barney cleaned up the kitchen and the area behind the counter.

"You're pretty darn good on that guitar, little lady," Mena said to Susan.

"Thank you. That was so much fun."

"Your singing has come a long way, sweetheart," Brandon said. "I had no idea."

"It was impressive," Darcy said. Mena tells me you want to learn how to play the fiddle. Is that true?"

"I would love to do that," Susan smiled.

Darcy leaned forward on the table. "I can teach you if you think you can commit some time to it."

Susan turned to Brandon with her jaw hanging down. "Oh, my gosh, Daddy. Can I?"

He laughed and looked at Trevor. "Do I have a choice here?"

"I'm guessing not."

Brandon looked back at Darcy. "Is giving lessons something you normally do?"

Trevor chuckled and smiled at Darcy.

"Brandon, I think I've been teaching ever since I left the conservatory."

"Conservatory?"

"Boston Conservatory. I graduated from Bellarmine College in Louisville and went to the conservatory. My folks thought I would play for the Cincinnati Symphony." She chuckled. "That didn't pan out for them. Life changed when I met this guy," she pointed her thumb toward Trevor.

Darcy began to write on a napkin.

"Impressive. You guys have any kids?" Brandon asked.

Mena's face turned solemn, and she put her hand on Darcy's arm. Darcy smiled and patted Mena's arm.

"We had two daughters, but they're no longer with us."

"Oh my. I am so sorry." Brandon looked at Trevor. "I can't imagine."

"We have two beautiful granddaughters, though. Twins. They are our sunshine and the main thing I miss about Kentucky. They're both going to Bellarmine now, in the music program. Their dad moved off the mountains of Eastern Kentucky to be near them in Louisville."

"Sounds like a good daddy," Brandon said.

"Oh, he is," Trevor said. "The best."

"My sister is going to go to Harvard," Susan said, grinning.

"Is that right?" Darcy said. "I bet you're all proud of her."

Brandon laughed. "Well, she hasn't been accepted yet. But she's a business geek, and that's what she's aiming for. Her name is Olivia. She's graduating from high school this year."

"That little girl wants to be a project manager," Deborah piped up. "She has her sights set on coming out here to work with her daddy. She'll be good at it, too."

"Well, if she's anywhere near as intense as this one, I'm sure she will do well," Darcy said smiling at Susan.

She handed Susan the napkin. "Here's my number, sweetie. Give me a call Monday, and we'll set up a time to get you started on that fiddle. Do you have a fiddle to learn on?"

Susan looked at Brandon. "Uh. No."

Brandon looked at Darcy and shook his head.

"Here," Darcy said, taking back the napkin. "Here's the number for a luthier in town. He specializes in fiddles and does all of my work now. He usually has some nice ones for sale. Don't buy cheap, Dad. Those are hard to learn on." She handed the napkin back to Susan.

Barney started turning the lights off. "Hey, Brandon," he shouted across the room. "When Emmett left, he told me to have you give him a call tomorrow. He didn't want to disturb you guys."

"Will do. Thanks."

Monday morning, Brandon walked onto the third floor and down to his office.

"Morning, Mena."

"Good morning, sir."

"Great time Friday."

"Yes, sir, it was."

He stuck his head in Deborah's office doorway. "Morning, Deb. I guess we better call the troops together first thing and debrief them on what happened in D.C."

"I agree. I'll round them up."

Brandon walked toward his office then stopped and turned to Mena.

"By the way, Mena. We're pickin' buddies now. I think we can drop the formalities. Just call me Brandon, okay?"

She blushed. "Yes, sir. But that's going to take some getting used to."

"Relax, Mena," Deborah shouted, overhearing the conversation. "He's not as important as he thinks he is."

"Hey!" Brandon shouted back. "Get to work."

They all laughed, and Brandon continued toward his office.

"By the way, Susan absolutely loves Darcy."

Mena chuckled. "Trust me. The feeling is mutual. I'll get the conference room ready."

All the department heads and project managers began filing into the conference room as Mena placed coffee pots on the heating plates and unboxed the pastries that had been delivered a few minutes earlier. Before long, there were many groups of employees huddled together in conversation. A loud roar filled the room. At the scheduled time, Brandon and Deborah entered and walked to their seats at the head of the long table.

"Good morning, everyone," Brandon shouted. "Can we get started, please?"

The two sat as Mena placed cups of coffee in front of them. The crowd began taking their seats, and the room became quiet.

"This is a good-news meeting, so everyone can take a deep breath and relax. Paul, how's that new baby doing?" Brandon smiled.

"Doing great, Brandon. Thanks for asking. Mom is fine. Everyone's fine."

Deborah smiled and nodded.

"Good. Good. Thanks, everyone, for being here. I know you're busy, but this is a pretty big deal, and we wanted to share it with you face to face—not in an email. As you know, Deb and I were in D.C. last week and got the go-ahead on something we're going to call PIE-D or Public Inclusive Efficient Design."

Brandon pressed a button on the remote control in front of him, and an infographic came up on the giant screens at both ends of the room.

"PIE-D is a program that will allow us to invite some of the greatest minds in the country to come together and design the features into the new city from the best of all leading-edge technologies. I know this may feel a little daunting at first, but we've determined, and the NTO in D.C. agrees, that the benefits far outweigh any potential risk. It will help give the citizens ownership of their new capital."

Deborah looked at Brandon, and they smiled at all the heads turning, looking at each other and murmuring.

"I know. I know," Deborah said. "What did we hire you for, right? It's a valid question to ask yourselves, but not to worry. You guys are still leading the design teams. But what we're going to do is find the nationally recognized experts in each of your disciplines and ask them to come onboard to be subject matter experts and a key resource on your project teams and what we'll call genius pods."

"The committee is willing to pay them for their time," Brandon continued. "But I have a hunch that if we approach them with an opportunity to become a part of building the foundation for a new beginning in this country, they'll want to do it pro bono."

Brandon noticed Jimmy wasn't at the table. He was sitting with some employees in one of the chairs that lined the wall—the gallery, they called it. His head was down in his phone, obviously texting.

"Mr. Dillon, are you with us?" He asked.

"Oh. Yes, sir. Sorry. Just a quick response to one of the contractors up on the beltway."

"When does all this begin?" one of the managers asked.

"We'll be getting an ad campaign going immediately with some brochures and invitation letters," Deborah said. "Of course, we need to build a list of potential candidates. So, we'd like you all to get your heads together on that and let us know who your choices are for your no-holds-barred dream team."

She pointed at Mena, who was sitting at the side of the table next to her, taking notes.

"Provide your lists to Mena as soon as possible, so she can compile them and start the mailing. We'll follow up with an email campaign, and IT will build a website to help get the word out. Right?"

She stared at the IT director with an exaggerated smile.

"Uh . . . yes, ma'am," he said. "I'll have a couple of my folks get with you on the details, and we'll start developing ASAP. We should have a prototype ready within the week."

Deborah nodded. "Perfect!"

The meeting continued with the leadership team discussing the status of each of their projects. As soon as they adjourned,

Brandon went back to his office and closed the door. He sat at his desk and stared out the window for several minutes before he was interrupted.

"Sir, uh, Brandon, Senator Wilhelm's office on line one."

"Thanks, Mena. I'll take it."

He gazed at the blinking red light for what seemed like an eternity before finally picking up the handset.

"Brandon here."

"Mr. McStocker, please hold for the senator."

"Brandon! How's it going out there?"

"Fine, sir."

"Have you told your team yet?"

"Just came out of the staff meeting."

"How'd they take it?"

"I saw a little concern. But they're big boys and girls. They'll be fine."

"It's a great idea, you know."

"Oh, I know, Senator. But it was all Deb. She's our resident genius."

"Well, you're lucky to have her."

"Yes, sir, we are. She's a good friend. Senator, is the investigation coming up with anything?"

"Not really. But your friends in the right-wing media sure are having a field day with the Sanders-family conspiracy theories."

"Yeah. I saw that. You think there's anything to it?"

"Beats me, Brandon."

There was a rapid knock on Brandon's door. Deborah walked in and closed it behind her. It looked like all the blood had left her face. Her eyes were red.

"Uh . . . I'm sorry, Senator. I have to go," Brandon said, staring at Deborah.

"Okay, Brandon. Listen, get back to me in a few days and we'll—"

Brandon hung up the phone mid-sentence.

"Deb? What is it?"

She began trembling and cupped her hands around the sides of her eyes and looked at the floor as if she was looking for something in bright light. Then she looked up, covered her mouth, and sat in the chair in front of Brandon's desk.

"Deb?"

"It's Cassandra."

"What about Cassandra?"

"Brandon, she's dead."

"What?"

"Brandon, she's gone."

"But, how?"

"Agent Simpson told Sonny it was a homicide. Murder–suicide, actually."

Brandon spun his chair and looked out the window. He couldn't speak.

"Brandon—I am so, so sorry. Sonny thought I should be the one to tell you."

He lowered his face into his hands. He wept for several minutes before popping his head up and spinning back around to his desk.

"What about Liv? Where's Olivia?"

"She's fine. She's with Anne McClellan."

"So, she knows?"

"Yes."

"I need to get Susan."

"Sonny just left for the school to pick her up."

"Oh, G—."

"Brandon—" She paused.

He looked up at her, tears flowing.

"Brandon, Liv is the one that found them."

"Them?"

"It was somebody by the name of Denny Cardoza. Apparently, he shot her then shot himself."

"Oh . . . no. Have Mena get Susan and me on a flight."

"Of course."

CHAPTER 20

After the funeral at Pastor Landry's church, the family and friends gathered at the cemetery for a small graveside service. Brandon stood to the side with his arms around Olivia and Susan, all three wearing sunglasses. Carl finished the service with a prayer, and the three of them stepped up to the casket and placed a flower on top of it. Deborah wore a black dress and a hat, crying behind her sunglasses.

Brandon looked up, holding his daughters' hands, and saw Senator Wilhelm on the other side of the grave, then turned to walk toward his limo, where Sonny was waiting. Deborah followed them. Sonny opened the doors to help everyone in, but Brandon stayed back. Once the ladies were in, Brandon turned to Sonny.

"Take them back to the hotel. I don't want them going to the house. Understand?"

"Yes, sir."

"I'm going to catch a ride to Wilhelm's office. I think Pastor Landry will take me. I'll text you when I'm ready to be picked up."

"Of course, sir." Sonny closed the doors. "Oh, and sir."

"Yeah."

"We learned this morning that it was Denny's car that had been following us."

A back window lowered. "Daddy, what are you doing?" Olivia asked.

Brandon nodded at Sonny and turned to Olivia. "Honey, I need to go see someone. I'll meet you back at the hotel later on."

"Daddy, can't it wait?" Susan shouted from the other side of the back seat.

Brandon looked at Deborah sitting in the front seat. She stared without saying a word.

"I have to go."

Sonny closed his door and drove away as Brandon walked back to the grave site.

"Carl, can you hang around a minute?"

"Of course, Brandon. Take all the time you need."

Everyone had dispersed when Carl walked away leaving Brandon alone under the green canopy by Cassandra's grave.

"Sweetheart, I am so sorry."

He put his face in his hands and fell to his knees, weeping. Carl watched him but didn't interrupt. Instead, Carl walked a short distance to his car and drove it back around to the curb near the grave site. He parked and walked around to open the passenger-side door. Brandon stood and brushed off his knees and shook his head, regaining his composure. Then he turned and walked toward Carl.

"I need a ride."

"I know."

"How did you know?"

"Sonny and the girls are already gone. Doesn't take a genius."

"Oh. Well, okay. Can you take me to the Capitol?"

"I can, but are you sure that's what you want to do right now?"

"I have to, Preacher. If you can drop me off, I'll have Sonny come pick me up."

"Okay, then. Let's go."

★ ★ ★ ★ ★

"Is the senator in?" Brandon asked as he entered Wilhelm's office.

"No, sir," the secretary said. "I'm afraid he's not. He was attending a funeral this morning."

"Yeah, I know. Any idea when he'll be back?"

"I don't know, sir. I'll be glad to leave a message for him."

"No, I'll wait."

"Sir, you're welcome to wait. But really, I don't know if he'll be in at all today."

Brandon sat on the long brown leather couch and stared at the door. "I'll wait."

After several minutes of silence, the secretary interrupted his gaze. "Can I get you a magazine or glass of water? Anything?"

"I'm fine. Thanks."

Brandon had sat motionless for thirty minutes when the senator arrived.

"Brandon. What are you doing here? I didn't realize you wanted to talk to me, or I would've hung around at the cemetery."

"That's fine, Senator. Do you have a few minutes?"

"Of course. Come in. Hold my calls, please."

"Yes, sir."

Wilhelm closed the door behind them, and Brandon sat on a couch in the office.

"What is it, Brandon?" Wilhelm asked as he sat in his armchair.

Brandon leaned forward and slammed his fist on the coffee table. Senator Wilhelm fell back in his chair, startled, and his mouth fell open.

"Brandon!"

"It's enough!" Brandon shouted. "I've had enough!"

"Brandon, I know this has been hard but please."

"Does the FBI have any idea who Denny Cardoza is?"

"I don't know, Brandon. Let them do their job."

"If they were doing their job, I wouldn't have been attending my wife's funeral this morning."

"Brandon, relax. Let me call the director and see if he can come talk to us."

Brandon turned his head and rested it on his fist, leaning on the arm of the couch.

"Yes, sir?"

"See if you can get the FBI director on the phone."

"Yes, sir. Will do."

"By the way, the president sends his condolences," Wilhelm said.

"Thanks. Deb told me that he sent a nice arrangement of flowers to the church. I didn't get a chance to see them."

"Sir, the director is on the phone."

"Stew, do you have some time to come over to my office and meet with me and Brandon McStocker? Yes. Yes, he is. Okay, great. We'll see you shortly."

Brandon lifted his head when Wilhelm hung up the phone. "Well?"

"He's on his way with the lead investigator. It'll take them awhile to get over here. You want to take a walk or something?"

"Not really. Why did they go after Senator Taylor?"

"I don't understand. What you mean?"

"I can almost understand why they wanted to get rid of Bob. I even understand why they wanted to use Cassandra to get to me. But why Senator Taylor?"

"Brandon, I don't know. I do know that she was a strong advocate of the president's push for the 28th Amendment. Maybe that has something to do with it. I don't know."

They talked for awhile before the secretary's voice filled the room from the intercom.

"Senator, the FBI director is here."

"Send him in, please."

The door opened, and two tall, dark-haired men entered the office.

"Stew, please come in and have a seat. Brandon McStocker, this is FBI Director Stuart Wilkins."

"Pleased to meet you, Brandon. This is agent Aditya Patel. He's been working the case."

"Thanks for coming to see us, gentlemen," Wilhelm said.

"Brandon, Senator, listen," Patel said. "I think we've been able to make a connection between this Denny Cardoza and the Sanders Foundation. We're just not sure yet. I have my team tracking it down."

"Did he kill Bob McClellan? Senator Taylor?"

"We just don't know, Brandon," the director said.

"We did find out that Cardoza used to work as a nurse down at George Washington University Hospital," Agent Patel continued. "We're looking into that as well. It's entirely possible that he was able to get his hands on some drug to do those murders. We're just not sure. I would hate to relax our investigation because of his death when you guys could still be in danger."

"I understand," Brandon said. "I just keep thinking about the conversation I had with Anne McClellan. It was Denny who visited Bob shortly before his death. Cassandra didn't say anything about a visit by a stranger."

"We're trying to piece it together, Brandon," Stew said.

"You know what else I don't understand," Brandon said.

The others all dropped their heads in unison.

"No, wait. Listen. Why did he kill himself after he shot Cassandra? I don't get it."

"Forensics is still going through evidence collected at the scene. It may take them a while to get through it all," Patel said.

"Brandon, you might want to be prepared for the genuine possibility that the president might want to sweep all of this under the rug," Wilhelm said. "At least for now."

"What are you talking about?"

"I know this is the last thing on your mind right now, my friend, but the president still wants Kéntro to be a success. We could be sitting on a tinderbox if all this gets out."

"Senator, what are you saying?"

"I'm saying let these gentlemen continue with their investigation, but don't expect it to be headline news. This is going to take time. You need to go home and get some rest. Gather your thoughts, and get Kéntro back on track. Can you do that?"

"I don't believe this. Are you serious?"

"Brandon, please."

He shook his head and looked outside through the windows in Wilhelm's office. He stood and walked across the room to look out further. The room was silent as the other men watched him.

"One more thing," Wilhelm said. "The president contacted Harvard and put in a good word for Liv. I think she was going to make it in anyway, but he sealed the deal. She's in."

Brandon turned away from the window and stared into Wilhelm's eyes.

"Is he trying to buy my silence?"

"Don't go there, Brandon, please. You know the president has all the respect in the world for you. Don't lose your trust in him now. The nation doesn't know about all of this nastiness yet. He just wants to protect them from it. It'll be much easier to get things done. Of course, Sanders is going to keep kicking up the dust, but lucky for us, the citizens are pretty media-weary these days and aren't paying much attention to it."

"Will Liv be getting an acceptance letter? I'm sure she'll be elated."

"I have it right here." Wilhelm walked over to his desk and picked up an envelope addressed to Olivia McStocker. "The president thought it would be nice for me to deliver it personally. But that was before—well, before recent events."

"I wish Cassandra had known."

"Gentlemen, I think we're done here for now," Wilhelm said to Stew and Agent Patel. He walked them to the door and shook hands with them as they walked out. He closed the door behind them.

"Brandon, are you going to be okay?"

"I'll be fine. With Liv going off to college, it'll just be Susan and me. That's just a little bit hard to wrap my brain around."

"I don't claim to understand what you're going through, Brandon. Take whatever time you need to pull things together. But you also have to know that the president is counting on you to get Kéntro done. If there's anything we can do, anything at all, to help you with Susan or anything else, please don't hesitate to ask."

"She'll be fine. She'll probably quit school as soon as she has me talked into it, but she'll be fine. She's a strong little girl. Once we get Liv on the job, you can bet Kéntro is going to get done. I have no doubts."

He turned and looked at Wilhelm with a smile. "I need to go, Senator. I'm putting my trust in the system, against my better judgment. But right now, I have to."

Wilhelm saw an unusual distance in Brandon's gaze.

"Go home, Brandon. Get some rest. Grieve for your wife."

"I'll be fine. I'm sure Deb is going to be there for me. She always is."

"She's a good friend, Brandon. Hard to come by. Don't blow her off."

CHAPTER 21

Brandon raised his head and looked at Susan sitting next to him and then scanned the thousands of people sitting around him at the Tercentenary Theater on the campus of Harvard University.

"There she is, Dad," Susan said, grasping Brandon's arm and pointing into the crowd of students in full regalia.

Brandon caught her eye just as her name was announced. "Olivia McStocker," echoed around the yard. Olivia looked away from Brandon and walked across the platform to receive her diploma. *She looks sad*, Brandon thought. But after she had her diploma in hand, a smile grew on her face. She turned, raised the diploma over her head, and pointed her other hand toward Brandon and Susan who were standing and cheering, also with their hands over their heads. Olivia laughed when she saw them, but tears were streaming down her cheeks.

"Dad, she's crying."

"I know."

Susan looked at Brandon. "Oh, no, Dad. *You're* crying!"

Susan started laughing, but her laughter quickly turned to tears as well. He put his arm around her and squeezed.

After the ceremony, Brandon and Susan made their way through the crowd to find Olivia.

"There she is," Brandon shouted, pointing into the chaos.

"Dad!" Olivia threw her arms around Brandon and Susan.

"Congratulations, sweetheart. I am so proud of you."

"Congrats, Sis," Susan said, kissing Olivia on the cheek.

"I can't believe they finally gave me an MBA," Olivia said.

"They didn't *give* you anything, honey," Brandon said. "You worked hard for that degree."

Brandon put his arms around his daughters and walked out of the crowd to the other side of the library. It was much quieter there, and they could chat on their way to the reception.

"Mom would've been so proud of you," Susan said.

Olivia stopped walking. "I just wish she had been there to see it."

"Oh, she was there, honey," Brandon said. "She was there."

Brandon put his arm around one of Olivia's, and Susan wrapped her arm around the other. They continued their walk to the reception.

"Dad, are you sure you want me to come to work at the firm? I don't want to cause any problems or upset anyone."

Olivia had interned there the previous summer. It seemed like a natural fit, but she didn't want to make any assumptions.

"Of course I want you there, sweetie. Everybody does. You know Aunt Deb loves you to pieces."

"I know. But then I don't think Jimmy warmed up to the idea of me being there very well."

"Jimmy's Jimmy. He'll be fine."

"Gosh, I don't know what to do next," Olivia said.

"I know it's overwhelming. But the first thing we have to do is get you moved back to Manhattan. We'll load up all of the boxes you packed and drive down to Fairfax so I can sign all the closing papers on the house, then we'll head west."

Olivia and Susan looked at each other and then at the ground.

"I know it's hard, you guys," Brandon said. "But I just don't want to keep renting the place out. It doesn't make sense now."

"I know, Daddy," Olivia said. "We just have so many memories there. Our whole lives, you know?"

"I know."

The elevator door opened. Brandon, Olivia, and Sonny walked out, and Sonny stepped to the side.

"Well, good morning," Cindy said. "Welcome back, Ms. Mc-Stocker. Congratulations."

"Thanks, Cindy. Good morning."

Brandon and Olivia walked toward the commons.

"Same place?" Olivia asked.

"Yep. For now. We kept that cubicle clear for you."

The cubicle where she worked during her internship was just outside the common area around the corner. She reached in and threw her purse and briefcase on the chair and continued walking with Brandon.

"Oh my gosh! Look who we have here," Mena shrieked.

"What!" Deborah shouted from inside her office, knowing who Mena was referring to.

Olivia walked into Mena's arms as Deborah came charging out of her office.

"Look here at Little Miss MBA," Deborah said. "I am so proud of you."

Olivia turned and hugged Deborah.

"Your mom would be so proud, honey," Deborah said softly in Olivia's ear. "So proud."

"Susan didn't come in with you guys?" Mena asked.

"No, she didn't want to miss any more work, so she went on in."

"We should all go up there and have lunch with her," Deborah said.

Brandon looked at his watch. "Sounds like a plan."

Olivia smiled and nodded. She caught a glimpse of Jimmy sitting at his desk as she turned to go back to her cubicle. Brandon walked into his office and closed the door behind him. He threw his briefcase on the table and sat at his desk. He leaned forward on his elbows, put his face in his hands, and began to weep. After several minutes, he spun his chair to look outside the window. He looked into the sky, tears on his face.

The *national cross*, the two interstate spurs between I70 and I80 that crossed at the new city, was almost complete, and the airport was about to be commissioned by the FAA for limited service. Substantial facility construction had begun, but there were still several major lawsuits to be resolved. Over the previous six years, Brandon had become a stranger to his own company. Deborah was running the show, and he knew it.

Just before noon, Brandon heard a tap on his office door and looked up from the drawings he had spread across his conference table.

"Yes."

The door opened slowly, and Olivia stuck her head in. She looked at his desk and then around the room until she spotted him on the other side at the table.

"Ready for lunch, Brandon?"

He smiled and shook his head. "I have to admit, that's going to take some getting used to."

"Yes. Yes it is." Olivia said, giggling.

Sonny drove the limo into Barney's parking lot and got out to open the door for Olivia on his side of the car while Brandon got out the other side. Mena rode with Deborah in her car, and they followed Sonny into the parking lot. Brandon looked at Deborah across the lot as she got out of her car.

"Jimmy didn't come with you guys?"

"Nope. Said he had some calls to make."

"Whatever. Sonny, you want us to bring something out to you?"

"No, sir. Thanks. I'm fine." He leaned against the corner of the building. He caught a glimpse of Susan through the window. She smiled and waved.

The others walked inside the diner. Susan looked up and smiled as she poured coffee for one of the patrons.

"Hey, Dad. Hey, Sis. Go ahead and have a seat anywhere."

Brandon saw Emmett sitting at the counter.

"I'll be right there," Brandon said to Olivia as he left the group and walked across the room.

"Hey, Preacher," he said, slapping Emmett on the back.

"Hey, Brandon. I was just thinking about you. How have you been?"

"I'm doing well, I suppose."

"How was your trip back east?"

"It was good. Being back at Harvard was surreal, but Liv's graduation was pretty awesome."

"I bet. Did you get things buttoned up with the house?"

"Yep. Done deal. You wanna join us over at our table?"

"Thank you, but no. I was just getting ready to take off. I need to get back to the church building. You three should come visit us Sunday."

"Maybe. Good to see you. We'll catch up soon."

"Let's do it." Emmett got up and walked toward the front door and waved to the others sitting at Brandon's table. They all waved back.

"See ya, Emmett," Mena shouted.

"How are you guys doing?" Susan said as she walked up to the table, pulling the order book from her apron pocket.

"Doing good, sweetie." Brandon said. "Busy here today?"

"Not too bad. The construction crews do keep us hopping, though."

"No doubt."

"Hey, everybody," Edna said. "Susie Q, you go ahead on your break so you can have lunch with your family. I'll get this."

"Are you sure, Edna? I don't want to leave you with this lunch crowd."

"Don't think a thing about it. Now sit down here." Edna slid a chair over from another table and put it next to Olivia.

"Well, okay. Hey, Barney, I'm off the clock!" Susan shouted then sat down.

Barney just waved his hand from behind the counter without so much as looking up.

"Let me know when y'all are ready to order," Edna said as she walked away.

"Susie Q?" Olivia laughed, leaning her shoulder into Susan.

"Yeah, well. You know." Susan smiled.

The ladies continued to catch up and laugh while Brandon stared out the window. He watched Emmett get into his car and drive away. He saw Sonny pacing slowly around the parking lot. His heart was full, knowing that both of his girls were with him now. His thoughts went back to the funeral. The girls seemed so strong. How did they do that? They were so young then.

He dropped his head and looked at the black-and-white checkered tiles on the floor. So many unanswered questions. Why Cassandra? Why would a scumbag like Denny Cardoza kill her? It made no sense. It had been haunting him since the day it happened.

"Hey, Dad?" Olivia said.

Brandon looked up and around the table. "Sorry. What?"

"Where did you go?" She chuckled. "I said, can we take a run up to the beltway? I'd like to see how things are going up there."

"Oh, sure, honey. We can do that." He noticed his food sitting in front of him.

Deborah stared at Brandon.

After they were finished eating, everyone stood and walked toward the door.

"This one's on me, folks," Barney said.

Deborah wrapped her arm around Brandon's as they walked. "You okay?"

"I'm fine."

"Well, I can tell by those dark circles under your eyes, you haven't been sleeping. What's going on?"

"Really. I'm fine."

Susan followed them out to the parking lot. "Hey, Sonny," she said, standing on her toes to give him a hug.

"Hey, buddy," he said.

"You take care of yourself. Try not to shoot anybody."

He chuckled and gave her a thumbs-up.

Brandon looked at her with a stern face. "Really?"

"Oh, Dad. Lighten up. I don't mean anything by it."

Deborah and Mena headed back down to the campus while Sonny drove Brandon and Olivia up to the construction entrance. Several miles after leaving the main road, Sonny stopped the car at a guard shack, where a man in a yellow construction hardhat and brightly colored vest held up his hand.

Sonny lowered his window. "Hey, Bert. How's it going?"

"Going good, Sonny. Mornin', Mr. McStocker. Hey, lookie here. Welcome back, ma'am. Have a good tour today." He waved them through the gate.

"Holy crap," Olivia said as they got to the top of a small rise in the terrain. The landscape opened up in front of them all the way to the horizon. Thousands of acres of dirt with hundreds of graders and dozers appearing as yellow specks appeared as far as the eye could see.

"This is amazing, Dad."

Sonny smiled at her in the rearview mirror.

"I mean Brandon."

Brandon looked at her and smiled. "We're making great headway now. The national cross is finally in place. You can go all the way through to Nebraska on both spurs. As much as I hated to, we had to force it with eminent domain in several areas. Deb is still dealing with some lawsuits."

"Is Jimmy doing anything?"

"He's coordinating the efforts of the project managers to integrate the plan. Why?"

"I don't know. He just gives me the creeps."

"What? I've never heard that one before."

"I don't know. It's like I make him nervous or something."

"He's fine. Hey, Sonny. Let's drive over to the airport."

"Yes, sir."

As they drove around the east side of the beltway, Olivia could see the new control tower in the distance. When they got closer, the hangars and runways came into sight.

"It's just about ready to go," Brandon said. "Cargo planes will start coming in next week. That'll step up progress tenfold. Deb has been pushing on this one really hard."

"Aunt Deb is a big help, isn't she?"

"Honey, right now, she is what's holding this project together."

"Are you okay, Dad?"

Sonny looked in the rearview mirror, and Olivia stuck her tongue out at him.

"I'm fine, sweetheart. Sonny, let's go into the center-city area."

"Yes, sir."

When they drove inside the beltway, new roads were under construction everywhere. Foundations for hundreds of buildings were being poured by the concrete trucks scattered around. Gray dust blew across the car, tinting its black color.

"Honey, I think it's time you take on some of these projects."

"Are you sure?"

"I think you're ready, don't you?"

"Uh, yeah!"

"We'll talk to Deb when we get back. I think she needs help with this center-city construction."

Olivia reached across the back seat and hugged Brandon. "Thank you, Dad—uh, Brandon."

Sonny drove back out to the beltway and around the south end, in the middle of where the two southern spurs joined the beltway.

"That right there"—Brandon pointed through the windshield—"is the site of the McClellan Center."

"McClellan Center?"

"The new headquarters for McClellan and McStocker."

"Are you serious?"

"I think your corner office will be right over there," he laughed.

"Dad, this is so exciting."

"This has been my pet project. I designed it myself. Of course, I thought your mom would be around to see it. But I do hope Anne will accept my invitation to speak at the opening ceremony."

"Wow! It sounds like you have this all planned out."

"I've been dreaming about it for years, honey."

"Ms. Anne will love it. Mom would have, too."

Brandon turned away and looked out of his window, wiping his cheek.

"Sonny, let's get back to campus."

Chapter 22

O livia sat in her cubicle reviewing a contract when Deborah walked in.

"Have you seen your dad this morning?"

"Actually, I haven't seen him all weekend. Since Susan and I got the apartment, we don't see him as much as we used to. Why?"

"He never comes in this late, at least not without calling. Something's not right."

Olivia called her dad's number, but there was no answer.

"I think Susan's working the breakfast shift this morning."

Olivia dialed again.

"Hey, Sis. Have you seen Dad lately? Really? No, he hasn't shown up here yet. Okay. I'm going to his apartment. I'll keep you posted." She ended the call and threw the phone in her purse. "I'm going to run over there."

"You want me to go with you?" Deborah asked.

"No. No. I'll give you a call when I get there."

Olivia got in her car and drove through town. She pressed the Bluetooth button on her steering wheel.

"Call Sonny," she said.

"Hey, Sonny, this is Liv. Are you with my dad? He did? Why would he tell you to take the weekend off? Okay. I'm headed to his apartment now. I'm getting scared. Can you meet me over there?"

Olivia parked just outside of Brandon's front door. She pressed the doorbell and knocked. After several seconds of silence, she knocked again. She looked around and saw his car in its usual spot.

"Dad!" she shouted while knocking more frantically. She could hear the TV.

She dug into her purse and pulled out the set of keys her dad had given her in case she needed to get in for anything. She unlocked the door and pushed it open. It slammed against the safety chain.

"Dad!"

She looked through the slightly opened door and could only see his legs stretched out under the coffee table.

"Daddy!"

She started throwing her weight against the door, crashing her shoulder into it over and over.

"Daddy! Wake up!"

Sonny arrived and, seeing the look on her face, he motioned her out of the way and kicked in the door.

"Daddy!"

She ran inside and looked around the room. The air reeked of alcohol. Brandon was unconscious, stretched out on the couch. There were beer cans strewn all over the apartment and a half-empty bottle of whiskey sitting on the coffee table in front of him. Olivia sat next to him, trying to shake him awake, slapping his face.

"Oh, Dad. Please wake up. Has this happened before?" she asked Sonny.

"No, ma'am. Not that I'm aware of."

"Call 9-1-1."

Sonny went back outside and made the call while Olivia wetted a washcloth in the kitchen sink and wiped Brandon's face and neck.

At the hospital, Susan and Deborah arrived at the same time and ran down the hall to the emergency room, where Brandon was. When Olivia saw them, she stood from the chair next to Brandon's bed and broke down crying in Susan's arms.

"He'll be okay," Deborah said, wrapping her arms around both of the girls.

A nurse walked into the curtained ER bay to check Brandon's vital signs.

"What's going on?" Susan asked. "What's wrong with him?"

"Miss, these are classic signs of alcohol poisoning. We're giving him IV fluids and oxygen. His breathing seems fine. We just need to keep his airway clear."

Olivia looked at Susan and held her arm.

"Alcohol poisoning?" Susan asked.

"There was a whiskey bottle on the table at his apartment. I didn't even know Dad drank. Has this happened before?"

"Never," Susan said.

They both saw Deborah shaking her head and staring at the floor.

"Aunt Deb, what's going on?" Olivia asked.

"Girls, let's go sit out in the hallway and talk." She ushered them out while the nurse continued to write on her clipboard. The three sat on a bench outside of the emergency room.

"Aunt Deb? What is it?" Olivia asked. "You're scaring us."

"Girls, listen. I didn't know your dad was drinking, either, but it doesn't surprise me."

"What? Why? What's wrong?" Susan asked.

Deborah looked down the hallway, staring into the distance, and rubbed the back of her neck.

"Look, back when Brandon first took over this project from Bob McClellan, it wasn't something he was striving for. Leading this project was way outside of his comfort zone. He hates the spotlight. But he stepped up, as he always does, and got it off the ground."

The girls nodded and listened with every bit of focus they had.

She continued, "When your mom died, his spirit left him. It seems like the only thing he had left to look forward to was your graduation from Harvard."

She squeezed Olivia's hand.

"I don't know how much your dad's been drinking, or even if he has before this. But I do know he has distanced himself from the project. His mind isn't with us most of the time."

"Mom would hate this," Susan said.

Olivia nodded and looked at Deborah. "What are we going to do?"

"I know what I'm going to do," Susan said. "I'm going to call Pastor Emmett."

Several days later, Brandon sat alone in his own car in the parking lot of Emmett's church. He stared at the cross on top of the steeple, trying to decide if he wanted to go in. While his mind wandered around his decision, he didn't notice Emmett pulling his car up on the other side of him. Emmett quietly walked around Brandon's car and tapped on the driver's-side window. It startled Brandon, but then they both laughed as Brandon lowered the window.

"Scared the crap out of me, Preacher."

"Sorry. What are you doing out here?"

"Truth be told, I was thinking about coming in to see you. I guess I'm committed now."

"Yes. Yes, you are. I've got all the time you need. Come on, let's go into my office and get some coffee."

Brandon greeted the church secretary as they entered the office complex of the large church building.

"How are you feeling?" Emmett asked.

"Oh, like an idiot mostly. An idiot that just got beaten with a baseball bat."

They walked into the kitchenette, where Emmett poured two cups of coffee.

"You can doctor it however you like."

"Black is fine," Brandon said, staring into his cup.

Emmett glanced at him. "You okay?"

"Yes . . . no . . . maybe . . . heck, I don't know . . . sorry."

Emmett smiled and shook his head.

"Want one of these donuts?"

"No, thanks. I probably wouldn't be able to hold it down."

"Let's go in my office, then."

Brandon followed Emmett through the door.

"Dang! Have you read all of these?" Brandon asked, looking around the room at the hundreds of books stacked on the cherry-wood shelves that lined Emmett's office walls.

Emmett chuckled. "Well, most of them, I guess. People give me books all the time. I'm not sure if they don't think I have enough knowledge or if they're hoping I'll validate something they read in one of them. It's all good. You read much?"

"Not really. Not for enjoyment, anyway. I have to read so much at work, I guess I don't much feel like it when I get home."

"I understand."

"I can't believe I've known you for all these years, and I've still never stepped foot in your church."

"True. You can't say I haven't tried. But, hey, I don't take it personally."

Brandon looked out of the large window behind Emmett's ornate cherrywood desk that sat along the only wall that wasn't covered by bookshelves. Emmett saw that he was getting lost in his thoughts.

"Have a seat here, my friend."

Emmett pulled out a chair from a small conference table in the corner of his office, wedged between the shelves. Then he walked over to his desk, picked up his Bible, and started back to the table.

"Brandon?"

Brandon hadn't moved. He seemed frozen, still staring out of the window. Emmett touched his shoulder.

"Brandon, come on over here and have a seat."

"Oh. Sorry, Preacher. I guess that robin out there caught my attention."

"I guess. So, Susan seemed pretty worried when she called me from the hospital. But she asked me not to come. How long were you in there?"

"They just kept me overnight. You know what, Preacher, I probably shouldn't have come. I don't want to waste your time. I need to get to work, anyway."

He started walking toward the door.

With a raised voice, Emmett said, "Brandon."

Brandon turned and looked at him.

"Sit."

"What?"

"Sit. If not for yourself, talk to me for the sake of your girls."

Brandon turned slowly, walked to the table, and sat across from Emmett. He put his elbows on the table and put his closed fists over his mouth.

"Brandon, Susan was crying when she called me. Does that tell you anything?"

Brandon's hands began to shake. He looked down, resting his forehead on his fists. His shoulders heaved up and down as he wept. Then he opened his hands and put his face in them, sobbing uncontrollably. Emmett remained quiet. After several minutes, Brandon tried to compose himself. Emmett reached over and took a box of tissues from one of the bookshelves and slid it across the table toward Brandon.

"Sorry," Brandon said.

"Nothing to be sorry about. You're safe here. Have you been drinking a lot?"

Brandon raised his head and glared at Emmett with his red, swollen eyes. He paused while he tried to figure out a way to answer the question without lying.

"Brandon. You just about killed yourself. It's not like you're keeping it a secret."

"I'm sorry, Preacher. I don't know what's wrong with me."

Emmett leaned forward and folded his arms on the table. "What do you mean you don't know what's wrong. Are you kidding me? You're leading the biggest, most politically charged project this country has ever seen, and oh, by the way, you lost your wife right in the middle of it, and you have two daughters and hundreds of employees to take care of. Try to chew on that for a minute, Brandon."

"I didn't ask for this," Brandon said. "I didn't ask for any of it."

"Do you want to quit?"

Brandon looked around the room. After a long period of silence, he looked back at Emmett.

"I can't."

"You mean you won't."

"I mean I can't. Bob McClellan won't let me."

"Brandon, the man is dead."

"Oh, I know. I haven't lost my mind. But he put his faith in me, and I made a commitment to his wife, Anne. And I certainly don't want to be a disappointment to my girls. Sorry."

"I get that. How did it feel, going back for Liv's graduation?"

"Surreal, mostly. Good. But everywhere I looked, I saw Cassandra."

The two continued to talk for over an hour. Emmett saw that Brandon was in such great pain that there was no way he was going to get through it anytime soon. They stood, and Emmett walked Brandon to the front door of the church.

"Brandon, look. We have a ministry here at the church called Celebrate Recovery. They meet every Friday night, and I think it would do you some good. One of their open-share groups is focused on the pain associated with the loss of a loved one. You should check it out. Will you do that?"

"I will," Brandon said. "I've got to do something."

★ ★ ★ ★ ★

The following Friday night at 6:00, Brandon walked into the foyer of the church, where he was welcomed by a few people sitting at a table loaded with information pamphlets. One of the ladies directed him to the fellowship hall, where dinner would be served before the main worship event, and the large group session would start in the sanctuary.

He walked down the hall and into the large room. He heard dozens of voices chattering and laughing. After a prayer was said over the meal, he went through the line, keeping to himself, and got a plate of food. He sat alone in the corner of the room and scanned the people while he ate. Some were obviously dealing with drugs and alcohol. Some may have been homeless. Many more appeared to be normal people he might see in his neighborhood or at the job site.

"Dad?"

He jerked his head around and saw Susan standing just inside the door to the room. He choked down the water he was drinking.

"Susan? What are you doing here?"

"I play with the band here on Friday nights. We were just in the sanctuary practicing."

She leaned down and hugged him and sat down next to him.

"I had no idea. I mean, I knew you had a gig every Friday night, but I had no idea you were playing at a church."

"This is where I've been playing. What are you doing here?"

"Well, after you reported me to Pastor Emmett, he suggested I give it a try."

"Shut up." She slapped his arm. "I didn't report you."

"Well, in any case, I'm here. I knew I had to do something. I'm sorry I disappointed you girls."

"Dad, you haven't disappointed us. We know you're dealing with a lot of crap, with Mom gone and all. I'm just excited that you're here. Please stay with it awhile. I think it'll help. Who knows, maybe you can start playing in the band with us, too."

CHAPTER 23

Brandon was lying on the couch in his apartment. The television was on, but the volume was all the way down. He awoke looking at the pizza box on the coffee table half full of stale pizza. Then he looked at the eight beer bottles sitting next to it. It occurred to him that the noise of his phone vibrating on the end table above his head is what woke him. He sat up and reached for the phone while scooting to the end of the couch.

"Yeah!"

"Brandon?"

"Oh, sorry. Hey Deb. What's up?"

"Are you okay? You sound terrible."

"I'm alright."

"Are you coming in today?"

Brandon took the phone away from his ear and looked at the time. "Crap. I don't know. What is today?"

"It's Thursday, Brandon, and the president has been calling here for you. He said you weren't answering your cell phone. What the heck are you doing? Where's Sonny?"

Brandon rubbed the sleep from his eyes. "Uh . . . Sonny . . . uh . . . oh, last night I told Sonny to take the day off."

"Brandon, you haven't been in all week. What's going on? Please tell me you aren't drinking again."

"Deb, call Wilhelm and the president both and tell them I'm taking some time off. How's Liv doing?"

"Liv is doing fine except that she's worried sick about you."

Someone started banging on Brandon's apartment door. Banging hard.

"Hang on. Let me see who's at the door."

Brandon got up and stumbled across the living room.

"Alright. Alright. I'm coming."

"Dad! Open the door!"

"Oh, crap," Brandon said throwing the latch over and opening the door.

Susan stormed in under his arm and into the living room. She froze in the middle of the room, and Brandon closed the door. She looked around at the mess but mainly at the beer bottles.

She turned to him with tears welling in her eyes. "Are you serious right now?"

"Deb, I think I better go. Let those guys know I'm out of pocket for awhile. You handle it."

He disconnected the call and threw his phone on the coffee table.

"Daddy, I thought this was over. What are you doing?"

"I just had some beer and pizza. What's the harm in that?"

Susan sat in the only chair that didn't have shirts or papers piled up on it. Brandon sat back down on the couch, leaned forward with his elbows on his knees, and stared at the floor.

"Why don't you go take a shower, Dad? You smell like a brewery."

He looked at her with piercing eyes and stood abruptly. He stormed into his bedroom and closed the door. When he came out about thirty minutes later, he was wearing a fresh T-shirt and blue jeans and was vigorously rubbing his wet head with a towel. He looked at Susan, who was still sitting in the chair. Deborah and Olivia were sitting on the couch. All three were staring at the beer bottles, not saying a word.

"What's going on?"

"Sit," Susan said.

Brandon picked up some books from one of the chairs and threw them on the floor. He sat and looked at Deborah and Olivia staring back at him.

"How long have you guys been here?"

"Just got here," Deborah said.

"Dad, this has to stop," Olivia said. "What's going on? I know you miss Mom. Dang it, we all miss Mom. Don't you know she would hate what you're doing to yourself?"

"Is this like an intervention or something?"

"No, Brandon," Deborah said. "This is the three people who love you more than anybody in the world pleading for you to get your head out of your rear end."

Brandon lowered his face into his hands.

After they spoke for almost an hour, Deborah finally said, "Brandon, look. Liv and I are holding this project together just fine. I'll call Wilhelm to tell him you're taking some time off. Stay out next week and pull yourself together."

"Do you want me to set up an appointment for you to see someone?" Olivia asked.

"No. I'll call Emmett."

"Daddy, why don't you come with me to CR tomorrow night?" Susan asked. "Please?"

"Okay. Okay."

There was a knock on the door.

"Now who is it?" Brandon said.

"I'll get it." Susan stood and opened the door. "Hey, Sonny." She stood on her toes and hugged him. "Come on in."

"I thought I gave you the day off," Brandon said.

Sonny looked at Deborah.

"I called him and told him his holiday is over," she said. "I also told him that he is to stay with you no matter what you say. You got that?"

"Sir?" Sonny said.

"Fine. But you know what? The sir, Mr. McStocker crap ends right here. Got it?" He pointed his finger at Sonny. "It's Brandon. You got that?"

"Yes, sir. Of course."

Brandon rolled his eyes, and they all laughed.

"Tell me Jimmy isn't the one holding down the fort."

Olivia smiled. "When we left, I asked him to take a run up to the inner city to check on a series of footings that are getting poured today. They're also drying-in the eighth floor of the bank building today, and I asked him to check on that for me."

Brandon looked at Deborah and then back at Olivia. "Oh, you did, did you? And how did that go over?"

"Well, he went," Olivia said with a smile.

"He went?"

Deborah winked. "He did."

"I've got to get to work," Susan said. "Barney's gonna have my head." She moved toward the front door, passing in front of Sonny, poking him in the chest. "Try not to shoot anybody."

★ ★ ★ ★ ★

Deborah met with the department heads in Brandon's office because everyone could fit in there more comfortably than in hers. She went around the room and got an update from each of them on the status of their projects.

"The airport runways, tower, and cargo facilities are in full operation and are accepting cargo supply flights on a routine basis. The passenger terminal is still under construction."

"The national cross is basically complete. Just waiting for some of the city streets to be finished before the ramps around and inside the beltway are done."

"Understood. Good work. The national cross is getting a lot of press."

"The power grid is coming online a little at a time with several of the planned substations up and running. The construction crews seem to have what they need with minimal generator use."

"Good."

"The financial center construction is coming along fine. No issues. The eighth floor is dried in."

"Nice."

"We have had a little bit of a snag at the McClellan Center site. The environmental folks were conducting a cultural resources survey in parallel with the building of the foundation and came across an archaeologically significant area. Looks like relics from a Pawnee or Wichita cooking station."

"Who knows about it?"

"The tribes already have the info, and the state's Native American Affairs office is on it."

"Dang it." Deborah looked at Olivia.

"As soon as we're done here, I'll run up and check on it," Olivia said. "That's my dad's . . . er . . . Brandon's baby."

"We couldn't hide it from the inspectors," the manager said.

"No, of course not," Deborah said. "I wouldn't want you to. I just wish we had gotten a chance to be ahead of it with the governor's office. Liv, after you gather what you need, you might want to head over to Topeka and pay a visit to Redman."

"Of course," Olivia said.

"Where is Brandon, anyway?" Jimmy asked.

Deborah looked around the room. "Brandon is going to take some more time off. He has complete confidence in everyone here, so we just press on."

Jimmy squinted and looked at Olivia.

"Jimmy, why don't you go back up and check on the financial center and see how they're progressing on nine and ten?" Olivia said. "You can ride with me if you want."

"Uh—maybe," he said. "I might have to wait until tomorrow. I know they have to jack the tower crane anyway."

After several more status reports, the meeting adjourned. Olivia stopped by her cubicle to pull her long brunette hair into a ponytail and put on her white construction hard hat. She walked to the elevator.

"Hey, Cindy. Can I get the keys to zero-two, please?"

"Sure. It was all fueled up yesterday."

"Good. Thanks."

Olivia exited the elevator on the first floor and walked out to the white company pickup in its reserved spot. She walked around to check the tires and then got in and left the Rathbone Hall parking lot, headed to Barney's.

"Hey, Sis," Olivia said, walking into the diner.

"Hey, Liv. Grab a seat anywhere."

Olivia took off her hard hat and sat at the counter.

"Hey, Boss. Coffee?" Barney asked.

"Please."

Susan finished wiping off one the tables and walked behind the counter.

"Headed up north?"

"Yep, I'm on a mission. Some issue at McClellan Center."

"Oh no. Dad's baby."

"Yeah."

"Hungry?"

"Not really. I didn't want to drive by without stopping in. Speaking of Dad, have you heard from him?"

"He texts me now and then."

"Yeah, that's all I get. I'm still worried about him."

"He texted me from Virginia yesterday," Susan said.

"What! What the heck is he doing in Virginia?"

"Beats me."

"Is Sonny with him?"

"As far as I know. But Dad didn't say."

"Well, I've avoided calling him. I don't want to push.

"Yeah, I know."

"When's your next gig?"

"I'm playing here Saturday night. Darcy's going to come play with me."

"Whoa, really? That'll be fun."

"Yeah, I'm looking forward to it. Come by if you can."

"Of course. I'll be here. I need to head out, kiddo."

"Okay, Sis. Be careful up there."

"See ya, Boss," Barney said. "Coffee's on the house."

"Thanks, Barn. I'll see you guys later. I might stop back by for lunch."

Olivia drove across the street and into the equipment yard, where the crew was staging the new cranes that were arriving. She drove around several lowboys before she found the foreman speaking to one of the truck drivers. She pulled up next to him and lowered the passenger-side window.

"Hey, Darrel. How's it going in here?"

"Well, hey there, Ms. McStocker. What brings you by here today?"

"'Liv is fine," she smiled. "I'm headed up to the city. Any problems with arrivals?"

"No, ma'am. Everything is showing up on schedule. Three more cranes are coming in just today. Exciting stuff."

"Yep, the city is sprouting up like a sunflower, blowing seeds all over the place."

"Your daddy is quite the hero around here. Haven't seen him around much, though."

"He's a busy man. He'll be up this way soon, I'm sure. Gotta run. Let us know if you run into any glitches."

"Will do—Liv."

She smiled and winked at him as she raised the window and slowly drove back onto 24 and turned north. After a few miles, she pulled off of the main road and around several barriers. When she arrived at the guard shack, she lowered her window and slowed

198

down. Bert recognized her and waved her through. She drove by him slowly and extended her hand.

"Mornin', Bert," she said as they slapped hands in their usual high-five greeting.

After she left the cross and entered the beltway going west, she sighed when she saw the many buildings under construction, changing the open fields into a real cityscape. For Olivia, it was a breathtaking sight. Interior roads and ramps were under construction all around her. Several of the contractors waved when they saw her. She pulled up into the dirt near the McClellan Center site and walked around to where a crowd had gathered at the other end of the foundation. She recognized several of the people from the local government offices, and a few were obviously tribal representatives.

"Good morning, Ms. McStocker. I'm glad you could come," the foreman said.

"Good morning. So what do we know?"

The foreman led Olivia over to the dig site and pointed out the relics they had uncovered.

"Wow," Olivia said. She turned to an elderly man dressed in traditional Pawnee garb and waved him over.

"Sir," she shouted. "Can you tell me what we're looking at here?"

He walked over to where they were, looking confused.

"Ma'am?"

"Sir. My name is Olivia McStocker, and I'm with the firm overseeing this project." She extended her hand to shake his. "And you are?"

"I am Chief Shiriki Anderson of the Pawnee Nation."

"Shiriki. What an interesting name! What does it mean?"

"Coyote."

Olivia smiled, still holding the old man's hand. "I love that."

The old man smiled back and dipped his head.

"Sir—Chief Shiriki—may I call you Chief Shiriki?"

He nodded.

"Chief Shiriki, can you explain what we're looking at here?"

"These are cooking utensils, and the large smooth object in the center is a mortar, used to grind corn. I suspect the pestle is nearby."

"Excuse me, ma'am," a voice came from behind them.

"Yes," Olivia said, turning to see who it was.

"I'm sorry to interrupt, ma'am. I'm Renee Lofton, and I'm with Project Archeology at K-State. This is Bonnie Miller with the state's historical society out of Topeka."

"Hi. Pleased to meet you," Olivia said, shaking their hands. "Renee, I'm so glad to have local help on this. What are we dealing with?"

"Unfortunately, this construction can't continue."

And there it is, Olivia thought . . . so strongly that she was afraid she might have said it out loud.

Olivia turned to the foreman and with a very deliberate tone, said, "Tommy, shut it down."

"Ma'am?"

"I want you to carefully back all of this equipment away from this site and park it until further notice. Can you reassign your people here to other projects?"

"Well, of course, but ma'am—"

"It'll be okay, Tommy. I'll let your company know what's going on, and we won't dock your performance metrics, I promise."

He shook his head and walked away from the circle. "Okay, guys!" the foreman shouted. "Let's get it outta here!"

Chief Shiriki smiled and looked at Renee. "This woman. She has power."

"Ms. McStocker, are you sure about this?" Renee asked.

"It'll be okay. Renee, can you and Bonnie join me for lunch down near the campus?"

"Uh, of course."

"In the meantime, do you think you can get a team up here from the college to lay this out and continue the dig?"

"Uh . . . sure," Renee said, looking over at Bonnie and shrugging her shoulders.

Olivia walked back toward her truck, and the small crowd that had gathered began clapping their hands. She shook her head and lowered her gaze to the ground in embarrassment, her long ponytail blowing in the breeze. When she got near her truck, she looked out across the field of dirt at the financial center going up a few blocks away. It looked like the crane jacking was going fine, but she wanted to see it up close, even if it was Jimmy's project. She drove around that way on her way back out to the beltway.

She stopped in front of the financial center site and waved for Renee, who had been following her, to come up to her side. "You know where Barney's is?"

"Of course we do. Love that place."

"Meet there?"

"Sounds good."

While driving back toward Manhattan, Olivia called her dad's work number.

"McClelland & McStocker, Mr. McStocker's office."

"Hey, Mena. Liv."

"Hey, Liv. How's it going up there?"

"Interesting, I suppose."

"How can I help you, hon?"

"I need you to try to get me in to see the governor late this afternoon. You think you can pull that off?"

"Well, I might have to call in a favor or two, but I think it's doable."

"Good. I'm going to meet with some ladies at Barney's for a working lunch. Shoot me a text when you know something?"

"Will do."

"Hey, is Jimmy still in the office?"

"No. He left shortly after you. Said he was headed up to the site."

"Really?"

"That's what he said."

"Hmm. Okay. Well, let me know what you find out. You want anything from Barney's?"

"No thanks. I'm meeting the kids for lunch."

"Oh, nice. I'll see you soon."

CHAPTER 24

Susan showed Olivia and her guests to the table in the corner of the restaurant. That table was typically used for such meetings where privacy was needed. Susan took their drink orders and left them alone.

"Thank you, ladies, for meeting with me. I'm going to need your help."

"Why were you so quick to shut the project down?" Renee asked. "I've never seen such swift action. You didn't put up a fight at all."

"It was the right thing to do. I have to admit, I was taken aback when you told me we couldn't continue, but I knew that in the end, it was an issue that we had to deal with. I know my dad well enough to know he wouldn't have fought this. There was no need to waste any more of the construction crew's time. There are other things they can be doing."

"You sure endeared yourself to Chief Shiriki," Bonnie said.

"Well, then there was that," Olivia chuckled. "That never hurts. He needed to know that his people and their heritage are important to us. So what can we do about it?"

"As I said before," Renee said, "you can't move forward with that construction site under these circumstances."

"There it is again," Olivia said.

"What?"

"*Can't.* You keep saying 'can't.'"

"It is what it is," Bonnie said. "We have nothing else for you."

"I think you do. What I'd like you to think about is something along the lines of, we can, if . . ."

Susan brought their drinks and took their lunch orders. The conversation continued.

"I'm not sure what the 'if' would be," Renee said.

"How much distance needs to be cleared around the original find?" Olivia asked.

"Well, that's pretty subjective," Bonnie said. "If we determine that nothing else is likely to be found after a reasonable search, we can probably get away with a protective corridor of about fifty feet. If the tribes agree to have the articles removed to a museum or university, we can probably get the project cleared with the state. But it's a drawn-out process, and a lot of ifs."

Olivia picked at her salad and drew a drink of iced tea through her straw. Then she stared out the window, thinking about her mom and how she loved history.

"Listen, I don't want to screw this up."

She thought about their backyard at the old house in Fairfax. Her mom loved the garden back there that she had nurtured for all those years.

"Cassandra's Garden," she said.

"What was that?" Renee asked.

Olivia didn't realize she said it out loud.

"Oh, I'm sorry. Something just came to mind. I have an idea I'm going to run by my boss."

Olivia's phone vibrated on the table.

"Excuse me, ladies." She turned the phone over and saw the text from Mena. *You're in! Appointment at 4.*

She placed her phone back on the table, facedown.

"I'm also going to bring the idea up to the governor. We may have a way around this yet," she said.

Olivia's phone began vibrating again. This time it was a call coming in.

"I am so sorry," she said, turning it over to see that it was Deborah. "I have to take this."

They both nodded and smiled.

"What's up? The news, no. Why? . . . Okay. Hold on. Hey, Susan, can you turn on the news?"

Susan changed the channel on the TV, and Olivia saw the Breaking News banner across the top of the screen and words scrolling across the bottom: "Kéntro closed down due to archeological find. Could cause cancellation." She saw Senator Sanders surrounded by his entourage on the steps of the Capitol building.

"You want me to turn it up?" Susan asked.

"No. I know what he's saying." Olivia looked back at her phone. "Oh, yeah. I just saw it. Have you heard from Wilhelm? Okay. I'm going over to see the governor anyway. Have they really shut the whole thing down?"

Renee, Bonnie, and Susan were all waiting to see some indication of an answer to Olivia's question. She shook her head, no.

"Okay. Have you heard from Dad—I mean Brandon?" She looked at Susan with a grin and shook her head. "Alright. Let me know. I'll head to Topeka straight from here. Yeah, I'll be fine. Don't worry about me."

Olivia disconnected her phone and put it back on the table. "This is getting out of hand. Ladies, I understand you can't help me right now, but I think you might be able to eventually. Can I come see you on campus tomorrow morning?"

"Of course," Renee said. "But I'm not sure what we can do for you."

"I'm not either . . . yet. I hate to break up this meeting, but I need to run. The meal is on me."

She looked at Susan and nodded.

Susan gave her a thumbs-up. "Yep. On the tab."

Within an hour, Olivia had gone by her apartment to change clothes, over to the campus to drop off the truck and pick up her car, and was on I70 headed east to the state capital. She was only about ten minutes down the road when her phone rang through the Bluetooth system in her car. She pressed the Answer Call button on her steering wheel.

"This is Olivia."

"Liv, Deb. Where are you now?"

"Uh . . . on 70 just headed to Topeka. What's up?"

"Honey, you need to turn around and get back to the office."

"Aunt Deb, what's going on?"

"There's been a terrible accident."

"Oh, my gosh. Daddy?"

"No. No. It's not him. The crane collapsed at the financial center and fell into the main structure."

"Oh, no! Is anyone hurt?"

"Nobody knows yet. I'm getting ready to head up there now. You need to get back here."

"I will. I will." Olivia pressed the End Call button on her steering wheel. She left the interstate at the next exit to turn around onto the onramp headed west. Her hands began trembling so badly she exited the interstate again into a rest stop. As soon as the car came to a stop in the parking lot, she leaned her head forward onto the steering wheel and started sobbing.

After several minutes, she lifted her head, removed the phone from her purse, and started punching numbers. She looked around the rest area to see if anyone might notice the tears streaming down her face. The phone at the other end began to ring.

"Pick up. Pick up. Oh, please pick up."

"Hey, sweetie. You okay?"

"Daddy—" Her crying became uncontrollable as she tried to explain what Deborah had just told her.

"Honey, where are you?"

She regained her composure long enough to tell him where the rest area was.

"Sweetheart, stay right there. I'm going to come get you."

Olivia was in shock. All she could think about was that she had just left the site a couple of hours earlier. Was there anything she could've done to prevent this? Had she missed something? Where is Jimmy? She stared out of the windshield and waited, her hands trembling. She couldn't get her crying under control. Finally, she saw the limo pull in behind her car. Her dad and Sonny both walked toward her.

She jumped from her car and ran into Brandon's arms. "Oh, Daddy!"

Sonny looked into the open door of Olivia's car and then scanned the rest area.

"Honey, Deb told me what happened. We still don't know anything, but several of our folks are heading up that way. The fire department and rescue crews are there now."

"Dad, it's my fault. I should have done something."

"Honey, none of this is your fault. I should have been there for you, and I wasn't."

Sonny rubbed Olivia's back, trying to help calm her.

"Come on. Get in, and I'll drive you back."

"Oh, no. What about my meeting with the governor?"

"Deb said Mena is going to take care of that." Brandon escorted Olivia around her car and into the passenger seat. He nodded to Sonny, and both men got in the cars and drove toward campus.

When they arrived, Brandon walked through the commons with his arm around Olivia. She was still crying and in shock.

"Deb!" Brandon shouted.

"Coming!"

"The governor's office said to call when we want to reschedule," Mena said.

Deborah followed Brandon and Olivia into Brandon's office, where they sat around the conference table. Deborah put her arm around Olivia, and Brandon closed the office door.

"What's the latest?" Brandon asked.

Deborah frowned at Olivia. "Four dead so far."

Olivia froze and peered into Deborah's eyes. "Aunt Deb?"

"I'm so sorry, honey."

Olivia dropped her head on the table, sobbing. "Oh . . . no . . . no!"

"Sweetheart, this is not your fault," Brandon said.

"Brandon, Jimmy just arrived at the site," Mena said over the intercom.

"Thank you. Get him on the phone, please, as soon as he can talk."

"Yes, sir."

Deborah continued to console Olivia as Brandon walked over to the window behind his desk and stared over the trees in the direction of Lebanon.

"I'm sorry," he said, his voice distant and shaky.

"Whoa. Wait. Brandon, this isn't your fault, either," Deborah said.

"Dad?" Olivia said, suddenly regaining her composure.

"I shouldn't have left you two here alone to try to run all of this."

"Brandon. You've been dealing with a lot. This isn't on you," Deborah said.

"She's been gone for six years. And so have I. I am so sorry."

Olivia looked at Deborah with her red eyes and stood from the table. She walked across the room and put her arms around Brandon's waist and laid her head on his chest.

Susan rushed through the office door. "Dad! Oh, my gosh!"

"Honey, what are you doing here?"

She walked over to Brandon and Olivia and joined in the hug. Deborah put her hands over her mouth, barely holding back her tears.

"I heard all the sirens then saw all the emergency vehicles screaming by the restaurant up toward the construction. Barney called his friend at the police station and found out what was going on. Was anyone hurt?"

Susan looked into Olivia's eyes and knew the answer. "Oh, my—"

"Brandon, Senator Wilhelm," Mena said on the intercom.

"That didn't take long. Thanks, Mena. Put him through."

"Senator."

"Brandon, what in the world happened?"

"At the moment, sir, I don't know. A crane collapsed, and I have four dead. That's the sum of what I've got. And back there?"

"Sanders and his henchmen have already gotten a hold of it and are planning to go live with a press conference in a few minutes. This plays right into their narrative."

"Excuse me, gentlemen," Mena broke in. "I have Mr. Dillon on the line from the construction site."

"Good, Mena," Brandon said. "Add him in, please."

"Hey, Boss."

"Jimmy, Senator Wilhelm is on the line with us. What do you know?"

"It's bad, Boss. When the crane fell, it went right through the main structure and took out most of the top three stories. Several guys jumped when they saw it coming. A few gas bottles exploded and started a fire on four. We've shut off the power, and OSHA just arrived with their command center."

"OSHA?" Wilhelm said. "I don't like the feel of this, Brandon. I'm going to get the FBI out there."

"Are you thinking it was a terrorist attack, Senator?"

"No, Brandon. Not a terrorist attack. But I'm not putting sabotage past these idiots out here."

"Boss. I . . . uh . . . I have to go."

"You okay, Jimmy?"

"Yeah. I just need to go."

"Alright. I'll head up there shortly," Brandon said.

"Thank you, Mr. Dillon. You be safe up there," Wilhelm said. "So, Brandon, I understand you've been out of pocket quite a bit lately. You okay?"

"I'm sorry, Senator. Yes, I've been out a lot. Frankly, I've had my head up my . . . anyhow . . . it's inexcusable. I won't let it happen again. Will you let me know if there's something going on out there that I should be concerned about?"

"I'll have the FBI contact you when they arrive."

"Okay, thanks."

Brandon hung up the phone and sat on the edge of his desk. Deborah, Olivia, and Susan were all staring at him.

"I'm so sorry, you guys."

He lowered his gaze to the floor.

CHAPTER 25

Brandon turned on the TV and sat at his desk just in time to see the Breaking News banner on the screen.

"Senator Sanders, can you give us an update on what's going on in Kansas?"

"Oh, jeez. Why are they asking him?"

"What's going on in Kansas is a disaster. We have to stop this charade once and for all," the senator said. "After all these years, not only are we still wasting the taxpayer's money, now we're losing lives over a senseless ego trip perpetrated by the president. He never should've been allowed to have this second term. We have to stop this ridiculous project now and get him out of office!"

"Tell us how you really feel, you . . ." Brandon couldn't hold back the explicative.

Susan dropped her jaw and threw a pen across the desk. "Daddy!"

The two sat in Brandon's office alone, watching the news. Susan still had on her waitress uniform and was sitting on a chair in front of her dad's desk with her shoes off and her feet propped up on another chair. She reached over the desk and picked up the TV remote control to mute the sound. Brandon looked at her with a squinted eye.

"Dad, are you okay?"

"I'm fine, honey. The guy's a jerk."

"Shut up," she giggled. "You know what I mean. Are you okay? That whole drinking ordeal freaked me out. I know you miss Mom. We all do. I'm even worried about Liv and all the balls she's trying to keep in the air. Are you guys going to be okay? Because listen, I need you guys. I can't have you going off the deep end. You just can't!"

Her voice cracked, and tears filled her eyes. Brandon stood and walked around his desk. Susan leaned forward and dropped her feet from the chair. Brandon sat in it, facing her, and held her hands.

"Sweetheart, I'm not going anywhere. I promise. And with your mom gone, I wouldn't be able to pry Liv away from you with a crowbar. Okay? You know your sister is upset over the accident, but she'll be fine. You know how strong she is."

They both turned their heads to look at the door when Mena knocked and quickly walked in.

"Brandon, I'm sorry to interrupt, but I just got off the phone with one of the attorneys, and the families are asking to meet with you."

"Are you sure? It's only been three days. The investigation is still going on."

"That's what she said."

"Okay. Thanks, Mena. Have you seen Liv?"

"She's in with Deborah, and the door is closed."

"Okay. I'd like her to be with me when I meet with the families. I'm guessing the president is going to come out for the funerals as well, so we'll need to get prepared for that. Will you ask her to come in when they're done in there?

"Of course."

"Thanks, Mena."

Mena smiled and winked at Susan as she turned to leave the office.

"You can leave it open," Brandon said.

The following day, Brandon, Olivia, and Sonny walked into the dining hall of the Green Valley Recreation Center. A man in a suit, obviously the attorney, was standing over a group of people sitting around two tables that were slid together. Sonny stayed by the door while Brandon and Olivia walked to the attorney to shake hands. Four ladies sitting at the table had been crying. Several children were sitting around gazing at the floor or into the distance across the room. One toddler was running from side to side, oblivious to anything the adults might be doing.

After shaking hands with the others, Brandon and Olivia sat at the table across from them. Brandon looked into each of their eyes, one by one. One of the teen girls took the toddler by the hand and led him out into the hallway. He was the only one making a sound.

"Ladies, my name is Brandon McStocker, and this is my colleague, Olivia. We manage the Kéntro Project. We are so very sorry for your loss."

One of the ladies lowered her head and began to weep. An older lady sitting next to her put her arm around her and continued staring at Brandon. Olivia's hands began to shake under the table. She placed one of them on her dad's knee trying to calm herself.

Brandon continued. "An investigation is underway at both the local and federal levels to get to the bottom of this horrible incident. We came today to address any questions you might have or simply to hear your concerns."

Brandon couldn't read the deadpan faces of the wives. The one who had been crying raised her head, drying her face with a tissue. Olivia was having a difficult time controlling her own emotions.

"So, ladies. Are there any ques—"

Olivia raised her hand from under the table and rested it on Brandon's arm, still shaking.

"Ma'am, are you okay?" Olivia asked, looking at the young woman who had been crying."

"Si. Estoy bien."

Olivia scanned the other women at the table. "And you guys? How are you doing?"

They shook their heads and looked down. Olivia looked up at the attorney and back down at the women.

"Is there anything you need right now?"

"Agua . . . water would be nice," one of the women said.

Olivia looked around and saw the kitchen area behind a stainless-steel counter. She stood and walked across the room and into the kitchen, searching for any sign of bottled water. She opened several cabinets before thinking to check inside the refrigerator. When she finally opened it, she found several bottles. She loaded her arms with them and grabbed a stack of Styrofoam cups on her way back to the table. Everyone's eyes were glued to her, including Brandon's. Sonny watched, holding back his tears.

Olivia opened one of the bottles and filled a few of the cups. She slid them across the table and sat back down.

"Can I say something?" the older woman asked.

"Of course," Olivia said. "Please. What is your name?"

The woman was nervous and looked around at the others before speaking.

"I am Madeleine. Maddie. We don't want you to stop," she said.

Brandon squinted.

"Excuse me?" Olivia said.

"We heard men on the news saying they wanted to stop Kéntro. They want it shut down. Please don't shut it down."

Brandon cleared his throat. "I don't understand."

The younger Latina lady began to speak. "My name is Maria. My husband. He was proud to be working on this project."

"They all were," another said. "I'm Gladys. Our men saw this as one of the most important projects they had ever worked on. They saw it as a service to their country."

Olivia jerked a tissue from one of the boxes on the table. She laughed through her tears. She reached across the table and held Maria's hand. The others reached over and placed their hands on top of theirs.

"It would be such a disservice to our men now after they've given everything," Maddie said.

Brandon put his hand over his mouth. He knew his lips were quivering.

"And you, ma'am?" Brandon looked at the woman who hadn't spoken.

"Ah . . . goodness. Shutting it down would be the stupidest thing you could ever do. Who were those idiots on TV, anyway?"

Brandon and Olivia looked at each other, eyes bulging, trying to hold back their surprised chuckle.

"Uh . . . what is your name, ma'am?" Olivia asked.

"Sally. Sally Miller. My husband was a steel foreman. He was planning to retire last year but wanted to stick it out longer when his company won a contract for Kéntro. He thought it was the coolest thing ever. Wouldn't miss it for the world."

"Well, Mrs. Miller—"

"Sally."

"Well, Sally," Olivia said, "your husband was a hero in my book. All of your men were. And you know what? So are you. Your bravery warms my heart. To be honest, I thought we were coming here to talk about a lawsuit."

She looked up at the attorney again. He shook his head and smiled.

Olivia looked at Brandon through her red, tear-filled eyes, and smiled.

He smiled at her and then at the ladies across the table.

"You all should focus on your loss now. Grieve them as you should," he said. "But there is no need for a lawsuit against us. We will take care of your needs. Everything. I will talk to the president personally. If he can't make something happen, we will do it from our funds. Liv here is my daughter. She lost her mother six years ago. One could argue that she lost her mother to this project as well. We know what it is like to lose the person who is the sun and the moon in your life. Since you are Liv's heroes, it only makes sense that we would take care of you financially."

"Sir, we don't want your money. We just want to see this city built."

"I understand. And I will use every ounce of my being to make sure that happens. I'm going to leave your names at the front desk at our offices on campus. For you ladies, my door is always open. If I'm out of town for anything, tell Cindy, our receptionist, that you want to talk to me, and I'll call you as soon as I can. I don't want you ever to feel like you're in the dark. Agreed?"

"Thank you, sir," the women said in unison.

They all stood and hugged. Brandon shook hands with the attorney.

"How did this happen?" Brandon asked.

"I've never seen anything like it," the attorney said. "You're a lucky man."

Brandon and Olivia walked out of the door, and Sonny fell in behind them.

"Oh, my gosh, Daddy," Olivia said. "Those women are amazing."

"I did not see that coming," Brandon said. "I'll tell the president that he has no choice now but to come to these funerals."

After they were all in the car and Sonny was about to exit the parking lot, Brandon looked at him in the rearview mirror.

"Wait! Stop!" Brandon shouted.

Sonny, startled, slammed on the brakes and glanced again into the rearview mirror.

"Dad, what!" Olivia shouted.

"Why were you going to see the governor anyway?"

Sonny narrowed his eyes.

"What?" Olivia asked.

"You were on your way to see the governor when the collapse happened. Why were you on your way to see the governor?"

"Oh, jeez, Dad. You scared the crap out of me. It's McClellan Center. There's a problem there.

"There is?"

Sonny shook his head and continued out of the parking lot.

"During excavation, they ran onto some relics. After quite a bit of careful digging, they found Pawnee cooking utensils and pottery, like a rock, formed mortar, and pestle."

"Well, dang. That'll shut us down."

"Not necessarily. I think there might be a way around it."

"I'm not even going to ask," Brandon said. "It's your deal, and I don't want to step in the middle of it now. When do you think you'll be ready to go see him?"

"I can go anytime. I'll ask Mena to set it up again. I shut it down myself, Dad. I asked the foreman to reassign the men working there for the time being."

"We need it get back on track if we can. But I'm sure you did the right thing."

Olivia punched the office number into her phone.

"Hi, Mena. Liv. Can you contact the governor's office, please? We need to try for that meeting again."

"Okay, thanks." Olivia tossed the phone back into her purse.

Brandon stared at her with a smile.

"What?"

"Oh, you."

"What about me?"

"Your mother would be so proud of you—the woman you've become. Heck, the leader you've become."

"Shut up."

"Honey, I can't believe how you've taken to this company and this project. It's like you've been here for years."

"Will you stop already!"

"I'm just sorry I haven't been available to you, to help you and Deb through all this. I am so sorry."

"Stop! Now you're gonna make me cry."

"Fine. I do want to know what you have in mind for McClellan Center, but I want you to get square with the governor first. Then tell me about it, okay?"

"Don't you want to go with me?" Olivia asked.

"More than you know, sweetie. But you've got this. I have a hunch you're going to be able to handle the governor better than I ever could."

A beep came from Olivia's purse. She pulled her phone out and read the text message out loud to Brandon.

"Governor tomorrow 11a.m."

CHAPTER 26

"Ms. McStocker," the governor said, holding open the tall wooden door to his office. "Please. Come in."

She smiled at his secretary as she rose from the chair and entered Governor Redman's office.

"Thank you, sir."

He closed the door behind them. "Please, Ms. McStocker, have a seat. Can I get you a beverage?"

"Oh, no, sir. Thank you. And please, call me Liv. I can't get past the fact that Ms. McStocker was my mother. Thank you for resetting this appointment for me, sir."

He smiled. "It was my pleasure, dear. I'm sorry we've had to shut down part of your project."

"Sir?"

"Well, you know. The collapse and then that archeological find. It's unfortunate."

"Sir, I think OSHA will clear the financial center to continue as soon as the investigation is complete. The relics at McClellan Center is what I came to talk to you about."

"Oh? How so?"

"Well, from what we can tell, the material that was found is of a limited quantity and is localized. It's almost like it was moved there from somewhere else for some reason. There are no structures around it as one might expect."

"Yes, but we don't know that for sure. Don't you think you should just abandon that location and try to build it somewhere else?"

"Uh . . . no, sir. I don't."

Governor Redman stood and began pacing back and forth. Olivia's eyes followed his every move. "Ms. McStocker . . . uh, Liv. Your father has tried to keep me away from this project from day one. Why?"

"Well, I don't know for sure, Governor. But I have a hunch."

"And what might that be?"

"Greed."

"I beg your pardon!"

"Greed, sir."

"Did you come here to insult me, missy?"

"Sir, Kéntro has been the biggest financial boon this state has ever seen. My father bent over backward to make it an equitable partnership with the state. And for that, you still refuse to come out publicly in support of the project. Why is that? It has been a rather lopsided partnership, if you ask me."

"Ms. McStocker, why are you here?"

"Well, sir. Not for that. I wanted to offer a solution for the relics that were found."

"A solution?"

"Governor, I would like to have the relics dug up by a team of experts and have them prepared for display. I want to have my team work on a modification to the design of McClellan Center to include a small museum adjacent to the lobby, where visitors can view the relics along with an audio-visual account of the Pawnee tribes that used to inhabit the area. I thought it would be nice if you would be the narrator on the recording. I know you can't just stop the dig, but I suspect you will be able to influence it."

The governor returned to his seat and smiled at her. He put his hand over his mouth and stared into the bookcase that rose above them in the corner of the office.

"A museum, huh?"

"Yes, sir."

"I thought you came here to pester me about sweeping the whole dig under the rug so you can press on with construction."

"No, sir. I don't think that would be fair to you or the people of Kansas. Certainly not to the Pawnee Nation."

They both sat quietly while the governor continued to stare at the books on the shelf.

He turned and looked at Olivia with a sternness she hadn't yet seen.

"Missy, are you trying to bribe me with this idea?"

"It's Liv, and no, sir, I'm not. Governor, we don't want to be adversaries. We want to be partners of the state on this. You know full well that when construction of the new city is complete, then K.D. becomes a federal asset, and the state is hands-off. But we want the state to be able to leave its mark. We've already preserved the center of the U.S. Geodetic Survey marker and that small park. Now, we want to preserve some of the American Indian history that lives here. Help us help you, sir."

Redman smiled and shook his head. He turned back to stare at the books some more.

"I bet your daddy is one proud man. And your momma. She died a few years ago, didn't she?"

"Murdered, actually."

"Oh, yeah. That was a terrible thing. Did they ever get to the bottom of that?"

"No, sir. Not really. They identified who did it, but he was obviously being controlled by someone else."

"You have a lot of your daddy in you. He was tenacious, too, when he started Kéntro. I admired him then, just like I admire you right now."

"I don't understand, sir."

"You're right, Liv. I was greedy. When I first learned about the project, I saw dollar signs and reelection written all over it. But what you people have done for this country is incredible. Thank you for coming over here to set me straight."

"I'm sorry about that, sir. I was out of line."

"No. No, Liv. You were honest with me. Something I don't get to see often. Don't back off now."

"So, will you help us?"

"Of course I will. When the president had the FTC drop the charges against Midwest Holdings several years ago, I knew how important it was to him."

"Charges, sir?"

"Oh, we had managed to get caught up in some pretty unscrupulous dealings that ended up in the headlines, and the feds had us over a barrel. Turned out, the president was able to use it as a bargaining chip. Draw up the plans for the museum and send them to me. I'll have the historical society ease off and will explain to them what a great opportunity they have. We'll get this partnership running like it should have been running all along. And tell your daddy to visit me. Maybe we can all have dinner one of these days."

"That would be nice, Governor. Thank you. I'll go share the good news with him now."

"By the way," the governor said, "are the families of the men killed in that collapse mounting lawsuits against you and the feds?"

Olivia smiled and her eyes filled with tears. "No, sir. Quite the opposite. My father and I met with the families, and their biggest concern was that we might stop the project. The strength and pride those people displayed were remarkable. Apparently, the entire workforce sees K.D. as an opportunity to serve their country. I don't think any of us saw that coming."

"That is pretty amazing. Do you think it would be okay to come out with my little entourage and visit the site?"

"Oh, Governor. I think that's a wonderful idea."

"Your daddy might hit me with a board or something," he laughed.

"You leave him to me."

★ ★ ★ ★ ★

Brandon had architectural drawings of K.D. spread across the large table in the conference room, refreshing himself on the overall layout. He knew it was time to begin construction on the new White House and Capitol building. A new state-of-the-art facility called The Defense Center was under development to replace the Pentagon. Construction was about to begin on that, as well. Several defense contractors had come together to design and install a technology infrastructure in the facility that would look like a futuristic science fiction movie.

"Hey, Dad," Olivia said as she walked in behind him and leaned over his shoulder to kiss him on the cheek.

"Hey, sweetie. How was your trip?"

"He wants to come visit the site."

"Say what!"

She chuckled. "It's true. He's completely onboard now."

Brandon squinted and sat in one of the chairs. "Do tell."

Olivia sat in front of him and explained the museum idea and what the governor said about it. She also described the governor's apparent change of heart.

"Honey, that's pretty amazing."

"I know, right? I even have a name for the new addition."

"And what's that."

"Cassandra's Garden."

Brandon raised his fist up over his mouth, and tears welled up in his eyes. He stared at her and shook his head.

"I guess she was right," Brandon said.

"Huh. She who? What are you talking about?"

"Deb came to talk to me while you were at the statehouse."

"About—?"

"Was she in her office when you came in?"

"Yeah, she's still there."

"Let's go pay her a visit."

They walked into Deborah's office together.

"Hey, she's back!" Deborah said. "How did it go?"

Brandon and Olivia sat down while Olivia explained everything that she had just told Brandon. Deborah was smiling at Olivia as she told the story but kept glancing over at Brandon, who was leaning his head on his fist, supported by the arm of the chair, a smirk on his face.

After Olivia explained everything, Deborah looked at Brandon. "See?"

"See what?" Olivia chuckled. "What are you guys talking about?"

Brandon sat up straight and smiled at Deborah. "Tell her." He reached over and closed the office door.

"Okay, you guys are freakin' me out here," Olivia said.

"Liv. Honey, I've decided it's time for me to retire," Deborah said.

"What! No!"

"Yes, it's time."

"Aunt Deb. No. You can't leave me," Olivia whimpered.

"Oh, she's not done yet," Brandon chuckled.

Olivia looked at him and back at Deborah. "What?"

"We want you to move into this office," Deborah said.

"I don't understand. Where will the new deputy—your replacement—sit?"

"Right here in this office," Brandon said.

Olivia glanced back and forth between them. "What are you saying?"

"Deb thinks you should be the new deputy."

"Wait. That's insane. I just got here."

"Sweetheart, you've already earned the respect of everyone in this firm," Deborah said. "The way you treated the situation at McClellan Center—the way you handled those families the other day—and today, bringing the governor onboard? You deserve this office."

Olivia sat motionless, staring at the floor. She put her face in her hands and began to cry. Brandon rubbed her back but said nothing.

"Why?" Olivia asked, raising her head, tears streaming down her cheeks.

"Honey, it's time for me to go back home to Virginia and spend time with my grandbabies. You can handle this."

"Oh, no! What about Jimmy?"

"Don't worry about him," Brandon said. "Besides, he lacks the people skills needed for this job."

"Won't the employees scream nepotism?"

"As Deb said, they already respect you and know what you do for this company. I'm pretty sure you won't have anything to worry about."

"Dang. When are you planning to leave?"

"Oh, I'll give it about a month to wrap things up. I'll start briefing you right away on the projects I have going. You can pick it up a little at a time."

Olivia turned her entire body around to look at Brandon. "Dad, how in the world are you going to survive without this woman? I mean, really."

Brandon smiled at Deborah. "I don't know."

"Come on, you guys. Stop it!" Deborah said. "You're going to make me cry."

"Come on," Brandon said as he stood. "Let's go get some of Barney's burgers. You hungry, kiddo?"

"I could eat."

It was almost dark when Sonny pulled the limo into the parking lot of the diner. Brandon and Olivia were in the back seat, and Deborah rode in front with Sonny. They all got out and walked inside. All but Sonny. He stayed in the parking lot as usual.

"Well, hey there!" Susan shouted across the restaurant. "Anywhere's fine. I'll be right there."

Brandon laughed.

"What's so funny?" Olivia asked.

"Oh, she just sounds like she's been a waitress all of her life at some old greasy spoon in South Alabama."

"You think she's been here too long already?" Deborah asked.

"I don't think you guys could force her out of here now," Olivia said. "She loves this place."

They sat around a table when Susan finally arrived. "What's up, y'all!"

Brandon snickered again. Olivia elbowed him in the ribs.

"What?" Susan asked.

"Don't mind them," Deborah said. "We are here to celebrate."

"And just what are we celebrating?"

"I am retiring, and McClellan & McStocker has a brand new deputy executive project manager."

All three of them jutted their arms straight into the air.

"Are you kidding me? Who?"

"Another McStocker," Brandon said.

Susan and Olivia both let out a piercing screech, demanding the attention of the entire restaurant.

"Sorry everyone," Susan laughed. "My sister is a rock star!"

The place erupted in laughter and applause.

"We'll do the official retirement thing in about a month," Brandon said.

"Oh, let's not make it a thing," Deborah said.

Olivia pointed at Deborah across the table. "It will, most certainly, be a thing."

CHAPTER 27

After several days, Olivia had things back on track. The design was being modified for the museum addition, and archeologists from K-State were excavating and preparing the artifacts at the dig site.

Each Monday morning, Brandon and Olivia visited the financial center to see how the investigation was going. They too wanted to get to the bottom of it, but they also needed to get the construction back in gear.

On the Monday before Deborah's retirement party, all three of them rode up to the site together in one of the trucks. First, they toured Deborah around the airport and then into the city, around McClellan Center, and finally to the financial center.

"Oh, that looks awful," Deborah said.

Two men in hard hats walked toward the parked truck. One of the hats had an FBI logo on it, and the other said OSHA. Brandon lowered his window.

"You Brandon by any chance?"

"Yes, sir. What can we do for you today?"

The two looked at each of them, then back at Brandon. "Should we talk privately, sir?"

"You can speak freely," Brandon said. "These two are part of the management team."

"Well, sir. You'll be getting the official report soon, but this was no accident."

"It wasn't?"

"No, sir. This was sabotage, plain and simple. We found that four bolts in the lower framing of the tower had been intentionally loosened."

"How do you know it was intentional?" Olivia asked.

"One, or sometimes even two, might loosen on their own, although it's extremely rare. But four? No," the OSHA inspector said.

Then the FBI agent said, "I've called in some people from my office to do forensics, but I think we can get out of your hair by tomorrow evening. The rest of the investigation will take place in the lab. We've got what we need here."

"Is it normal to allow the construction to continue with an investigation underway?" Brandon asked.

"Not really," the OSHA inspector said. "Apparently, the governor got involved and convinced our bosses that we should clear out. No harm was done, though. I think we do have what we need."

Brandon looked at Olivia and smiled.

Deborah patted Olivia on the back. "You did it."

"Well, thank you, gentlemen," Brandon said. He handed them each a business card. "If there's anything we can do to help, our offices are on campus."

Brandon raised his window to keep out the dust and drove several blocks through the city to where the government buildings were to be built. Stakes, strings, and flags were everywhere. The surveyors were hard at work, laying out foundations.

"We need to get back," Brandon said. "But before we leave, I want to show you something."

He drove a few more blocks until, through the windshield, they saw some trees and a couple of small structures rising from a bed of green in the distance.

"Is that what I think it is?" Deborah asked.

"What?" Olivia asked.

"Oh my gosh, it is!" Deborah shouted.

Brandon stopped the truck in front of McClellan Center, and a cloud of dust engulfed them from behind. After it cleared, they opened the doors and got out.

"It's a heck of a place for a park," Olivia chuckled. "I didn't even realize this was over here behind this wall of boards."

"This is it," Deborah said. "Oh, Brandon. I can remember the first day we stood here like it was yesterday. But it sure looks different sitting here with all this construction around it."

"Once we get a real park and visitor center built up around it, it'll be a magnificent tribute to the little town of Lebanon," Brandon said.

"I can't wait to see it then," Olivia said.

"Let's get back and plan that retirement party," Brandon said, smiling at Deborah.

"Oh, gawd. Give me a break." Deborah punched him in the stomach.

★ ★ ★ ★ ★

Friday morning, Olivia arrived at the office and walked into her cubicle. Brandon walked in behind her.

"Where is everything?" he asked.

"You're asking me? What did you do?"

"What? I didn't do anything," he chuckled.

Olivia pushed him out of the way and walked around the corner to Deborah's office. Deborah was hanging the last of Olivia's photos on the wall—a picture of Cassandra.

"What are you doing?" Olivia asked.

"Nothing."

"Nothing?"

"Nothing."

"You're not gone yet, ya know."

"I know."

"Where's all of your stuff?"

"What's mine is in my car," Deborah said. "What belongs to the company is still right here, waiting for you to deal with it."

"Gee, thanks. When do you head out?"

"My trailer is packed, and tonight, I'm staying at a hotel. I'm headed east in the morning."

"You could stay with me," Olivia said.

"No. I'm saying all of my goodbyes today and will be hitting the road dark and early in the morning."

"This makes me so sad."

"Don't be sad. You have a world to change. I have grandbabies waiting for me."

Jimmy walked by with a deadpan look on his face, rounded the corner, and kept walking toward the reception area.

"What is with that guy?" Olivia whispered.

"He's just Jimmy. Heck, he thought he should have had my job when your dad first took over. I don't think he ever got over it."

"I sure am gonna miss you."

"I'll miss you too, sweetheart. But you can visit me when you come out to Fairfax."

"Gosh, I don't know when that would be."

Deborah smiled. "Sooner than you think, I suspect. Oh, and don't forget, the genius pods are meeting again next week. We'll have people coming in from all over the country."

Later that evening, a crowd gathered at Barney's. Susan had set up a small stage area, where her guitar was sitting out on top of its case. Trevor and Darcy had their instruments against the wall. Sonny was walking around in the parking lot. When Deborah finally walked in, everyone cheered and popped confetti over her head. "Happy retirement!"

"Oh, my goodness. Thank you, everyone!" she shouted. She turned and looked at Mena. "Did you have to invite the whole town?"

"Hey, these are your friends. That's not my fault," Mena laughed.

Barney handed the food across the counter: vegetable trays, chicken platters, potato salad, coleslaw, and meatballs.

"Hey, Preacher," Brandon said. "Can you start us off with a prayer?"

Emmett bowed his head as the room got quiet. Everyone stood to face him and bowed their heads as well. He asked for a blessing for the party and for Deborah and then said grace over the food.

Everyone yelled *amen* in unison, and the noise resumed. Susan walked to the stage and started tuning her guitar. Trevor and Darcy saw her and walked up behind her. Darcy picked up her fiddle, and Trevor opened the case for his old open-back clawhammer banjo.

Susan unmuted the small sound system and stepped up to the microphone.

"Thank y'all for coming tonight to help us celebrate my Aunt Deb's new chapter. We're gonna miss her, but not before we get her dancin'."

Darcy began shuffling the bow across her fiddle as Susan and Trevor joined in to kick off a fast dance tune.

"Yeehaw!" somebody yelled as the dancing began. Someone else pushed Deborah into the middle of the floor that had been cleared for the purpose. Hordes of people squeezed onto the make-shift dance floor and began clogging and swinging their partners.

Brandon looked out the window and saw Sonny in the light of the sign, peering back into the restaurant. Emmett walked up to Brandon from behind and put his hand on his shoulder.

"So, how has CR been going for you?"

"Hey, Preacher. It's been going well. But I think that tower collapse did a number on me."

"Yes, a catastrophic event like that can certainly get your attention."

"I'm sorry I put you through all that, Emmett."

"Think nothing of it, my friend. It's what I'm here for."

"If it's okay with you, I'd like to join your church, Preacher. I think the girls would like that as well."

"Brandon, you don't know how it warms my heart to hear you say that."

Susan, Darcy, and Trevor continued to play several more fast tunes before finally slowing it down so the waltzes could begin. Everyone had finished eating, and Barney had cleaned off the tables, but the music and the dancing continued.

Brandon looked out of the window again and noticed Sonny talking to someone. After a few minutes, Brandon realized it was Jimmy. Jimmy eventually walked inside and looked around at all the people.

"Hey, Boss."

"Hey, Jimmy. I'm glad you could make it," Brandon said.

Jimmy's eyes were bloodshot, and Brandon noticed how stressed he seemed.

"You okay?"

"I'm fine. Why wouldn't I be?"

"Just wanted to make sure. Are you hungry? Want something to eat?"

"No, I'm fine." Jimmy looked around in every direction.

"Who are you looking for?"

"Nobody, Boss. I'm fine."

He drifted off into the crowd, and Brandon lost track of him. Deborah walked out of the crowd of dancers toward Brandon, fanning herself with her hand, trying to catch her breath.

"Okay folks, we're going to take a little bit of a break," Susan said. "Don't go away. There'll be more dancing in about fifteen minutes." Then she walked away from the microphone.

Brandon heard screams, and the crowd rushed back away from the stage. Brandon and Deborah lunged forward to get in front of the crowd and saw Jimmy with Susan in one arm, holding a gun to her head with his other hand.

"Jimmy! What are you doing?" Brandon shouted.

"Jimmy, stop it!" Deborah said.

Brandon stepped forward again and raised both of his hands in front of him.

"Jimmy, please. Think about what you're doing. Stop this."

"Stay away," Jimmy shouted. "I'll shoot her."

Susan closed her eyes, clenching the tears out of them. She held Jimmy's arm with both of her hands, hoping he wouldn't strangle her.

Olivia walked out of the restroom and saw what was happening. She was afraid to speak but slowly walked to the front of the crowd, motioning for everyone to move back.

"Jimmy, what's the matter?" Olivia asked.

"You! You're the matter!" he screamed, trying not to cry.

"Jimmy, what did she do?" Deborah asked.

"You, too!" he shouted. "Get back!"

The front door chime rang, but nobody could see who walked in. Brandon turned and saw Sonny slowly walking through the crowd with his gun drawn and down to his side.

Brandon looked into his piercing eyes. "Sonny, I—"

"It's okay, sir. I've got this."

Susan relaxed some and smiled at Sonny.

"Jimmy, is there something you need to tell us?" Olivia asked. "I don't understand what's going on."

"Jimmy!" Brandon shouted. "Are you the one that tampered with the tower crane?"

Jimmy didn't say anything. He looked around and continued to hold Susan at gunpoint.

"Jimmy, tell us it isn't so," Olivia cried.

"I had to!" Jimmy cried. "I didn't have a choice. I couldn't get out."

"Get out of what?" Deborah asked.

"I was trapped. Just like that guy that killed Mrs. McStocker and Bob McClellan and Senator Taylor!"

"What are you saying?" Brandon shouted.

"Jimmy, lower that gun and let Susan go," Sonny said.

"No! I can't."

"Come on, Jimmy. Tell us what's going on," Deborah said.

"Shut up! Just shut up! Everybody just shut up!"

Susan stared into Sonny's eyes.

"Hey, Susan, Remember what you keep telling me not to do?"

"Sonny?" Brandon said.

Susan nodded subtly and turned her face away.

Sonny pulled the trigger. Screams erupted as the bullet struck Jimmy squarely between the eyes only inches from Susan's head. He fell to the ground in a lifeless heap. Susan froze with her hands over her mouth and began crying uncontrollably. Sonny pointed his gun toward the ground as Brandon ran up and put an arm around Susan to usher her away. The room fell silent.

Sonny reholstered his handgun and shouted, "Is everyone okay?"

"Police are on their way!" Barney shouted from behind the counter.

Sonny stood still with a look of shock on his face. Susan left her father's arms and walked toward Sonny.

"You okay?" he asked.

Without saying a word, she fell into his arms, dropped the side of her face into his chest, and sobbed.

He smiled and looked down on the top of her head. "I'm sorry, baby girl. I guess you told me not to do that."

She smiled through her tears. "I'll make an exception."

"I need to call this in," Sonny said, motioning for Brandon to take Susan.

Chapter 28

A White House staffer met the black limousine when it arrived in front of the door. He helped Olivia and Brandon exit the car. Senator Wilhelm stood nearby to welcome them.

"Senator, this is my daughter, and now deputy, Olivia Mc-Stocker."

"Well, I've heard a lot about you, young lady," he said, extending his hand.

"It's a pleasure to meet you finally, Senator. You can call me Liv."

"Alrighty, Liv. Let's go up and see the president. Brandon, how have you been?"

"Doing well, sir. And you?"

"Oh, still kicking. Beats the alternative, you know."

They arrived outside of the Oval Office, where they waited for several minutes.

"Can I get you all anything to drink?" the receptionist asked. They declined.

Finally, the door opened, and the president walked out.

"Hello, hello. Come on in."

Olivia's eyes grew as she walked into the Oval Office in front of her father and Senator Wilhelm.

"Who have we here?" the president asked.

"President Richland, this is my new deputy PM, Olivia Mc-Stocker."

"McStocker?"

"Yes, sir. She also happens to be my oldest daughter."

"Hello, Olivia. It's a pleasure to meet you. Welcome to the team."

"Thank you, sir. It's a pleasure to meet you as well. You can call me Liv."

"Okay. Liv it is, then. Have a seat. Coffee or water, anyone?"

"None for me, sir," Wilhelm said.

The others shook their heads and sat in the chairs across from the president.

"I heard about the tragedy out there. Is everything okay now?"

"I think so, Mr. President. But we certainly still have some unanswered questions," Brandon said.

"The FBI director is here, sir," a voice said on the intercom.

"Show him in, please," the president said.

After he entered the room, the president said, "Brandon and Olivia McStocker, this is FBI Director Stewart Wilkins. So, Director, what's the latest?"

"Well, sir, as you know, we've pulled Agent Sonny Langston off of assignment pending a full investigation of the shooting incident."

"Uh, yeah. About that—"

"Liv, honey. Easy," Brandon said.

"No, it's okay, Brandon. Ms. McStocker, uh, Liv. Please, continue," the president said.

"Sir. With all due respect," she said, looking at Wilkins, "I can give you all the investigation you need. Your agent Langston saved my little sister's life. I think that's about all you need to know about that."

Brandon stared at the floor and smiled, shaking his head.

"Stew, listen," the president said, "I know you have your protocol, but I've known Brandon here for a long time, and I would trust him with my life. If Liv has even half of his character, I'd say you know about all you need to know about the incident. He obviously means a lot to this family. Do you think we can expedite that investigation and get him back on the job?"

"Of course, sir. Consider it done."

Olivia smiled and nodded at the director. "Thank you, sir."

Brandon lifted his head with a grin. "Yes, thank you, Director. We do appreciate it."

"So, have we been able to find out any more about Mr. Dillon?"

"That's still a little bit of a mystery," the director said.

"Clearly, somebody had something on him," Brandon said. "Him and Denny Cardoza, both. I'm guessing whoever killed Bob McClellan was dealing with the same thing."

"Wait a minute," the director said. "That hasn't been ruled a homicide."

"I never wanted to believe it was," Brandon said. "But now, with all this going on, I don't doubt it for a second. Can't we dig a little deeper into Senator Sanders' dealings?"

"Really," Olivia said. "Every time I see that guy on TV, the hair stands up on the back of my neck. He's just creepy."

"Well, we can't investigate everyone on the hill who happens to be creepy," the president said, then laughed.

Olivia blushed and looked at Brandon.

"We can't start a full-fledged investigation into a senator without Congress knowing about it," the director said. "But I'll start looking for any low-hanging fruit to see if there may be some leads we haven't considered before. We have Mr. Dillon's home computer in forensics now. We'll look through his work computer as well."

"That's perfectly fine with me," Brandon said. "It's all yours."

"I will say that I'm just not sure how much more of this drama the NTO can handle," Wilhelm said. "The other day, they were considering how to back away from Kéntro gracefully."

"No!" Olivia shouted.

"Liv," Brandon said, grabbing her arm.

"We can't give up on this now. We just can't," she said.

"Liv, we're getting a lot of bad press on this thing," the president said. "You know I would love nothing more than to have Lebanon, K.D. up and running so we can get this monkey off our backs. But convincing the NTO is a different story."

"They are starting to unravel," Wilhelm said. They were trying to figure out how to cut their losses and determine their options for repurposing such a monstrous ghost town. They mentioned trying to sell it back to the state. Then they thought maybe the university could use it. I feel like I might be losing control of them."

"That would be a heck of a campus," the president said.

"Gentlemen, stop," Olivia interrupted. "Please. I sat and cried with the wives of the four men who were killed in that crane collapse. I told them to their faces that there was no way I would let this project be scrapped. I wish you could have seen the look on their faces when they told me how proud their husbands were to be associated with such a move. Those men gave their lives for this. This isn't just about moving offices across the country. People see this as a shift in the attitudes of this country's leadership. Don't you see that?"

"Hold on now, Liv," the president said. "Nobody is canceling anything. Not yet anyway. We need to show some real progress and successes out there. I know we've already got a lot of skin in the game."

"Sir, we did get a call from the governor out there a couple of weeks ago," the director said. "He asked that we pull our team off of the site and help get OSHA to do the same. Darnedest thing I ever heard."

"Wait. Redman is onboard now, after all these years?"

"It would seem so, sir," Brandon said. "Thanks to a goodwill visit by my deputy here."

"I'm surprised he didn't try to find a way to make money off of the accident," the president said.

"He has had a change of heart," Olivia said. "I proposed a way to get past an archeological issue that we ran into. We worked out a plan that was good for everyone."

"I heard about that find. So, you got him past that, huh?"

"Yes, sir. I think we're all pulling for the same thing now."

"Dang. That ol' coot never ceases to amaze me. There may be hope for him yet."

"Brandon, could you two be ready to address the NTO Committee while you're in town?" Wilhelm asked.

Olivia looked at Brandon and dropped her jaw. "Uh . . . Brandon, can we do that?"

"When can you set it up?" Brandon asked.

"I think they're planning a session day after tomorrow. How about it?"

Olivia nodded.

"If you can get it set up," Brandon said, "I guess we'll do it. What's the message?"

"How about full speed ahead," the president said. "And Mr. Wilhelm, try to get an impromptu full Senate hearing. Not just the NTO."

"Uh . . . yes, sir."

That night, Brandon took Olivia to a restaurant for dinner. They discussed the presentation for the Senate hearing.

"Daddy, I thought I was going to pass out. A full Senate hearing? Are you serious?"

"Honey, it's the same as a committee hearing. Just a few more people. That's all. You'll do fine."

"What do you mean, I'll do fine?"

"You don't think I'm going to do the talking, do you? That was always Deb's job."

"You're just messing with me, right?"

"It'll be fine. We'll work on it tomorrow. You know, your mom loved this place. We came here all the time."

"Really? It looks like someplace she would love."

"Yep. She did. Hey, you know what. Let's finish up and go pay a surprise visit to Anne."

After they had finished eating, they drove to Anne McClellan's house in Fairfax. The porch light was on when they pulled into the driveway. When they got out of the car and walked up the front steps, Brandon saw Anne pull back the drapes to look out of the window.

"Hello!" he shouted.

"Well, I want you to look at who we have here," she said as she opened the door. "What a nice surprise. Come on in here. How are you doing, Brandon?"

"I'm doing great, Anne. You look good."

"Oh, I try. Who is this beautiful young lady?"

"Hi, Ms. Anne. I'm Liv."

Anne's jaw dropped as she put her hand over her mouth. "My word. Little Olivia? That's you?"

"Yes, ma'am. It's little ol' me," she chuckled.

"Well, come here and give me a hug. My goodness, what a beautiful young woman you've grown into. Let's go in the kitchen. You two want some coffee or iced tea or something?"

"No, Anne. We're fine. Thank you," Brandon said. "We just left the restaurant and thought it would be nice to stop by while we're in town."

"You're not here to stay, then?"

"No, we were here for a meeting today, and then we were asked to stay around a couple of days for another one."

"Does it have to do with Kéntro?"

"As a matter of fact, it does, Ms. Anne," Olivia said.

"How is it going out there?"

"Anne, Bob would be so proud of what his dream has become."

"Oh, he didn't do it. You all have made it happen."

"It's still his vision, Anne. Always was, always will be."

"He always referred to it as the real American dream," Anne said. "Everyone in D.C. had lost sight of what freedom meant and who they worked for. He just wanted to restore the honor that was lost."

"Daddy, that's it," Olivia said.

"That's what?"

"That's the message. Lebanon, K.D. is all about the real American dream. That old banner about our *why*? Let's update that."

Brandon smiled and took Anne's hand into his own. "He's still speaking to us, isn't he?"

"I'd sure like to think so. How's Cassandra? Did she come with you?"

Olivia put her hand over her mouth and tears welled in her eyes, shocked that Anne didn't remember. Brandon smiled.

"Cassandra is no longer with us, Anne."

"What? What do you mean?"

"She died almost seven years ago."

"Oh, my goodness. I am so sorry. How did she die?"

Brandon and Olivia both looked at the floor. Then Olivia turned away.

"Did they kill her just like they killed my Bobby?"

Olivia's head spun back around, and Brandon snapped his head up to look at her.

"What? Anne, do you think Bob was murdered?"

"Well, of course, I do. You don't really believe he had a heart attack, do you?"

"I had my suspicions, but I had no idea you thought that way."

"Brandon, he hated keeping the Kéntro Project hidden from you. He hated it so much it made him sick. But he knew there were forces inside D.C. that would fight it with every ounce of power they could muster. He didn't want to put you and your family in danger."

"Apparently, they have power somewhere because they have people outside of their organization doing the killing for them. They seem to have some kind of control over people."

"Well, dear. You'll get to the bottom of it. I know you will."

"The FBI is working on it. I'll let you know if they come up with anything."

"Ms. Anne," Olivia said. "We've started construction on our new office building out in Kansas. I hope you don't mind, but Dad wanted to call it McClellan Center, in honor of Bob."

"Oh my." Anne blushed and began to cry. "What a beautiful gesture, sweetheart. That's just lovely."

"It's our pleasure and our honor to do it, Anne," Brandon said. "Hopefully, you can come out and see it when it's done."

"Oh, I sure hope so. I surely do."

"I guess we better get back to our rooms for the night," Brandon said. "We have a full day ahead of us tomorrow. But you gave us what we needed. Or at least, Bob did. We're going to try to do right by his idea of the real American dream."

CHAPTER 29

The gavel slammed onto the block that sat in front of the chairman. "We will call this hearing to order. Senator Wilhelm, you've been sworn in, is that correct?"

"I have, Senator. We all have."

"Very well. I understand you are here to convince Congress not to scratch our plans for moving the nation's capital. Is that correct?"

"That is correct, sir."

"Who is testifying with you?"

"This is Brandon McStocker and his deputy, Olivia, from the firm of McClellan & McStocker Engineering Services."

"The firm that is heading up the Kéntro Project?"

"Yes, sir."

"Very well. You may proceed with your opening statement."

Wilhelm looked at Brandon to his right. Brandon looked at Olivia to his right.

"Your honor, I would like to start—"

"Wait. Wait. Wait. Miss, this isn't a courtroom. You may refer to me simply as Senator or Mr. Chairman."

"Of course. I'm sorry, sir."

"Okay, that works, too."

A chuckle came from the crowd that had gathered in the chambers.

"Senator, I think this body would be fools to shut this project down now."

Brandon reached his hand over onto Olivia's arm.

"Ms. McStocker, might I suggest that you watch your tone during these proceedings."

"I'm sorry your honor . . . er . . . Senator, sir."

"Continue."

"Senator, I would ask that this body remember back to a time when moving our capital meant everything to this country. Bob McClellan, my father's partner and the CEO of Mack & Mack at the time, said it best. We have lost sight of the real American dream. The dream of freedom. Freedom to make choices. Choices that allowed us to make America a better place. Washington, D.C. has become a place where power is purchased and traded, not for the sake of the citizens of this country, but for the sake of the power brokers in this city. We've tried for years to vote out the corruption, but when the fox is guarding the henhouse, the rules are constantly changed to serve only the power brokers. Ladies and gentlemen, Washington, D.C. is no longer about serving this nation. Washington, D.C. is all about serving Washington, D.C. We knew when the 28th Amendment was ratified that it was time to rip the nation's capital out from under this system of self-preservation and the out-of-control growth.

"In the new city, Lebanon, Kéntro District, our designs include a total square footage of office space that is about a third of that now available in D.C., while still utilizing the twenty square miles authorized by the amendment. Lebanon, K.D. will be able to breathe, and it will belong to the citizens again.

"We have been meeting with the great minds and thought leaders of this country to come up with the perfect plan for infrastructure. The national cross is complete. The beltway in the center of it is complete. The airport is complete. The track is being laid now to interconnect with a major railhead in Kansas City. Mack & Mack will be moving into our new facility in about six months. We will be able to begin the relocation phase for federal facilities within the year. Do you want to allow all of that to go to the highest bidder? Worse yet, do you want to mothball it?"

A cheer erupted in the chambers. The chairman slammed the gavel down again and again.

"Quiet. Quiet. Hold it down, please. We'll have order in these chambers."

Olivia slid the microphone across the table in front of Brandon. He slid it over to Senator Wilhelm.

"Does the panel have any questions for Senator Wilhelm or Ms. McStocker?"

The room fell silent.

"Nobody? Really?" The chairman looked to his left and his right for reactions.

"Okay, if nobody is going to speak up, I will," Senator Sanders said. "Why are we even here? This entire project is a sham. A power play for the president to get his name on something. I think we should vote to shut it down now."

Olivia stood and reached across the table and grabbed the microphone from in front of Senator Wilhelm. There was feedback in the room from her handling it so roughly.

"Easy, hon," Brandon said softly.

"Mr. Chairman, may I have a word with the senator?"

The chairman smiled. "You certainly may, Ms. McStocker."

"Thank you, sir. Senator, I just wanted to make it perfectly clear to you and to this body that there is nothing in that city that carries the name of President Richland. Nothing! I knew I wanted to be part of this project when I was a kid. I worked my butt off to get through Harvard Business School because of men like President Richland who merely want to return the real American dream to the people of this country. Rest assured, sir, that President Richland has no ulterior motive here. If self-preservation were his mission, this project would have died years ago."

All of the other senators on the panel turned their eyes to Senator Sanders.

"Do you have anything to add, Senator?" the chairman said.

"I do not, Mr. Chairman."

Olivia pushed the microphone away from her as she sat down. It slid all the way across to the front of the table and fell off onto the floor with a loud boom that filled the chambers. She cringed in horror. Another loud cheer erupted. Some people stood in the gallery, cheering as if it were a football game. The vibe in the room might have led one to believe that's exactly what it was.

A senator from the other side of the panel pressed his button and spoke. "Mr. Chairman, I move that we strike this entire proceeding as though it never happened so these fine people can get back to work."

"I second," another voice said.

"Motion moved and seconded. All in favor signify by saying aye."

"Aye!"

"All opposed?"

Senator Sanders sat red-faced and silent.

The chairman grinned. "Thank you, Senator Wilhelm, for your time. Mr. McStocker, Ms. McStocker, thank you. Ladies and gentlemen, this hearing is adjourned."

He slammed the gavel on the table one last time, and the entire room jumped to their feet in jubilation.

Brandon and Olivia arrived back in Kansas the following afternoon. When they walked out of the terminal into the pickup zone, they saw Sonny leaning against the limo, smiling like he just got away with something big.

"Well, look who's back on the job," Olivia said.

"Good to see you, Sonny," Brandon said extending his hand.

Olivia put her luggage down and reached up on her toes to hug him.

"I understand you may have had a little to do with it," Sonny said.

"It wasn't fair!" she said, poking him in the chest.

"Let's go to the office, Sonny," Brandon said.

Sonny put the luggage in the trunk and closed the doors behind Brandon and Olivia. As soon as he got in the driver's seat, he looked in the rearview mirror and caught Olivia's attention.

"So, little Miss Livvy is a star," he said.

"Little Miss Livvy? What the heck are you talking about?"

Somebody posted your entire speech at that hearing on Facebook and YouTube. It's blowing up. It has almost three million views already."

"Say what!"

"Now, that's funny," Brandon said.

"Shut up!" Olivia shouted. "It wasn't a speech. I didn't even have anything written down."

"America's new sweetheart," Brandon laughed.

"Will you shut it!"

"No. All kidding aside, sweetheart. You did a great job in there."

"You really did, Liv," Sonny said. "I've watched it like ten times already. You need to run for president."

"Okay, now you guys are out of control. Just get me to the office."

Sonny reached over the back of his seat and slapped Brandon's hand.

Olivia shook her head and rolled her eyes. "You guys are killing me."

When they arrived back at the campus, the three of them rode the elevator to the third floor. When they arrived, Sonny stepped to the side.

"Hello, Cindy," Brandon said.

"Welcome back, Mr. McStocker." Then she smiled at Olivia. "Fist-pump, girlfriend!!"

Olivia reached across the counter and met her halfway. Sonny covered his mouth and bent over. He couldn't control his laughter. Brandon turned around and narrowed his eyes at Olivia.

"Sorry, Dad—uh, Brandon. Shall we get to work?"

They rounded the corner into the commons, and Olivia threw her purse and jacket onto the chair just inside her office door.

"Hey, Mena. How's everything?"

"Way too quiet with you guys gone. Nobody around."

"Sorry about that," Olivia said. "It was a fun experience, but I hope we're staying around here now for awhile."

"Great job on that speech, kiddo."

"It wasn't a speech! Gah!"

"It sure sounded like a speech."

"That's what I thought," Brandon said, walking into his office. The phone rang.

"McClellan & McStocker. Mr. McStocker's office."

"Oh, yes. Mr. McStocker will take the call." Mena covered the mouthpiece with her hand. "Senator Wilhelm's office."

"Put him through." Brandon walked quickly into his office and to his desk. The phone barely rang when he picked it up.

"Senator. Just got in. What can we do for you?"

"Turn on the TV!"

"Sir?"

"Your TV. Turn on your TV!"

"Turn on the TV. Yes, sir." He looked through his door to make sure Mena heard him.

Mena reached for the remote and turned the TV on in the commons. Olivia sat on the corner of Mena's desk. Brandon hung up the phone and walked out of his office. The first image they saw was that of Senator Sanders in handcuffs being escorted out of the Capitol building along with four or five other people, presumably his staff. The screen split, and there was an image of his wife, also in handcuffs, being escorted out of their home in Reston, Virginia.

"What the heck is going on?" Brandon said. "Turn it up!"

Susan walked in off of the elevator and turned to slap Sonny in the stomach.

"I'm not even going to ask," she said.

"Better not. Never know," he laughed.

"Hey, Cindy. Are they down there?"

"Yep. Just got in."

Susan walked down the corridor as if waitress uniforms were a normal thing at the firm of McClellan & McStocker. She rounded the corner and saw everyone glued to the TV.

"What in the world—"

"Apparently, the FBI's investigation has uncovered something pretty serious," Brandon said.

An excited reporter began to speak. "We've just gotten word from an FBI spokesperson that the Sanders Foundation has been making deals with several federal agencies to confuse and even destroy the Kéntro Project. Several murders have also been linked to Sanders through forensic evidence retrieved from the computer of a recently deceased employee of McClellan & McStocker, James Dillon. These murders reach all the way back to the beginning of the project when Bob McClellan, the CEO of the firm at the time, was found dead in Fairfax. According to our sources, the murders were an organized attempt to break the leadership of the firm and stop Kéntro."

"Holy crap!" Susan said.

Olivia turned and looked at Brandon. "Dad, is it over?"

"You mean this was aimed at me? If all of this sticks, I think it just might be, Liv."

Mena looked at her phone. There were no lights blinking. "Brandon, did you hang up on Senator Wilhelm?"

"Oh, crap. I guess I did. Oops."

Mena, Olivia, and Susan laughed.

"Nice going, Dad," Susan said. They laughed even harder. Tears of laughter turned into tears of joy and then tears of the memories Olivia and Susan had of their mother. Brandon lowered his head, thinking of his friend, Bob McClellan.

Mena's phone rang again.

"Uh-oh," Olivia said. "I bet it's the senator calling to fire you."

"Oh, hush," Brandon laughed.

Mena answered. "McClellan & McStocker. Brandon Mc-Stocker's office."

She smiled.

"Hey there, stranger. Let me put you on the speaker. We're all right here."

She pressed the button. "It's Deborah!"

Everyone shouted, "Hey, there!"

"Hey, there, Deb," Brandon said. "How's the retired life?"

"It's great, my friend. I'd recommend it to anyone. I was just watching this breaking news. So, they finally got that son of a—"

"Apparently so," Brandon said. "I knew his wife was a criminal from day one. Wouldn't surprise me he if was working for her. I just can't figure out what they were holding over the heads of Jimmy and Denny Cardoza that would cause them to commit murder."

"Family," Olivia said.

Brandon, Susan, and Mena looked at Olivia.

"What do you mean, Liv?" Deborah said over the speaker.

"It had to be money or family. But Jimmy was paid well. My gut tells me their families were being threatened. It would also explain why Jimmy was so jumpy all the time."

"Could be," Brandon said. "But I also know that when Bob passed, Jimmy wanted that deputy spot so bad he could taste it."

"That's true," Deborah said. "You don't suppose he killed Bob just to get the deputy spot, do you? Hopefully, it'll all come out in the investigation. Listen, you guys. I need to get off of here and do some baking. You guys have a city to build."

"We miss you, Aunt Deb," Olivia said.

"I miss you all, too, sweetheart. Bye now."

Mena pressed the speaker button to hang up the phone then turned the TV off with the remote. The room was silent, and the four of them stood motionless.

"Well," Susan said. "Uh . . . I guess I need to get to work. What are you guys going to do now?"

Brandon smiled. "Like the woman said, we've got a city to build."

CHAPTER 30

After six months, massive, ultra-modern, glass buildings had risen from the fields of north-central Kansas in record time. After the Sanders Foundation story broke, the depth and breadth of the corruption in Washington, D.C. was confirmed, and both houses of Congress, indeed the entire nation, stood once again behind President Richland and the Kéntro Project. Huge corporations that had been involved in the shared vision through the hugely successful PIE-D program were now helping to fund Kéntro and were getting even more involved in the genius pods.

Brandon, Olivia, Susan, and Mena sat behind the podium on the grandstand that was erected in front of McClellan Center. A crowd sat in front of them, looking up at the grand twelve-story building that was born in Brandon's dream.

It was dedication day, which included a national prayer vigil in Lebanon, K.D., where over two million people poured onto the beltway and surrounded the new capital city. Several hundred large monitors and sound systems had been mounted in strategic locations around the beltway so the attendees could watch the celebration proceedings. Just before the speeches were to begin, a chain of people holding hands started to form in a long line that eventually became an unbroken circle around the entire length of the beltway. A news reporter onboard a helicopter broadcast the images on live television. All of the local stations were live-streaming the event on the Internet for the entire nation to experience. The sight was breathtaking from the air. When the crowds noticed themselves being broadcast on the massive video walls, a loud cheer erupted.

This moving show of support and unity was infectious, and the entire country was one again. The image on the screens switched to a large band on the lawn of what would eventually become the new Capitol building. The National Anthem played, and everyone on the beltway began to sing. The power of the song was deafening as everyone sang at the top of their lungs with an exuberance that had rarely been displayed in the previous twenty years.

After the song was over, the scene on the monitors cut to Pastor Emmett Cleveland standing at a lectern next to the old geographic center monument near what used to be the town of Lebanon. The monument stood in the middle of the front yard of McClellan Center. Brandon, Olivia, and Susan were standing behind him. Many dignitaries were seated in front of them, including the entire cadre from both houses of Congress. President Richland sat in the first row with his wife, children, and grandchildren. Senator Wilhelm and his family sat next to the president. On the other side of Brandon sat Anne McClellan holding hands with Deborah Blanchard. Susan smiled at Sonny, standing on the edge of the platform, hiding behind his sunglasses. She gave him a thumbs-up, forcing a smile from him.

Pastor Emmett adjusted the position of the microphone. "Ladies and gentlemen, will you please join me in the blessing of a new beginning for this great nation?"

He, along with everyone at the monument as well as the multitudes surrounding the city, bowed their heads. Traffic throughout the inner-city streets came to a stop. All construction had already been shut down for the day.

"Most gracious Heavenly Father, we come to you today as a fresh new nation. We offer ourselves, renewed in the unity that you prayed for. We come before you to recognize Your dominion and Your strength. Lord, we petition you for your renewed presence here with us. We welcome you back into our schools and our government buildings. As a nation of sinners, we ask for Your forgiveness. Here we are but straying pilgrims, God, and only through You will this nation be great once again. Not for our selfish gain, but to be Your light—the city on a hill for all Your glory. It is with this new hope that we ask your blessing on this new Lebanon, Kéntro District, that we might accomplish all things through You, and that we will serve this nation from these structures built on the foundation of Your love. As a nation of renewed spirit, we ask a special blessing on this body that sits before me, that they may serve, not from a position of power and privilege, but from a position of humility and love. As a nation of many cultures, many traditions, and many faiths, we come before the one God in recognition of our need for You and only You, to provide the cement that holds us together as one tribe, endowed with the freedom You intended for us from the very beginning. While we honor all of the states of this great nation and the flags that fly over them and the men and women who have fought and often died for our earthly rights, we reserve our highest honor and glory for You, O Lord. We stand at the center of our newly formed national cross and ask these things in the name of Your Son, Jesus Christ. Amen."

Over fifty clergymen from many faiths stood on the other side of Pastor Emmett and bowed to acknowledge the prayer and show a sign of unity.

Susan walked to the lectern and picked up her guitar from its stand. She began finger-picking a slow roll and started singing a song that she chose for the occasion.

"Oh, beautiful for spacious skies. For amber waves of grain. For purple mountain majesties. Above the fruited plain!"

Never had such a well-known song been so perfectly suited for a time such as this. Again, everyone sang at the top of their lungs, all the way around the beltway. When it was over, deafening cheers erupted, and Susan returned to her seat. Brandon stepped to the microphone. When the crowd quieted, he began.

"As my former and current deputies can attest, speaking in front of people isn't something I do. Not willingly, anyway. But today is a special day. The city that rises before us, while indeed authorized by Congress, was the dream of one man. The man whose name we have proudly placed upon this beautiful facility: my friend, Bob McClellan."

A cheer erupted from those on and around the platform while the senators and members of Congress rose to their feet. Brandon stepped back from the podium, turned, and smiled at Anne. When the cheers quieted, he continued.

"Mrs. Anne McClellan, Bob's widow, is with us here today." He continued speaking through the applause because he knew she would be embarrassed by the attention. He hoped to quiet it quickly.

"Anne lost her husband, and I lost my wife, Cassandra, in the pursuit of this dream. But when I look out over this shining example of unity, I see the magic that Bob saw. I see the love that Cassandra saw. Today is dedicated to them. Not only to them, but to others we have lost in pursuit of this dream."

He turned and nodded to the four ladies sitting behind him. He pointed to them.

"Behind me sits Maddie, Maria, Gladys, and Sally. Their husbands were killed in the tragic collapse of the tower crane just over there, where that beautiful financial center has literally risen from the ashes. It would be an understatement to say that these families were devastated. They could have gone to court and probably could have been awarded millions of dollars. But when my daughter, Liv, and I went to visit them just after the incident, they didn't want to talk to us about a lawsuit. They wanted to tell us how proud their husbands were to work on this project."

Brandon was having a hard time holding back tears. Olivia and Susan didn't even try to hold them back.

"What Liv and I saw was how proud these women were, and are, of their husbands. What I want to say here today is how proud Liv and I are of these women, along with all of the other men and women who have been touched by Bob's dream.

"What Bob saw was bigger than this day. What he saw was even bigger than this new city. What he saw was the real American dream. He saw a damaged nation, a nation with a broken heart, and he wanted to see it put back together.

"Now, I want to introduce you to the man who shared Bob's vision for a new beginning. He has traveled a very rough road to get to this city, and I am beyond elated that he finally made it.

Ladies and gentlemen, the president of the United States, Andrew Richland."

Everyone jumped to their feet, applauding and screaming. The screams from the millions who surrounded the city on the beltway were deafening.

"Andy, Andy, Andy, Andy," they shouted in unison. When the crowd had quieted, the president was in front of the microphone and holding up his hands.

"Thank you, Brandon—you and this wonderful McClellan & McStocker team, members of Congress, and distinguished guests. Thank you. While on my way out here this morning, I was able to stop and have breakfast with Brandon and his two beautiful daughters. What an amazing example of integrity they are. Something fascinating that I learned while we ate was that we sat at the very table where much of the planning and brainstorming happened for Kéntro. We were sitting in the back corner of Barney's Diner."

The crowd broke out in laughter and applause. The president continued his speech while Brandon sat between Olivia and Susan. They each had an arm wrapped around his. His mind drifted back through the years after he had taken over the project—the stress he lived through—the friends and the enemies he had made along the way. When the president's speech was over, he introduced Governor Redman. The governor's speech was a little longer, but Brandon could tell, his accolades were sincere. When the speech was over, the governor turned to walk away and caught Brandon's gaze. They both smiled and nodded. It was done.

When the celebration was over, it seemed to take hours for the chatting and handshakes to end and the crowds to disperse. The construction crews eased back into position to make preparations for the next day of work. Brandon gave Deborah and Anne a hug, then took each of his daughters by the hand and walked into the new facility, McClellan Center.

The foyer was massive, the floor as shiny as new ice. The daylight streamed in through the gigantic plates of glass. The museum that Liv designed herself was at the west end of the foyer—a large opening in the wall, where local Pawnee relics hung on display beneath small spotlights against black walls. Over the opening was a large wooden sign that read, "Cassandra's Garden."

The three walked into the elevator, Olivia and Susan still holding on to their father's arms. When they reached the twelfth floor, they stepped off into their new corporate headquarters. Everything was new and shiny—virtually untouched.

"Hey there, Sonny," Brandon said. "You beat us up here."

Susan let go of her dad's arm and fell into Sonny, wrapping her arms around his waist.

"Hey, bud. Thanks for not shooting anybody today," she said.

Olivia shook her head and stepped away from them into the middle of the new reception area. She closed her eyes, pointed her face straight up, and started spinning.

"Finally. Our new home," she said.

Sonny stayed by the elevator while the other three strolled down the empty, cavernous office complex. When they got near the end, Olivia looked into her new office.

"God, I love this!"

Susan looked in after her. "Wow! You go, Sis!"

They continued to walk together into the end office—Brandon's new office. They walked across the shiny tile floor, past the enormous desk, and to the window that stretched from wall to

wall, floor to ceiling. They held hands and walked up to it together.

"Whoa. Daddy, this is incredible," Olivia said.

Susan raised her free hand to cover her mouth. She couldn't
hold back the tears. What they saw was a breathtaking panorama
of the new city. The dream of Lebanon, K.D. was spread out before their eyes, across the beltway and all the way to the airport.

Susan tried hard to speak and could only barely get the words
out. "I wish Mom could have seen this."

"She sees it, sweetheart. Trust me. She sees it," Brandon said.

They stood in silence for several minutes, staring out across
the city. Many of the federal buildings were still under construction. Lights were starting to come on in the skyscrapers against the
sunset, making the view even more breathtaking.

"Oh, I forgot to mention something," Brandon said. "One of
the private industry smart guys that we had in a genius pod? It
turns out, he owns a recording studio and record label in Nashville. He was quite impressed with your singing today. He wants
to talk to you about it."

Susan turned to Brandon, her mouth gaping open. "What!
Dad, are you messing with me?"

He laughed. "Not at all."

"Oh, my gosh!" Olivia shouted.

Olivia and Susan jumped into each other's arms behind Brandon's back, screeching with excitement, bouncing up and down.

"Let's go tell Sonny," Susan said. "Thank you, Daddy!"

They danced back toward the elevator leaving Brandon standing alone, still staring out across the city. He was smiling, but a
tear came to his eye.

"What do you think, Cassandra? You love it, don't you?"

He thought quietly for several more minutes, then sighed a deep breath.

"Bob, my friend. We did it."

Brandon heard someone behind him. He turned to see who it was.

"Liv! Susan! Is that you?"

He caught another glance at someone clearly sneaking around in the shadows.

"Hello! Who's there?"

He ran out of his office and around the corner. He saw who it was, and they both froze.

"Cindy? What are you doing up here?"

TERRY STAFFORD RECOMMENDS

Strings of Faith

A musical dream. A family tragedy. Can one fiddler fight through the pain to stay true to her own melody?

Darcy has two great passions in life: fiddling and family. But when she and her husband learn they're unable to have children, the music she once loved only amplifies the pain in her heart. Her soul only begins to sing anew when an everyday miracle brings her hope for a child back to life.

But when the path to motherhood causes discord in her marriage and separation from her faith, Darcy must decide if her desire for a family is worth the overwhelming sacrifice. And when her lifelong dream of winning a national fiddling contest comes back into focus, she'll face her biggest challenge of all. Against impossible odds and unimaginable heartache, can Darcy rediscover her passion for music to overcome the scars of tragedy?

Strings of Faith is a toe-tapping Christian fiction novel that will sing to your soul. If you like family drama, journeys of self-discovery, and the healing power of music, then you'll love Terry Stafford's melodic tale.

Pick up a copy of *Strings of Faith* to fill your heart with a tale of musical healing today!

Contact Me

You may contact me directly at terry@terrystafford.com.

Join my email list, check out my many resources, and request coaching through my website at TerryStafford.com.

ABOUT THE AUTHOR

Award-winning author, Terry Stafford, came to writing in the second half of life. He uses his fiction to weave tales of music for readers who miss the good ol' days. Having a Master's Degree in Management as well as a background in the US Navy and later with NASA as a senior project manager, Terry saw how his experience could bring order out of creative chaos in his own writing life. He knows creatives often feel like scatter-brained writers and helps them become prolific storytellers. Terry lives in California's beautiful San Joaquin Valley with his wife, Gail. Both talented musicians, you can find them attending bluegrass music festivals or playing with the praise band every Friday night for the Celebrate Recovery ministry at their church.

A free ebook edition is available with the purchase of this book.

To claim your free ebook edition:

1. Visit MorganJamesBOGO.com
2. Sign your name CLEARLY in the space
3. Complete the form and submit a photo of the entire copyright page
4. You or your friend can download the ebook to your preferred device

Morgan James BOGO™

A **FREE** ebook edition is available for you or a friend with the purchase of this print book.

CLEARLY SIGN YOUR NAME ABOVE

Instructions to claim your free ebook edition:
1. Visit MorganJamesBOGO.com
2. Sign your name CLEARLY in the space above
3. Complete the form and submit a photo of this entire page
4. You or your friend can download the ebook to your preferred device

Print & Digital Together Forever.

Snap a photo

Free ebook

Read anywhere

Printed in the USA
CPSIA information can be obtained
at www.ICGtesting.com
JSHW022214140824
68134JS00018B/1055